LeRoi

LeRoi

MEL MATHEWS

FISHER KING PRESS

This is a work of fiction. Names, characters, places, and incidents either are the product of the author's imagination or are used fictitiously, and any resemblance to actual persons, living or dead, business establishments, events or locales is entirely coincidental.

Fisher King Press
P.O. Box 222321
Carmel, CA 93922
www.fisherkingpress.com
1-800-228-9316

LeRoi

ISBN-13: 978-0-9776076-0-0
ISBN-10: 0-9776076-0-7
LCCN: 2005937566

Woman cannot be contained.
Real or ethereal,
She cannot be harnessed.

Chapter 1

Friday

My MG overheated, blew a radiator hose was all, I hoped. By some stroke of luck it happened within a mile of a remote service station on the desolate highway. It had to be pushing a hundred degrees outside when I coasted into the station. The wind was beginning to pick up as the branches swayed and the leaves rustled in a lone oak tree that was rooted twenty feet opposite the barbed wire fence in a dry grassy field just east of the station. Across the street was a diner. That was it, a service station and a diner plopped right in the middle of miles of dry hills rolling off in all directions, and a bumpy, worn out highway running east and west that connected similar sparse settlements like a dot-to-dot game along this landscape that was leading me home.

It's harder than hell to get any mechanic to look at an MG. They know that with something as little as checking the oil, the back bumper will probably fall off, the mechanic getting the blame. The wrench at the service station told me that he couldn't look at it until after lunch, said it needed time to cool off before he could do anything anyway. I guess I needed the cooling off time, too, so I headed for an iced tea and lunch at the diner across the highway, if it looked safe.

The diner had a gravel driveway with a couple of old telephone poles laid out about ten feet from the front door and two plate glass windows that made up the front of the faded white building. The west corner had been damaged by a wayward vehicle, the remnants of the past having lived on, un-repaired. The telephone poles must have been an afterthought to protect the diner from the potential of another run-in.

I opened the door and walked in, my presence announced

by the un-oiled creaking hinges. Without looking around, I walked to the coffee counter, slid into the end seat next to the cash register and ordered an iced tea with lots of ice. I guess the woman who was sitting in the booth behind me was immune to the non-smoking section that she was sitting in; I wasn't.

"Excuse me, I wonder if you could put your cigarette out?" I asked, assuming she knew that it was a non-smoking section.

She ignored me. A few minutes later she lit up again and set the just lit lipstick-coated Virginia Slim into the slot of the amber ashtray. I stood up, walked around to her booth, grabbed her pack of smokes and the ashtray and walked out the front door. I dumped the ashtray and stepped on her lit smoke; then, I dropped her pack and stomped them as well. I walked back inside.

"Who the hell do you think you are?" she asked, sliding her pink polyester two-ton ass out of the booth.

I slammed the empty ashtray down on the coffee counter and sat down looking straight ahead. I could feel her breathing over my shoulder.

"Lady, you don't want to find out!"

That was enough for her. I could hear the remnants of spoiled little bastard as the door swung shut.

A petite pony-tailed brunette walked up with the iced tea pitcher to refill my glass.

"Can I have some more ice please?"

"Sure," she answered, turning to the ice machine behind her and scooping a glass full while I admired the sculptured tilt of her finely proportioned ass-end. "I'm sure Flo will be out in a minute," the brunette said, as she turned around with my ice.

"Who's Flo?"

"The boss-lady."

"What does she want?"

"You'll have to ask her yourself."

Flo walked up behind the sweet little brunette. "Sarah, could you catch that back booth with some decaf?"

Flo wouldn't have been half bad in her day. She could have passed for Sarah thirty years earlier. She wore very little make-up behind her black-rimmed reading glasses that rested about halfway down on her nose and were clipped to a strand of cheap miniature pearls that hung around her neck. Her eyes were hazel with bluish flecks, and she had long straight brunette hair held up in a clip. Her hair had the gray that accompanied a fifty-five plus year old woman. She was tan, trim and took care of herself, in spite of the gravity that age had introduced. She wore cotton pants and a simple uniform-type, button-up-the-front blouse. She looked like a boss-lady should look, in control.

I waited for Flo to go first.

"Howdy."

"Hi," I answered, before taking a swig of tea.

"Purdy hot day, huh?"

"I can stand the heat. It's the stray cigarette smoke that sets me off."

"So that gives you the right to run off one of my regulars."

"I asked her to put it out."

"Did you ask her or did you beat around the bush with some rude indirect comment?"

"Lady, I don't know who you are or what's on your mind, but I really don't need any more crap today."

"Well kid, right now you're in my diner, and you're runnin' off my patrons..."

"Oh great," I muttered.

"I've dealt with your kind for years, so let's just cut to the quick."

I'd run the weak one out the front door, but now I had one who wasn't going to scare off quite as easily. I guess it would be pretty hard to throw the queen out of her own palace.

"Look, lady, I'm sorry if I offended anybody here, but I've got some problems. My MG is broken down across the street," I said, knowing that the mechanic waiting for it to cool would have come up with a pretty damn good excuse for not being able to work on it by the time I returned.

"So what?"

"Besides that, I keep playing telephone tag with Janie, one of my lady friends."

Flo stood there and stared at me dumb-founded.

"It's her birthday this Sunday, and I need to get her address so I can send her a birthday card. Jenny's coming this weekend, and I won't be able to sneak a phone call to Janie. Well, now that

I think about it, I probably can get that done. Anyway, things just aren't falling into place today."

"Would you like some chocolate milk little boy, or how about your ass wiped?

I just stared at this piece of work as I noticed a shadowy figure looking on from behind the kitchen window.

"Yeah, you heard me. In this cafe the world doesn't revolve around you."

"I don't expect it to," I flashed back.

"As a matter of fact, for you, I think it has a way of stoppin' all together. There's not a waitress in the world, let alone any other woman, who will ever live up to your demands. We just can't sit in front of you all day waitin' on or guessin' your every need, demand, or desire."

"What?"

"You heard me Mr. Needy-Needy-Never-Enough-World-Ought-to-Revolve-Around-Me. It never has, and it never will. Besides, gettin' around doesn't sound as if it's a real problem for you anyway."

"What do you want?"

"Get over it."

"Get over what?"

"Bein' a helpless little boy who is trapped in a grown man's body."

"Wha..."

"I see your kind stumble into this place all of the time. Grow up. Get over it," Flo interrupted.

"Get over what?"

"Feelin' sorry for yourself and shruggin' your crap off onto some woman with a cigarette or any other woman for that matter."

"It was a non-smoking section!"

"I'll bet you're one of those that doesn't like to be told no."

"No I'm not."

"I'll bet that great big word NO pierces your heart every time you hear it."

"You think I'm too sensitive?"

"I think you overreacted. If you'd have given her a chance, she'd have put out the cigarette."

"She lit up a second smoke after I asked her to put the first one out."

"Did you ask her to put it out a second time?"

I stood up and reached into my pocket for a couple of bucks, threw them on the counter, stumbled out of that beehive, and then walked back across the street to check on my car.

I only went in there for a goddamn glass of iced tea and to try to unwind. Now I had this self-righteous mama trying to tell me how to act. Who in the hell did she think she was anyway and how in the hell did it go from me not putting up with the used cigarette smoke to me not respecting women. That's all I needed, another run in with a die-hard feminist who felt responsible for defending the rights of all womankind. God I hoped my MG was up and running.

"How do things look?" I asked, standing a few feet back, not wanting to take up too much of this guy's space.

"Not good."

"What did you find?"

"Well your radiator's got troubles for starters, and its either goda be repaired or replaced."

"Doesn't sound so bad. Why can't we run it down to the radiator shop and get it worked over?"

"What radiator shop you have in mind?" he asked, cocking his head back, pulling off his glasses and then crossing his arms over his embroidered name patch that read 'Okie'.

Great, a mechanic with an attitude: they loved it when you needed them, made them God. God was wearing a pair of dark blue coveralls and was pushing sixty if he hadn't made it yet. His graying sandy-brown, Brill-creamed hair was combed back and parted to the side. When he looked at me, his left eye drifted away in the opposite direction. It was obvious that this glass-eyed son-of-a-bitch who couldn't see straight liked to argue.

"I don't care which one you use. Who's the quickest?"

"None of 'em are the quickest because we ain't got one."

"So what do you do for your radiator repairs?"

"Send 'em out."

"Can't we just drive it over to the next town?"

"No, we can't just drive it over to the next town because there ain't a repair shop in the next town either, and because

I'm the only one here. This is the only gas station fifty miles in either direction. I can't just up and leave."

"What do I do?"

"I'm gunna pull the radiator, clean it to make sure it is repairable, and ship it out."

"How?"

"UPS, and they've already been here today, so cool your jets kid. Besides, I don't know that that's your only problem. Your water pump has a leak, and, as dry as you ran this little hot rod, it wouldn't surprise me if you cracked the head."

"Hell, I was less than a mile from here when the hose blew, how could I have a cracked head?"

"Son, I don't break 'em, I fix 'em, and this one's not gunna be fixed overnight. If I were you, I'd make sleepin' arrangements. It'll be at least a week before I've got your radiator back and whatever other parts I'll have to order."

"Hell, I haven't got a week. I got a girl coming to my place for the weekend."

"Well, maybe you better think about havin' her meet you here."

"Mister, I live in California. There's no way in hell I'm gunna get her to drive twenty hours for a weekend roll in the hay."

"Well kid, looks like you've just had a change in plans. I can fix your car, and I'll get it out of here as quickly and inexpensively as possible, even if you are one of those impatient hotshot Californians."

"So that's as good as it gets, huh?"

"That's as good as it gets, and you might as well start trustin' me right now. You don't have much choice. You can tow it to the next town, but you know as well as I do that not many mechanics will even pop the hood on this British tub to check the oil. Count your blessin's, I've owned a couple myself, so you can be damn sure I've had my practice wrenchin' on these moody critters."

"Fuck," I thought, but kept it to myself. "All right, any suggestions on a room?"

"I'd see Flo across the street at the diner. She runs the place, lives upstairs and usually has a room to rent."

"What other possibilities are there?" I asked, realizing that

I'd been fighting with my new landlord and had yet to even fill out an application.

"If that doesn't work, I might be able to set you up on a buddy's cattle ranch, but the accommodations won't be nearly what they are across the street, plus you'd probably have to work, and you don't appear to be the type that likes to get too dirty."

I wanted to stomp the cocky old man's little toe along with the rest of his smart-ass self, but I needed him just like I needed Flo across the street. I had to shut up and start kissing both of their asses. As I waited to cross the highway, a semi roared by, leaving me in a whirlwind disarray to match my frustration and anger that was rapidly turning into helpless despair.

Days like this that made me question why I left my hundred thousand dollar a year company job selling John Deere Tractors. I always had a new Chevy extended cab Silverado that drove more like a touring sedan than a pickup truck. I had traded it all just to be able to sleep in as late as I damn well pleased and for the freedom to do business on my own terms.

I walked back in to the coffee counter and sat down. Sarah was scooping some more ice. I watched her until she turned around and then shifted my gaze to the daily special board.

Fish and Chips with a cup of clam chowder for $4.50, tea or coffee included, had been scribbled in pink and blue chalk on the blackboard. Friday in Five Points was just about the same as anywhere else.

"Hungry?"

"Yeah, I'll try the special."

"Tea?"

"Yes, please, with…"

"Lots of ice," Sarah interrupted.

"You got it. Is Flo around?"

"She's upstairs. I can call for her."

"Only if she's not busy. I don't want to bother her."

"I'd say you've all ready done that."

"I'm sure I have," I said, feeling like a fool for having argued with the woman.

"Can't see what a little more could hurt. Let me get your soup and then I'll go after her."

I had bothered her, but there was no changing the past,

even if it was only twenty minutes earlier. I didn't have much of a choice. Okie was right; I wasn't into punching cattle. A few minutes later Flo walked back up to the coffee counter.

"Well, look who's back for dessert," she said with a smart-ass-now-I-gotcha grin.

"Okie across the road says you might have a room for rent."

"Sounds like Okie across the road probably had more bad news than just that for you kid. Things got to be pretty shitty if you're back here for a room."

"Yes ma'am, I guess you could say that." I answered, wanting to tell her to fuck off in the worse way.

"Why does this not surprise me? Okie is always stickin' me with your kind. I guess it isn't his fault that guys like you always end up broken down in those good-for-no-more-than-fifty-miles-from-home British sports cars that you try to run away from life in."

"Lady, I know I seem to have left what little courtesy I have back at home, but I really would appreciate any help you could give me."

"Yeah, I got an extra room. Sarah, will you show him upstairs when he's finished lunch?"

"To the non-smoking room?" Sarah asked with her back to me facing Flo. They both broke out in a giggle.

"I guess we'll have to try to be nice to him," Flo said, as she turned from Sarah to me.

"How much for the room?"

"I don't know yet. Depends on how many more of my patrons you run off."

CHAPTER 2

Friday

After lunch I walked back to the service station to get my duffel, laptop, and cellular phone. Okie was at the gas pumps.

"I just need to get my goods out of the car, and I'll be out of your hair," I told Okie as he watched me walk up to the station.

"I'm gunna need some money."

"For what?"

"For fixin' your rig. What do you think?"

"You haven't done anything yet."

"And I won't if I don't have parts to repair it. No money, no parts, no fixed car."

"Can I put it on my VISA?"

"Cash or a local check," Okie muttered.

"How much you want?"

"Couple hundred; I've got to pay the radiator man, and that'll be at least fifty bucks. The rest ought to cover the water pump and hoses."

I reached for my money clip and handed him two crisp hundreds. "Do I get a receipt?"

"If I had a receipt book you would, but I don't, so like I said, you're gunna have to learn to trust me."

About all I trusted Ol' Deadeye for was slipping it to me, but I didn't have a choice. "OK, I'll talk to you tomorrow."

"You can talk to me, but it won't do you any good. I don't wrench on Saturday or Sunday unless it's a quick fix just to keep a car on the road. Otherwise, I clean the shop and take care of stuff 'round the house."

Okie lived about two hundred yards behind the gas station in a mobile home that appeared to have been moved right into where a house had possibly burned down. It made sense. The yard and everything else he needed was in place, so instead of trying to restore the remnants of the past, he had done the smart thing. He moved into a new home. I hoped that he had more faith in his trade than he did in his domestic repairs. He had faith in something though, because it was a wonder that the whole damn station hadn't gone up in flames when his house had. Okie and I were done doing business for the weekend, so I hoofed it back across the highway to the diner.

The lunch hour had passed and the place was empty with the exception of two old men in the back booth who were playing gin. Sarah was waiting for me when I walked in with my duffel and portable office.

"Would you like me to call a bellhop?"

"A bellhop won't work for what I have in mind," I said grinning.

I followed Sarah toward the stairs, curious to know what she was really like after she had showered off Flo's influence.

"I've always heard that it doesn't make much difference to you Caliboys."

"Well it's your lucky day. You don't have to hear about us Caliboys second hand anymore."

"More like unlucky."

"You've got yourself a real live one now," I answered, following her up the stairs.

"Like I said, unlucky."

"You get to see first hand what pulls the rope of this Caliboy. If you're lucky it might even be you."

"A true California dreamer."

"Dreams come true."

"Well it's time to wake from this one," Sarah said, as she stepped up onto the second floor.

There was something about Sarah that I liked, maybe more than just something. She was sassy but wholesome. I was looking forward to finding out what exactly it was about her that was so enticing. She was in her mid-twenties, about five-four with long dark brown hair in a ponytail. She wasn't one of those anorexic looking model types, but she damn sure wasn't overweight by any standards either.

Sarah had natural beauty. If she wore make-up, I couldn't tell, and it was quite apparent that she took her health seriously. She was full of energy—almost too much energy. I say too much energy because that's what attracted me to her but also scared the hell out of me. I doubted my ability to keep up with a woman like her, to keep her happy.

"This is your stop. There's no key, and it only locks from the inside with a dead-bolt."

"Well now, how do you know that?"

"It's where I stayed when I first arrived."

"Broken down car?"

"I wish," Sarah said, as she turned to walk back downstairs.

I decided not to probe too quickly. That was one thing that always seemed to scare them off. Although, I'd been known to use the scare tactic to see how quickly they spooked just to cut through the crap and save myself a lot of time and grief. I walked in and set my goods on the bed.

The room was about fifteen by fifteen with a double bed, a dresser, and a desk with a red rotary dial trim-line phone. I looked for the phone jack so that I could access my e-mail to do business from my new loft, but it was the old style wiring. The room had wooden floors and an area rug. A few pictures with American Indian motifs hung from the walls. I had my own private bathroom with a huge cast-iron bathtub, the type with claw feet. I wouldn't be taking a shower for a while.

There was a small bookshelf with a handful of paperbacks. None seemed to reach out and grab me. Still, it wouldn't be long before I picked one up to pass time. The room had two windows that came together in the northwest corner. I could see Okie piddling around his shop across the street to the north. I thought of how I'd like to shoot the grumpy old fucker and put him out of my misery but needed him too damn much. I looked west to watch the remnants of the sunset melting into the dusk of the rolling brown hills and decided on a hot bath to soak off the weather I had collected while driving the convertible.

I toweled myself dry before stretching out on the bed, exhausted from the day and relaxed from my steaming bath. The bath was good for my aching bones as well as my aching mind that had been fighting everything that had happened that day—actually, everything that had been happening for most of my life. I could never nap, but felt as if I had no choice, as if something else had taken over. I woke around seven that evening and after watering down my hair and combing it back, I went downstairs to see if I could get some dinner.

"Where's Sarah?" I asked, greeting Flo.

"Just missed her. Why?"

"I don't know. I guess if she's gone it's too late to eat?"

"Well things don't just stop because Sarah gets off work."

I don't know why I expected Flo to have changed her attitude; I was the one who had had the hot bath and nap.

"Can I get a French dip and a green salad, please?"

"What kind of dressing?"

I wanted to ask her what kinds of dressing she had, listen to her rattle them off and then ask her to repeat them, but I was too scared of her.

"Do you have Catalina or French?"

Flo just looked down her glasses over her nose and in a disgusted wake-up-dumb-ass you're-stranded-in-the-middle-of-nowhere look shook her head from side to side.

"I'll have the house dressing," I conceded.

Flo scribbled my request onto a pale green ticket, tore it from the book, snapped it under the clip of the chrome order-up wheel and spun it around.

"Order Jimmy. French dip, no fries. I'll take care of the salad on this side."

Jimmy was at least six and a half feet tall, but hunched over to six feet, having had to duck under everything for the last forty-two years of his sixty-year life. Jimmy wore a white faded T-shirt that was starting to unravel from wear, not over-washing. Under his tan colored, Big Ben work pants spurted his black Reebok tennis shoes that housed a pair of size fourteen feet. He had a grease-stained dingy white apron that for most people would cover their knees, but for Jimmy hardly cleared his waist. The slender face housed his deep, sad looking blue eyes, and his bridged nose made his eyes appear to be sunk further back into his head than they really were. With arms as long as Jimmy's, there wasn't room for another cook.

Jimmy slid my French dip under the hot lamp and slapped

the bell a few times, summoning Flo, but there was no sign of her. I finished the last few bites of my salad with the ranch style house dressing and decided that next time Flo was going to have to give me a bigger choice of dressings. Jimmy stretched his neck through the opening above the counter out into the dinning room to see if he could spot Flo.

I watched Jimmy's Adam's apple bob around over my French dip. He didn't shave it very well or couldn't shave around it and the graying whiskers protruded out around it like grass that grew out from under and around a rock. I waited for him to say something, knowing that if he did, he'd end up dipping his goiter in my au jus sauce. Not a peep came out of Jimmy, nor was there a sign of Flo.

A few minutes later, Flo walked in through the front door. She headed straight over to my sandwich, picked it up and set it down in front of me. The thought crossed my mind that this old bitch was testing me. Maybe she had walked out the back, around to the front and just stood there watching to see how I handled having to wait while my French dip went stale. I wasn't certain if she was actually fucking with me, but my mind sure wanted to believe it.

"Been putting out a fire?" I asked.

"Is it cold?"

"In here?"

"You know what I mean."

"No, its fine." The French dip was still warm, and if I hadn't watched it sit there, I never would have guessed it had been under the hot lamp for more than a minute, but 'its fine' was all I was giving her. I had no intention of fighting her, but I also wasn't about to rave about how delicious the dip was either. Besides, I'd lost a good portion of my appetite watching Jimmy's goiter dangling over my plate. I could only stomach about half the meal and pushed the rest aside.

"Eyes bigger than your belly?"

"Just like a hungry little boy who piles it on before his siblings have a chance at it," I said, indulging her.

"Sounds about right for you."

We both smiled at each other for the first time.

"Dessert?"

"Whatcha got?"

"Bread pudding with loads of California raisins."

"I'll pass on the dessert, but I would like a cup of coffee."

"Cream?"

"Low-fat or non-fat, please."

Flo reached into the refrigerator below the counter, pulled out a pint of half-and-half, and set it down next to my coffee.

"You'll have to pour it from the carton."

"Exactly how I do it at home."

I drank my coffee contemplating what I could possibly do for the evening and what I'd be doing if I were home. I thought about asking Flo for some suggestions, then reconsidered. I wasn't in the mood for another one of her smart-ass answers and didn't want to open myself up to another one of her attacks.

Instead of hanging out and drinking more coffee than I should, I decided to return to my room, to hang out with myself. Since there was no television, I tried to settle on a paperback, hoping to get lost in the drama of some other fool less fortunate than myself. Getting lost in the life of some fictional character in a paperback would have been great, but shuffling through the books, all I could find was the happily-ever-after-fairytale stuff that I'd given up on long ago. It was close to eleven when I decided to walk downstairs to look for the newspaper. Flo was sitting at the coffee counter when I stumbled off the last step.

"Whatcha need?"

"Couldn't sleep. Why are *you* up at this hour?"

"Tryin' to balance this checkbook, but now you made me lose my place."

"Sorry."

"Guess I need a break anyway. What's your excuse?"

"Don't know."

"This place too quiet for you?"

"Maybe. I feel... I don't know, maybe a little rejected tonight."

"Rejected?"

"Yeah, Janie never called back with her address and Jenny never called to get directions to my place for tomorrow, even if I won't be there," I explained as I went over to the coffee pot.

"And you don't have any others at your beck and call out

here either, do you?"

"Sure doesn't look that way," I answered, pouring a decaf.

"Guess I feel a little lonely, too."

"Yeah, problem is, when you're stuck out here, there's not many ways to escape it."

"I don't know. Something's not right, though."

"You're needy."

"I'm not needy."

"Yes you are."

"Bullshit."

"You're lonely."

"What?"

"You'd like to have a woman, but without any obligations."

"Without any obligations?" I asked.

"You don't want to have to fake it anymore! You don't want to worry about losing her because you can't fulfill her every wish and desire."

"I'm not worried about that."

"Yeah you are, but you don't want to get lost in her."

"I what?"

"Like tryin' to get your mother's attention, even if it was just a fleeting response."

"Don't drag my mother into this shit."

"I'm not."

"Yes you are."

"You just need to look at how you relate to women."

"How's that?"

"How many kids in your family?"

"Four boys."

"No sisters?"

"No sisters."

"No wonder you don't know how to have a woman in your life."

"Bullshit."

"Kid, I've seen a whole lot of grown men just like you that have a little boy trapped inside of them. A little boy who still runs the show."

"Yeah, right."

"The way you relate to a woman and the type of response

you usually get is like dope. If you don't get your fix, you go away mad, and if you do get your fix, you wake up in the next day longin' for more."

"You've lost me." I said, thinking about all the idle time Flo had for watching Oprah and reading self-help books.

Flo put her stack of bills and checkbook back into the clear Tupperware container, snapped on the blue lid and slid it under the counter below the cash register.

"I think we've had about as much of each other as we can stand for one day."

"I think you're right. Maybe even a little more," I answered, thinking about the suffering I was going to endure while the MG recuperated.

"Pleasant dreams," Flo said, walking back into the kitchen.

"Yeah, you too," I answered. Pleasant dreams; hell!

I headed up the stairs. When I walked into my room, I could see the lights from the parking lot shining inside. My boyhood bedroom had windows that came together in the northeast corner. I had no American Indian art dangling from my walls, but for some reason this place was stirring up old memories. I put on my sweats and a loose T-shirt before crawling into bed and drifting off.

Mom had once sent me to my room for something that I'd done wrong. I was pissed off, sitting on my bed that was under both windows. I got a pencil and left a note that said that I had run away, opened the window, and crawled under the bed. Not long after that, my mother started calling for me. When I didn't respond, she came looking for me. I watched her feet coming towards my bed, a few seconds passed before she discovered my fugitive status and proclamation of freedom from her tyrannical rule.

Mom climbed up on my bed and stuck her head out of the window yelling for me. I let her carry on for a few minutes with her idle threats and realized that she loved me in spite of herself, and I started belly laughing. I don't think she spanked me that time, but she damn sure didn't run off to cut me a piece of chocolate cake. I caught myself actually laughing out loud, but soon the image of Flo starring down at me through her glasses came back to me.

Flo was right; I'd had all of her that I could stand for one day. In fact I think I'd had enough of her to last a lifetime. Who made her the queen shrink anyway?

Chapter 3

Saturday

I slept soundly, once I got to sleep. I dreamed about a few old girlfriends, but nothing exciting. Of the fleeting passionate and erotic dreams that so rarely blessed a lonely night, my lovers appeared as unknown figures to me. I never remembered the details of seduction from or towards any of these images, but always recalled how after we had symbiotically melted together making love, she always seemed to evade me, leaving me in pursuit.

My waking life was usually the opposite. After making love to a woman, I ran like hell. There had only been a couple of women in my life with whom I had actually let myself go.

Lying in bed, I tried to plan my day. After emptying my bladder, I found my watch. It was eleven-thirty; I had slept long and hard. I wasn't hungry but needed coffee. It could be six in the morning or twelve noon when I woke up, but I always needed coffee. I slapped my John Deere hat on and walked downstairs.

"Well, well, well, look who we have here," Sarah greeted.

"Morning," I mumbled.

"For another ten minutes."

"For you, but mine's just started. Could I get a cup of coffee please?"

"I don't know, could you?" asked Sarah, as she filled my cup.

Some of Flo was oozing out on to Sarah, and she didn't wear it well. Flo didn't wear it well either, but she had been wearing it so long that her smart-ass suit was the only thing left that fit her.

"Thanks Flo... I mean Sarah. I'll bring the cup back down later."

I didn't raise a peep out of Sarah, so I knew that I'd jabbed her.

"I'll be back down in a while for lunch, after the regulars have left. That way I won't run off my mouth and anymore customers." I announced.

I went up to my room and drew a bath, emptying some shampoo into it for the bubbles. It never bubbled up like real bubble bath, but it was close enough to serve my needs. I climbed into the hot bath and stood in it for a minute waiting for my nerve impulses to register. Standing there naked, I looked up, discovering myself in the full-length mirror on the back of the half-open bathroom door. I took in the image of a standing, six foot, hundred-and-ninety pound bullfrog, long skinny legs and a fat-bellied short body. Good thing there wasn't a fly buzzing around the room.

I looked old: my bare-ass naked self, the hairy, long white legs, which ran up into my skinny thirty-eight-year-old buns. I stared at my shriveled up thing that in my mind never quite measured up. On top of my hips sat the hairy white skin of my sucked in belly. I had developed the habit of sucking it in and puffing out my chest when I was in Little League. After a game my mother told me that I had bad posture and needed to stand up straight. I thought that my midlife crisis goatee gave me character, but the two-day shadow around it really seemed to age me. I just shook my head and decided that it was probably safe to dunk my ass cheeks, and in I went soaking for about fifteen minutes to loosen up my stiff back.

I pulled a red cotton pocket T-shirt over my wet head, stepped into Levis and a clean pair of white, cotton, ankle high socks, before pulling on my Tony Lamas. I didn't care so much for country music, but my Tonys went everywhere I went. I remembered stepping off a 727 in a mid-January Michigan snowstorm in my cowboy boots on a trip to visit my brother years earlier; not once did they leave me busted ass on the black ice. I had sold several million dollars worth of tractors wearing my Tonys, and I'd be damned if I was going to give up a pair of boots that fit and had served me so well.

I shaved my shadow and ran an old vent brush through my thinning, but not-yet graying hair. After brushing my teeth, I let my Tonys lead me down to the coffee counter for Sarah to take my lunch order. There was no sign of Sarah or Flo when I sat down. I could see Jimmy's dingy white T-shirt and apron floating around behind the opening to the kitchen.

"Where's the girls?" I asked, hoping that he could hear me. Jimmy didn't respond.

"Dono," Jimmy finally answered after a couple of minutes had passed.

"Can I order some lunch?"

"What'll it be?"

"You pick. Whatever it is, just no onions and no bell peppers."

"What do you want?"

"Not to have to decide." And I didn't want to have to either. The women were gone, and as much as I hoped Sarah would be there, Flo not being there made up for my loss. I could eat my meal in peace. No words, no thinking, just peace and quiet. Someday, heaven, for me, would simply be peace and quiet.

A few minutes passed and Sarah came walking up to the counter, back from where the pay phone hung on the wall just outside the bathroom door. She walked with her head down and her arms crossed as if there was this come-on-snap-out-of-it dialogue going on inside of her.

"Here she is Jimmy. Hey Sarah."

The "hey" drew Sarah out of her trance and she looked up, shifting from a blank stare to a fake smile and then she quickly looked away. I could see where the tears had dried on the flesh just below her cheekbones. I wrestled with trying to rescue her with some words or keeping my mouth shut. Right then one of Jimmy's long arms delivered a steaming hot plate of something onto the stainless steel counter.

"Order-up." Jimmy wasn't boisterous, but the silence that hovered with Sarah's return made the words bounce through the diner.

Sarah set my lunch in front of me and quickly poured an iced tea with lots of ice and put it next to my plate along with napkin and silverware. What was on my plate wasn't offered on the menu. It was a T-bone steak with the juices still running out of it, a heap of steaming hot white rice, and a nice sized stem of broccoli. It was something that I might have fixed for myself on one of my semi-annual cooking sprees. One thing was certain: I didn't know about the rest of them, but the guy back in the kitchen was my friend. The best thing about it was that Jimmy told me so without having said a single, empty word.

I cut into my steak and savored it, curious of what was going on with Sarah. Where had she come from, and of all places, why was she here? What ran her or what was she running from? Something was causing her pain, but I had to fight rescuing her from what I believed I could rescue her from: her experience. The fix-it role had adopted me early on in my life and seemed to have stuck with me. I knew how to be in the world by fixing things, like other people's broken down machinery and broken down hearts.

Jimmy knew exactly what I needed, nourishment: the nourishment of a big fat juicy T-bone, not someone else's empty words. That's when I realized that Sarah could probably use the same.

"What time you off Sarah?" I asked instead of prying into her condition.

"Depends on the day."

"Today."

"I mean it depends on how busy we are."

Right then Flo walked up. "Looks like we're all caught up around here. I can handle it until dinner if you want to take a few hours Sarah."

"Good, I've got some things to do."

"Why don't you try to be back by five-thirty?"

"OK, thanks Flo."

Flo had the uncanny knack of busting up any potential fun that I could dream up. Damn, she pissed me off! It was as if she was sitting back there waiting for me to cross the line, walking in right before I could take that final step. The place was starting to seem like jail. Sarah grabbed her purse from under the register and hurried out to her blue Volkswagen Jetta.

"What's up with you, sleepy?" Flo asked.

"I'm rested and fed, just can't figure out what else to do with myself now that I've died and gone to heaven."

"Oh, you're a smart guy. I'm sure you'll figure it out," she said, standing cross-armed behind the cash register.

"What do you do to rent a car around here?"

"You borrow one."

"I see. What do you do after you've borrowed one and you can't get a date?"

"Leave her the hell alone," she said, staring down at me.

"Just checking."

"That will get you checked right out of here."

There wasn't a sweet bone in Flo's body. If there was, I'd yet to stumble across it.

"Flo, if you know of someone who's got a car I could use, I'd be happy to pay them some rent."

"There's an old white Chevy half-ton out back. Keys are by the back door," she answered, with her back to me, looking for something below the kitchen window.

"Thanks Flo."

"I mean what I said about Sarah," she reminded in a sharp tone, her back still to me.

I grabbed the keys from a hook and swung out the back door like an excited teenager ignoring his mother's advice. Getting the keys for the pickup was like drawing a get-out-of-jail free card. I didn't know where I was going, but I wasn't going to stick around that damn diner all day.

The truck was low on fuel, so I pulled into Okie's for gas. There was no distinction between self-service and full service, so I got out and pumped my own fuel. The quicker in and out of there, the less chance I had of starting a fight with the grumpy old fart. I filled the truck with twenty bucks worth and walked inside to pay.

"How much you get?" Okie asked, without looking up at me.

"Twenty even," I answered, throwing a twenty down on the counter. I grabbed a pack of gum and fished around in my pocket for change.

"Don't worry about it."

"About what?"

"The gum. It's on the house."

"Thanks," I said, leery of his generosity.

I walked back to the pickup, unsure of what had gotten

into Okie. The only conclusion that I could come up with was that he either had gotten laid or had been relieved of one of the aging toxic turds that the constipated old fart had been toting around inside him. Maybe the first led to the second. After checking the oil and finding it full, I started the pickup and pulled out of the station. When I gassed it to get on the highway it choked, backfired, coughed a little more, and then it was smooth sailing from then on. I drove west with no agenda.

I didn't have anywhere to go. I wasn't going home, and I didn't know anyone to go visit, so I just drove. I drove for a couple of hours, in and out of places just like where I was stranded. They all seemed to have a diner or a burger stand, a post office, a market or a gas station. Sometimes the market was the gas station; sometimes it was the other way around. The scenery just didn't seem to change. I guess Okie wasn't lying to me about running out and getting the radiator repaired. I had driven well over a hundred miles and there was no sign of a welding shop, let alone anyone who specialized in radiator repairs. I finally gave up and turned around to head back to wherever the hell I was staying.

The day wasn't much different than any other day in my life, even if I was a thousand miles from home. In one way or another, many of my days had been spent driving around in circles. Home did have a familiarity to it. I knew my way around, and I knew people. I had friends, even if I didn't pass much time with them. It was just knowing they were there, that I could hang around with them for a while, that was most comforting. So, here I was, stuck out in the middle of never-never-land, and I didn't have the comfort of running over to a friend's place for a thirty-minute bullshit session.

Most of the drive back, I kept thinking about how I was supposed to be with Jenny that weekend. I was thinking about her tits and how I wasn't to get a hold of them. Jenny was my twenty-one-year-old lover who I had met at a title company when I was selling a piece of property. An airplane ride to the coast for dinner and the rest was history. She was beautiful and she was built, but she lacked passion when it came to sex. I didn't know if it was because of me, because of her age, or because she just hadn't come into her own yet, but her tits helped make-up for what she lacked.

I also reflected on a few other old loves, wallowed in a longing that I just couldn't seem to shake. It was dark, well after nine when I got back to the diner. Flo was sitting in one of the big booths long ways as if she was lying on a couch watching some old black and white movie on television.

"Welcome home," Flo said, sitting up as I walked in.

"Home?"

"Welcome back then."

"Thanks."

"So the old bomb didn't fail you?"

"It choked up when I pulled on the highway after I gassed it up across the street, but after that she ran fine," I answered, walking up to the booth where she was sitting. "Probably picked up some water in his gas."

Flo shrugged off my last comment and asked: "Where'd you go?"

"A hundred miles from nowhere."

"I know where you left from. Where'd you go?"

"Like I said, a hundred miles from nowhere."

"Find anything of interest?" Flo asked, trying to coax a conversation.

"Can't remember."

"Get lost?" Flo asked.

"In my head. I should be home with Jenny right now," I answered, deciding to sit down across from her.

"What's so great about Jenny anyway?" she asked, standing up and walking over to the television that was mounted on the wall in the corner of the room.

"Can't really say," I lied, wanting to say her tits and hard young body.

"You really miss Jenny, or is it because you're stuck out here?" she asked, standing on a chair so that she could switch off the TV.

"Stuck I guess," I answered, thinking about the last time Jenny came over for the weekend. I ended up having to entertain her the whole damn time. I mean, it was one trivial question after another: such as what to eat or where to turn and the topper: "What's tortellini?" Man it wore on me. Most people didn't even bother themselves with concerns like Jenny's. It was as if she couldn't think for herself. She looked to me for approval or answers. She was a fine person and all. I wanted the best for her, but there was such an age difference, and my heart wasn't so keen on turning a girl into a woman.

"Stuck is what I thought," she said, walking back for the booth.

"I wouldn't mind being with her." Jenny's youth had a way of making me feel young. It felt empowering to have a younger woman looking up to me, sleeping with me. It was that she-wanted-me thing.

"I bet you wouldn't."

"She's safe."

"Safe?"

"Don't have to invest my heart."

"I see," she said, looking out the front window.

"Not with her anyway."

"Why not?"

"Too young. Maybe with a woman a few years older."

"Then do it."

"What?"

"Find a woman a few years older," she said, turning her gaze from the window towards me.

"I'm looking."

"You'll meet one that'll serve you."

"Serve me? I don't want that," I answered, confused.

"I mean you'll come together, serve each other."

"Doesn't sound like fun to me."

"I mean you won't take from each other. You'll give," she said, looking out of the window again.

"Sounds like a fairy tale," I answered, thinking here we go with that give shit. I'd rather be alone than have to worry about taking care of a woman.

"It won't be a duty. You'll want to."

"I'll believe it when I see it," I answered, thinking that it would have to be a whole lot different from anything I'd had before. I knew how to live alone. "I've learned how to steer clear of a mess."

"You also know how to miss out on life," she said, as a semi blew by on the desolate highway.

"I bet money that you pushed."

"Pushed?"

"Pushed the women in your life. Tried to make them into what you needed them to be," she said, pulling off her glasses and letting them dangle around her neck.

"So what if I want a woman to be a certain way."

"You're crazy."

"No I'm not."

"You can't make a woman fit into your idea of what she should be."

"I know. That's why I'm alone," I answered, unsure of what she was trying to make me into being.

"They develop over time."

"What does?" I asked, going over to the coffee pot.

"Relationships."

"Oh, relationships," I said, shifting into the world of relationship and pouring myself a stale cup of coffee. "Want some?" I asked.

"You have to allow them to become what they will," she said, shaking her head no to the coffee.

"I see," I answered, walking the coffee pot back to the burner, not really understanding and growing tired of her sermon.

"They're developed by lettin' people be true."

"True?" I asked, sitting across from her. True, truth, I'd heard these words a hundred thousand times; they had a hundred thousand different meanings.

"Yeah, like you and me right now," she said, pulling away from the table and leaning against the back of the booth.

"We're developing a relationship?"

"Sure! It may not be a love affair, but it's most certainly a relationship."

"This isn't a relationship."

"Probably the most honest one you've ever had with a woman."

"I don't know if I'd call this honest."

"Why not?" she asked, crossing her arms and pressing deeper into the back of the booth.

"I'm too damn scared to be honest with you."

"Why?"

"I can't afford to be. You'd boot my ass out of here."

"Tell you what, be honest with me, and I won't kick your ass out of this place."

"Yeah, right."

"You'd like to tell me to fuck off right now, wouldn't you?"

"I'm not that stupid."

"There, see?"

"What?"

"You view everything with the idea of gain or loss in mind," she answered, leaning forward and resting her forearms on the table.

"So what," I said, leaning back into the booth.

"You edit. Tell people what they want to hear, or what you think they want to hear."

"So you're saying I can tell you to get fucked anytime I feel like it?"

"Yep," she said, looking me dead in the eye.

"And you won't boot my ass out of here?"

"Nope," she answered, continuing her stare.

"So what if I told you that I'd love to get busy with Sarah?" I asked, testing the water, unable to hold back my grin. Flo was right, I had spent most of my life editing and being accommodating. Maybe this was a chance for me to fight with a woman without really having anything to lose beside a rented room and a place to eat while I waited for the constipated old fart across the street to get my MG repaired.

"I told you, leave Sarah alone," she warned in the same sharp tone that she used when she threw me the keys to the Chevy earlier in the day.

"See!"

"What do you really care if I run you out of here?" she asked, walking over to the stairs.

Flo was right about asking me what I had to lose. I had nothing better to do than stick around this place and fight with this old broad until she ran me off. She couldn't tap my bank account, and she couldn't cut me off because neither of these was on the chopping block. Big deal if she did give me the boot.

It would be like I had broken down, she didn't have a room, and I ended up poking cattle in my Tonys. Besides, she was an interesting study; I just might learn something. Other than being her sparing partner, she appeared to be a woman without an agenda. If she had one, I couldn't see it.

Chapter 4

Sunday

Jimmy was sitting at the counter, sipping something out of a stainless steel milk shake tumbler and reading the classified section of the Sunday paper when I walked down for my late morning coffee. The television was on, but muted so that we didn't have to suffer through the half-time bullshit session sports announcers get so excited about. There was another kind of silence; actually more like tranquility, not another soul was in the place.

"Morning Jimmy."

"Mornin'." Jimmy didn't bother looking up.

"Where's everybody?"

"Where you should be." Jimmy belly laughed.

I walked behind the counter and poured my own coffee. I didn't say anything. I wasn't sure if I should.

"Church," Jimmy said, after he'd finished laughing.

"Church?"

"Yep, every Sunday. Place don't open 'til noon."

"No shit? Man, I'd have never guessed that one."

"Best not to guess nothin' 'round this place."

"Guess you're right about that." I looked over at Jimmy who was grinning wide, but not turning to let me see him.

"You hungry?"

"Not yet, but curious as hell."

"I bet you are." Jimmy started to belly laugh again.

"What's the deal with Sarah?"

"Ran away from a husband."

"For?"

"I don't know. Maybe she was tired of gettin' banged up."

"Good enough reason for me."

"Maybe."

"You don't think a beating's reason enough for leaving?"

"It's a plenty good reason to run, but I really don't know if that's why she left him. Could've been about anything," Jimmy said, as he continued to cruise the classifieds. "But I'm sure it wasn't all him."

"Like maybe she was screwing around on him?" I asked.

"Could be, but I think it had more to do with a little yippin' dog."

"Oh, she's not one of those women who brings every stray dog she comes across back home is she?"

"More like maybe she could be one of 'em," Jimmy said, as he turned the page.

"What do you mean?"

"You know, one of them mutts that's always nippin' at your ankle. Pissin' and moanin', nothin's ever good enough."

"OK," I said, getting the picture Jimmy was painting.

"It doesn't give a man the right to hurt someone, but women do have a way of provokin' a man at times," Jimmy reminded.

"Yeah, I hear you."

"They can drive you right to the edge."

"I had my chance when I was married, but didn't do it. Let the opportunity slip past me."

"What are you talkin' 'bout?" Jimmy asked.

"Prozac. Had a sinus infection, so my doctor called in an antibiotic and the goddamn drug store filled it with Prozac."

"They what?"

"Filled my Ceclor prescription with Prozac. The same drug company makes both and the pharmacy got the bottles mixed up when they filled my prescription. I took that shit for three days. Thought I was going wacky."

"How'd you figure it out?"

"Went and got the prescription bottle and poured the pills in my hand and read P R O Z A C. That's when I called my mother. She's a registered nurse. Asked her if Prozac was generic for Ceclor."

"No shit?"

"No shit, and I missed my chance. I could have put my mutt

to sleep, pleaded postal and walked. Hell, I could have even written a book about it afterwards. I wouldn't be here today traipsing across the country peddling tractors if I'd have been smart enough to let the Prozac take over."

Jimmy looked at me this time when he started grinning. "You're a half crazy little fucker aren't you?"

"Only half Jimmy. Just like everybody else."

The blue Jetta pulled in up front. Flo got out, and Sarah drove off. Flo waltzed up to the front door all dolled up in her Sunday duds. She almost seemed to float in, but when she saw us sitting there her feet hit the ground and her angelic glow faded to a what-the-hell-are-you-looking-at stare. She didn't say a word, just walked right past us and up the stairs.

"Don't you want to know nothin' 'bout Flo?"

"I wasn't really thinking about her Jimmy."

"Maybe you should start."

"Later, Jimmy, later."

"Just don't say nothin' about church to her. You can cuss and you can scream. You can make a royal red ass of yourself all you want, but stay away from her churchin'."

"How about a cheeseburger, Jimmy?"

"You got it."

Jimmy stood and walked into the kitchen, tied on his short-waisted, dingy apron and fired up the grill.

I heard Jimmy. I knew that he was serious about Flo and church. I wasn't all that curious about it anyway. I wouldn't have brought up her religion knowing how private and what a foundation church could be for people. To screw with their foundation was like robbing them of their inheritance. People get real pissed when you screw with their inheritance, real or ethereal.

I ate my cheeseburger and decided that it was time to go drive around in circles for a while. I drove back across the street for gas. I pumped another twenty bucks worth and walked inside to settle with Okie.

"What have we got today?"

"Another twenty," I answered, setting a bill down on the counter in front of Ol' Deadeye, thinking about how much money this old fucker was dragging out of me.

"Where ya headed?"

"Don't know."

"Just burnin' gas, huh?"

"You got it," I answered, without giving him anything else. I didn't like the crusty old fart. All I wanted was gas. I didn't want to have to justify my fuel burning habits. What the hell did he care; it was another twenty in his pocket. I gassed the truck, pulled on the highway, and it backfired again. That's when I realized that my car might be stuck there, but I wasn't. There was nothing keeping me from buying gas elsewhere, even if it was fifty miles out of my way.

I didn't have to drive a hundred miles to feel lonely. I felt it before I left. I also felt agitated and had gotten that way between the time I had left the diner and fueled the truck. Something had set me off, and I think it was that fucking Okie. I was trying to figure if it was something he'd said or if it was just the fact that he had the power of getting or not getting my MG repaired. Following fate, I took the first northbound road that looked like it might be paved for more than just a hundred feet.

I was hoping it would lead me to a blue Jetta, but instead it dead-ended at a cattle guard with barbed wire fences on both sides. I drove over the crossing and kept going north on the dirt road. I drove another five miles and there it was: a river. There was a Ford truck parked along the riverbank. It was dry where I had come from, and it appeared to be just as dry across the river. It was rangeland, summer rangeland, clad with remnants of scrub brush. The river cut through the middle of this high dessert with a few small trees and bushes sprouting from its banks, but it was mostly gravel and small smooth boulders, few of them bigger than a bowling ball. Occasionally I spotted a larger boulder big enough to serve as a seat for a tuckered out angler. Walking along the river, I came across a man in his mid-sixties just stepping out of the water in his neoprene waders.

"Do any good?"

"Raised one here and there."

"What kind of fly?"

"Muddler's all I fish with."

"What size hook?"

"A two hook."

"That's a damn big fly."

"Not for a damn big fish." The fisherman grinned, and I knew that his eyes, hiding behind his polarized find-the-fish-in-the-water sunglasses, had to be twinkling.

"That's what I like to hear. What kind of wading boots you got on there?"

"They're spiked. Tungsten carbide spikes," the angler explained.

"I've got felt bottom wading boots."

"Yeah, they're good in most rivers, but its mossy here, and the water moves pretty fast through some of these chutes. Fast water and mossy boulders is what sold me these spiked boots."

"Can you get by without them?"

"You can do anything you want kid, but now you know everything I know."

"Where are the fish holding?"

"Muddlers, big muddlers, and fish them anytime of the day you like; spiked boots for the mossy boulders in the fast water. As far as where the fish are, you'll have to find that out for yourself," the old boy explained in a matter of fact tone.

"Thanks, good luck."

"There's a hardware store about fifty miles west on the highway that sells the spikes. They'll take your money, wet or dry. They don't care."

He was my kind of angler. No need to exchange names or pleasantries. In the world of fishing, names didn't really matter. What mattered was the information a guy was willing to share, and I'd received plenty of it. It was a pretty safe bet to fish a muddler pattern, and spikes were not an option. What I respected the most about this guy was that he didn't reveal were he'd been catching fish. If he had, I wouldn't be fishing a muddler and the fifty-mile trek to the hardware store wouldn't be on my agenda.

Thanks to my father, I'd been fishing since I was old enough to hold a fishing rod, but I'd only been fly-fishing for a few years and very infrequently. What I enjoyed so much about fly-fishing was my inexperience. I didn't know what I was doing, and I didn't feel the need to master it. I'd just grab my gear and go when I felt like fly-fishing. I'd usually stop at a local tackle shop to ask a lot of dumb questions about the local fishing habits and get sold the stuff that nobody else was stupid enough to buy.

When I hooked a fish on a fly, it wasn't because I knew what I was doing; it was because the fish gods were smiling on me. I wish I had learned to approach the rest of my life like I did my fly-fishing.

I had found my church. Now all I had to do was get to the trunk of the MG for what fishing gear I'd thrown in before I left home and visit the hardware store before the next worship service. I spent most of the afternoon scouting the river. I started feeling hungry and decided to head for the diner. On the drive back I realized that the river had washed away my loneliness and agitation, at least for that service.

When I got back to the diner, Flo was sitting in her booth watching the Wheel of Fortune.

"Hi Flo."

"Hey kid, what's up?"

"Fishing! I found the river."

"Didn't know you were into fish."

"I'm hot and cold, depends on what else is in my life. Looks as if I'm gunna go into it all the way for a while."

"Sounds good."

"Where's Jimmy?"

"He left. Things were slow, so I gave him the boot early. Why, you hungry?"

"Starving, but I wanted to take a hot bath first."

"There's stuff for sandwiches. Help yourself when you're ready. Just make sure you clean up afterwards."

"OK, I'll be back down in a while."

It was getting too easy. I had a truck to drive, a place to fish, a place to sleep, a place to eat, and I was stuck, so I didn't have to worry about work. I guess I could have worried, but it wasn't going to change anything.

I squeezed some shampoo into the bottom of the tub and turned on the bath water as hot as my old buns could take. I soaked until I couldn't take the heat any longer. I looked out of the north window while toweling myself dry. My agitation from earlier in the day returned. I hung the towel over the door to dry, and slipped on a pair of sweats so that I could go down to make my sandwich. Flo was still watching television, the Sunday night movie.

"You hungry, Flo?"

"No. Help yourself, though."

It was going to be kind of fun. I hardly ever waited on myself. Ninety-nine times out of a hundred I was sitting on the other side of the coffee counter. I found some cheese, the white kind with seeds and wrapped in red wax coating. I found a turkey breast already sliced, so I dragged that out of the big stainless steel refrigerator along with the container of cottage cheese. I dropped a couple of wheat bread slices into the toaster. When the lightly toasted bread popped up, I grabbed it and laid on a thin slice of cheese, then over it, the turkey breast. I dropped another thin slice of cheese over the turkey and slid the whole concoction into a toaster oven. I found a plate and scooped a mound of cottage cheese to one side, minus the parsley or wilted lettuce leaf that usually accompanied it.

The toaster oven dinged, and when I opened it, the smell of freshly toasted bread and melting cheese almost made me forget the old prick across the street. I walked over and sat down in the booth opposite Flo.

"Smells pretty tasty."

"It's the cheese," I answered. My grandmother used to get cheese like this from the Dutch bakery. Sometimes after church she'd slice some up for us. We always had our dessert before lunch. When she had cheese, she'd slice some of it up, too.

"Want coffee?" Flo asked.

"Sure, thanks."

Flo got up and grabbed two cups and the pot. She poured the cups and then set the pot down on the table.

"How's your dinner?"

"Great. What's hard to swallow is that goddamn Okie across the street and my MG."

"Yeah, it's your will," Flo said, and then laughed a short nervous chuckle.

"My will?" I asked, paying more attention to her laugh.

"Still willin' yourself to be somewhere you're not."

"So."

"So what can you do about it?" she said, her nervous chuckle shifted to an impatient laugh. I could sense her frustration with me again.

"Not a thing. Just wait, I guess," I responded, not to spur her aggravation.

"That's right. Okie knows his business. Take a back seat for awhile."

"Yeah but..."

"Yeah but nothin'. Just slow down. You don't know the first thing about that little hot rod. Just let him fix the damn thing for you."

"I just wish he..."

"Quit wishin'. I know it's hard to sit back and not be in control, but..."

"But..."

"Stop it!"

"So he can screw me?"

"That old fart isn't gunna screw you. Just worry about that fish for a change."

"Fish and forget the car, huh?"

"Leave Okie alone. It's one thing if he needs to talk to you, otherwise, stay out of his way."

Chapter 5

Monday

I woke up feeling lonely the next morning. I had called Janie earlier in the week and hadn't heard from her since. A good number of the women who had come into my life were born in September. My high school sweetheart's birthday was the next day. Jenny, my current lover, the ex-wife—Shelly, and Lauren, the biggest heartbreak of my life, also had birthdays this month. I had even married Shelly in September. They'd all passed from my life, but impulsively I continued to read their horoscope every morning just to see how my day was going to go.

Thoughts of Lauren still invaded my mind and weaved their despairing threads around my heart even though we had been apart for over four years. I just couldn't shake off the "what if" of Lauren. It had a way of making me feel very lonely and doubt my ability to be enough of a man for her or any woman. Why didn't Lauren fight for me? Was I of value to any woman? I often found myself in that what-can-I-do-to-make-her-love-me complex.

I ran the bath even though I had just bathed the night before. I liked to take a bath at night to soak away the day's tensions, and enjoyed one in the morning to bring me back to life. On this particular morning, I was bathing to limber up and to soak off the slime that I had accumulated during the night. Sometimes I woke up that way; other times it could just be a scent, a sound, or the smile of another woman that sent me back to an old love. I guess it didn't matter when or how it happened as much as it just happened. I was getting better at catching it though. I caught it early that morning, scrubbed it off, and watched it swirl down the drain of that big old bathtub, slurping for one last gasp of air. I had fishing to do, and there was no way in the world to catch a fish with the bittersweet scent of an old love's perfume oozing from me. I dressed and headed downstairs.

Jimmy was carting in the produce through the back door from the delivery truck's biweekly drop off.

"Morning Jimmy."

"Mornin'." Jimmy looked at me with a puzzled stare. "What's your story, up this early?"

"Fishing."

"Don't give me that fishin' shit."

"Really, I stumbled on the river yesterday. Talked to a guy who was fly-fishing. There're some big trout out there."

"You see any?"

"No, but who cares?"

"I've been around these parts for years and haven't seen trout of any size come out of that river."

"You ever fish that river, Jimmy?

"Once."

"Get any?"

"Sure didn't, but that don't mean much either. Give it a try."

"Oh, I will."

"Tell you what. You bring fish back; I'll clean 'em and cook 'em."

"Fair enough," I answered, knowing that I wouldn't be bringing my catch back to the diner. I was a catch and release man.

I had to get my spikes and muddlers, so after hopping into the Chevy, I headed for the hardware store several miles west of the diner. I drifted off, back to my spill at Cable Crossing on the North Umpqua River eleven years earlier. I hadn't forgotten that brush with death. I was almost mid-river when I went down. The water was just over my knees, and every step I took closer to the luring hole on the other side of the river, the stronger the current became. I turned around to Tom and Kent, my fishing partners, and yelled to them, asking something about what they thought of fishing that deep hole on the other side of the river. Tom just kind of shrugged. What I was really asking was if he thought it was safe, but the words came out differently because I didn't want to appear a coward.

The steering wheel of the Chevy started jerking, pulling me to the right. My tire was already over the shoulder. Instead of horsing it back and possibly rolling the truck, I let off the brakes and gas pedal, coasting to a stop. After a few deep breaths, I pulled back onto the highway and proceeded to drive back on track, back to my ride down the Umpqua.

Two more steps after talking to Tom I went down. I stood up and went down again. When the current pulled me down the third time, there was no riverbed to support me. I had been whisked into one hell of a deep hole; the kind where the river narrows and the only way water can flow is downward. I had been swept into an underwater canyon. There were no white water rapids, just fast spinning, swirling water funnels that liked to suck wader-clad, heavy-booted, foolish fly-fishermen down to an underwater grave. My salvation was that my waders had torn an hour or so earlier. I had decided to take them off and just use the heavy wading boots.

My lips and nose were the only parts of me above water, and I remember thinking to myself, twenty-seven years old and this is it. That's when I made my deal with God about giving up anything and everything if I could just get out of this one. Then the will to live took over, and I started to fight. As fate would have it, my fighting was in the form of swimming with the current, not against it, and I made it to a small rock sticking up out of the Umpqua. The current was so fast that I couldn't hold onto what I believed to be my salvation and was swept back into the rushing waters. I was finally pushed into a back eddy and was gently swirled onto a cluster of rocks. I pulled myself out of the water, my left hand in a death-grip still holding the fishing rod. Tom and Kent had been helplessly stumbling down the jagged riverbank trying to help me, willing me to escape dry and unscathed and standing next to them on shore.

"You saved the rod!" yelled Kent in amazement from down river.

"Fuck the rod!" rolled off of my tongue unconsciously.

I wore a fanny pack, and inside were some personal items, along with my mother's camera that I had borrowed. I was lying back on a rock, trembling, trying to catch my breath. Tom was the first to catch up to me. It had been just over a year since I had gotten out of rehab. I pulled out a one-year sobriety medallion from the drenched fanny pack.

"Are you all right?" Tom asked

"Guess I get to go for year number two, huh?" I said, grinning and trembling with the medallion pinched between my thumb and index finger of the hand that hadn't been gripping the fly rod. It was July 5th, 1988. I ate spaghetti that night and it was the sweetest meal that I had ever tasted. I remembered the meal like it was yesterday, but the deal I made with God was still sitting at that dinner table, wrapped up in the napkin I used to wipe the spaghetti sauce from my face that night.

I promised to give up everything just for another chance at life, but I walked away from that promise just as I had walked away from death that day. What was so different on July 5th, 1988 than any other day, except for the few drops of death I had breathed in while sucking for air on my ride down the Umpqua? The difference was that almost every day, besides that day, I had taken life for granted. I had forgotten what it was like to savor every single strand of spaghetti that I slurped up that night. My passion and zest for life were left crumpled up in that napkin. I had to get spikes and get back into the water. I had to catch something.

I woke from the daydream of my ride down the North Umpqua when I stepped from the white Chevy pickup after parking in front of the hardware store. It was a newer style metal-sided building and had windows running the length of the entire north side with two side-by-side aluminum framed glass doors right in the middle. In the window to the right of the door there was an announcement printed on red construction paper about a rigatoni-feed that was to take place the following Saturday, benefiting the local T-ball league who were in need of uniforms. There was nothing in the window to the right except for specks of fly shit and a BB hole that some kid had probably shot up on his late night rounds.

Inside there was an old wooden desk just to the left of the front doors with a two-burner industrial style coffee maker, the back of the machine facing the window. Placed in the window next to the coffee pot was a cork-type bulletin board with a few business cards and fax paper copied cartoon that somebody had sent the hardware store. There were a few chairs and a wooden bench circled around the coffee pot that supported the ass-ends of four or five locals. I had to walk through the camped out locals in order to get to the counter at the back of the store. They carried on as if I hadn't even walked through the middle of their conversation. According to the remnants of the forum that I made out on my way to the back counter, it seemed that the hardware store doubled as city hall.

A thin brunette woman with a few strands of gray dragged on a cigarette, I guessed her to be in her mid-forties. She looked up at me from behind a computer screen sizing me up; although, she and the local ass-ends had actually sized me up long before I walked through those double doors.

"How can I help you?"

"I ran into a guy on the river yesterday. He said you might have some fishing gear."

"We got some. Whatcha lookin' for?"

"For starters, I'm gunna need an out-of-state license." That put an end to the local's rhetoric. Now that they had the potential for a new drama with a foreigner, they could set aside their own gossip for something fresh.

"We got one-day, three-day, or full season licenses. We're out of the ten-day passes."

"How much for a three-day or full season?"

"Three-day is twenty-two, full season is sixty-eight bucks."

"What about spikes and muddlers?"

"Got the slip-on spikes, kind that ties up over your boots. I've got a few muddlers, but I don't know what you plan to do with muddlers."

"Same thing I plan to do with everything else I'm here for."

"Spikes and a license will keep you dry and without a fine, but the muddlers I've got here are so old that the glue's crystallizin' and the hackle's fallin' out like old Duane Fairmore's locks. Isn't that right, Duane?"

"Yeah, whatever you say, Julie. You're right Julie. You're always right."

"I'll take what you've got as long as it's a two hook or bigger." That got the old farts up front percolating again. I could hear them snickering about another Californian chasing his high hopes halfway across the nation.

"OK, I've got half a dozen number two muddlers. Since they're fallin' apart, I'll give them to you. Now I need to know what size spikes you want."

"Eleven."

"You sure? Seems to me that those boots aren't all the same."

"I've got them in the truck. Should I get them?"

"Probably be best."

"I'll be right back."

I walked up front and through the middle of the ass-ends. They were quiet, hardly moved. When I walked back with my boots, I think they were all still on the same breath of air they had inhaled when I walked outside. I thought about pouring a cup of coffee just to cause a discomfort and then shied away from the idea and walked back to Julie.

"Let's see what you've got there," Julie said, as she took my boots and then sized them to the spikes. "Size twelve. These ought to work just fine. Now, what did you decide about a license?"

"I'll take the season pass," I answered. It usually proved cheaper in the long run; I'd gone through three-day fishing licenses in the past like candy.

"OK, I need you to fill out this form." She rang me up on a real old-fashioned, bronze-colored cash register. "That'll be eighty-eight bucks."

"Can I put it on a credit card?"

"Depends on two things. It has to be a Visa or MasterCard, and it has to be good. I don't have any of those electronic scanner devices, and I'm not gunna sit on hold for thirty minutes to find out that you're a flake."

She didn't bat an eye as she watched for my reaction. I handed her the MasterCard. She tripped the old mechanical imprinter with my card inserted under the carbon copy duplicate charge form.

"All I need is your signature right here." She pointed to the X she had marked on the signature line.

"Say, do you have any straw hats?"

"Should be one left up on the rack over where we got your

spikes."

I walked back over to where she had pointed. "Great, I'll just pay for this with cash. How much?"

"Five bucks."

I laid a five down on the counter. "Thank you very much."

"Thank you. Good luck." I walked back through the ass-ends who were still sitting in the center of city hall. Just as I was on my way out, Julie hollered: "Hey mister, you want your carbons?"

I stuck my head back inside the door, and instead of answering back to Julie I looked to the ass-ends. "Did you guys hear what she said?"

"She's worried that you might want your credit card carbons so you don't get ripped off," one of them answered.

"Why would I be worried about that around here?" I asked, with a puzzled look of naive innocence and then let the door swing shut before anyone could respond.

I walked to the truck without looking back and tossed my newly purchased goods on the seat and climbed in. I'd have liked to pour myself a coffee and bullshitted with the locals, but I knew better. I was a local myself, and I knew how I treated lost souls who stumbled into my life looking for directions. I knew what it was like not to want to make new friends, especially when all they wanted was to take and give nothing in return. It's that phony friendly how's-it-going-good-old-buddy-old-pal-you-don't-mind-if-I-fuck-your-daughter-now-that-I've-got-to-know-you-over-the-last-ten-minutes-do-you attitude that made me want to grab a great big aerosol can of insect repellent and beat the guy over the head. With locals like these guys, you got to know them if, and when, they were ready.

I started the truck and headed back in the direction from where I had come. I was tired. I had only been awake for a few hours, but I was still tired. For some reason, being a stranger in need of something and walking into a place like that hardware store had zapped me. Since the river was only a few miles west of the diner, I decided to go back for a late lunch and then head out for an evening run at those big browns and rainbows. An hour later, I pulled into the diner and headed in to get refueled.

I sat up at the coffee counter. Jimmy was back in the kitchen, and Flo was working the floor. Flo walked up, scooped a glass full of ice, and poured my tea.

"Heard you went fishin'."

"Haven't made it that far yet. Had to drive to the hardware store in Tranquillity to pick up some gear."

"Julie get you fixed up?"

"You know her?"

"I've got occasional hardware needs, too."

"Yeah, I guess you would know her. I got the gear I needed, but, no, she didn't get me fixed up." I picked up my iced tea and took a drink to hide my smile.

"You want lunch?" Flo asked, ignoring my comeback.

"Yeah, I'd like a tuna melt on wheat and a scoop of cottage cheese."

Flo wrote up the order and snapped it under the clip of the wheel just as Jimmy was approaching the window. Flo turned her back on the wheel and started wiping up the counter a few chairs down from me where two older men had just walked away having finished their afternoon coffee. Jimmy looked out of the window, nodded his head and winked at me behind Flo's back. My sandwich was ready in no time. Flo plopped it down in front of me and refilled my ice tea.

"Where's Sarah?"

"Her day off. Why?"

"Just wondered. I hadn't seen her."

Flo didn't respond and went back to the vacuum cleaner that she had turned off after being interrupted by someone wanting to order a late lunch. I ate while she vacuumed. I hated noise and hated the stale smell of vacuum bag dust that the cleaner re-circulated every time the thing was fired up because the damn bag hadn't been changed since it was new. I finished my tuna melt, and if it hadn't been for the noise and that real fine, stale dust that crept up into my nostrils and down the back of my throat, lunch would have been just fine. A few minutes later, Flo locked the handle into the upright position and crisscrossed the electrical cord around the plastic ears that were bolted to the chrome tube that separated the vacuum cleaner from its handle.

"Can I get you anything else?" Flo asked, as she walked up

after putting the vacuum away.

"No, that'll do it. Hey, Flo, what's the scoop on Sarah? I mean what's her story?"

"Sarah's story doesn't concern you," she answered in the usual sharp tone that accompanied my Sarah inquiries.

"Look, I respect you keeping an eye on Sarah. I'm just curious about her, that's all."

"Oh, so now you've developed a little respect, have you? Don't give me that respect shit. You just want to weasel your way closer to Sarah. I told you to leave her alone."

"I can't help it if I'm a man, and I think she's hot. Big deal."

"You just want to mess with Sarah because you're stuck here and she's the only thing around that you've got to chase."

"So what?"

"So get her yourself. I'm not gunna help you run off my help."

"I'm not gunna run off your help."

"If I give you the skinny on Sarah, you'll just weasel your way into her and then you'll hit and run."

"I just want to get to know her a little."

"You don't want to know Sarah. You just wanna play with her while you're stuck out here in the middle of nowhere."

"You don't know what I want."

"I know your kind."

"My kind? Come on, you mean men, period."

"If Sarah is just another toy-thing for you, you can hit the road right now."

"What are you trying to protect her from?"

"Assholes like you who don't know what they want. One day you want this, the next day you want something else."

"Yeah, right. You think I'm only interested in Sarah because she's wounded."

"I think you're only interested in fuckin' Sarah."

Fuck Flo and her self-righteous insights. I decided to act like the lying, conniving little boy she was accusing me of being.

"Yeah, yeah, yeah. Hey, Flo, what's Flo short for?"

"Florence, after my grandmother. My real name's Emmaline, but my father started calling me Flo when I was still a baby," she answered, looking confused.

"Emmaline? Hell, no wonder he nicknamed you Flo." Now I had her back on the school playground where I could be the conniving, insulting, rotten hurtful little bastard that she was accusing me of being.

"What's wrong with Emmaline?"

"What's wrong with your mother and your father?" I asked; it was now my turn to deal the parent card.

"Nothin', wha…"

I knew I had her when she started to stutter. "I'm sure that your mother was the one who wanted to name you Emmaline, and your dad just went along with it instead of fighting your mom. Then he called you what he liked, and your mom got her way."

"You arrogant little bastard. You don't know a thing about my parents."

"You're right about that, but I do know that naming your daughter Emmaline is real close to naming your son Penrod."

"Fuck you! It's no where near being named Penrod."

"You're the one who asked for honesty. Just being honest," I flipped back at her.

"You spoiled brat, you don't know the first thing about honesty," Flo fired back.

"Through your eyes," I answered, slapping back a dose of her medicine.

"You know how to lie and manipulate, but you don't know the first thing about being real with a woman!"

"Yeah, whatever you say."

"You're a wounded little boy or some knight in shining armor around women. You seek out the wounded ones who you can manipulate, women that need to be rescued."

"You're all wounded when it serves you."

"You're a self-centered little bastard!"

"I'm sure it has something to do with my mother."

"Yeah, I know why you're the way you are, and it's time to get over it."

"Yeah, whatever." Now I had her really humming. I hadn't pissed off a woman that good for quite a while. It was nice to know that I still had it in me. What I really liked about pissing them off was walking away from them right in the middle of a fight. Walking away when they're screaming robs them of any power they think they have over a man.

"I need a break," I announced to deliver the last punch.

"You need a brain, not a break," belched out Flo.

"No, wrong again. I need to catch a fish." I got up and walked to the pickup, climbed in, fired her up and headed for a weekday-afternoon-church-service out on the river.

It worked. I was tired of giving in to Flo. I was tired of her righteousness, thinking she had all the answers. I'd be damned if I was going to cave in to her view of me. She didn't know me as well as she wanted to believe she did.

Chapter 6

Monday Afternoon

I wasn't more than a half a mile from the diner when I crossed paths with the blue Jetta. I didn't hit the brakes, but I let off the gas to slow down as I watched her in the rearview mirror. Sarah pulled into the gas station. That's when I decided that the old bastard was going to snooker me out of another twenty bucks, so I whipped the half-ton Chevy around for a fuel stop. Sarah was just slipping the nozzle back into the gas pump when I pulled into the other side of the fuel island. It was just like that old fucker to make her pump her own gas. She watched me pull in, and instead of walking off to pay for fuel, she grabbed the window scrubber and started washing her windshield.

"Hi there," I said, walking up to unscrew the gas cap.

"Oh, it's you. Hi there," Sarah replied in the innocent-girl-playing-dumb routine.

"I was headed out to the river and noticed the low fuel gauge; decided to gas up instead of chancing the night out in the middle of nowhere."

"Thought I just passed a truck like this one," she said, smiling just to let me know that she was on to me. "What's out at the river?"

"A fish," I said, looking away from Sarah and into the window of the service station. The old fart was leaning cross-armed on top of the red crank-type candy dispenser that collected quarters for the Seeing Eye dog foundation. He was staring right at me.

"A fish, huh?"

Sarah's "huh" is what woke me. "I'm sorry, Sarah, couldn't hear you," I said, wishing the old fucker would just mind his business, particularly the business of getting the goddamn

MG fixed.

"A fish, huh?" Sarah repeated.

"Yeah, stumbled on the river yesterday. Ran into a guy fishing out there. Decided to try my luck." I walked over and grabbed the other window scrubber and went to the passenger side of the Jetta's windshield.

"Oh I can get that."

"I'm sure you can," I said, picturing the way she had reached and dragged that squeegee across her window had told me she could "get that" and a lot more. I watched her go up on her left tiptoe and swing her right leg back out in the air about half a foot off the ground reaching for the center of the windshield and then come back down. Sarah had an ass-end to die for. If I owned that gas station I'd have been paying Sarah fifty bucks an hour to be washing windows. She'd have a line of traffic a mile long backed up along that desolate highway waiting to pay the old bastard for his overpriced gas.

"Thanks," Sarah smiled, her head cocked to the side a little. A sparkle in her eyes glimmered like a candle flame that had just been creased with a light breeze.

"My pleasure," I nodded

"Well, I better go pay my bill," she said, grabbing the wallet out of her purse that was lying on the front passenger seat of her car. I watched her glide on in to settle-up with the old fart. She wore those faded Levi's like a party dress, I'm telling you. All that I could think about was finding a good enough reason to celebrate helping her out of them, until I looked and saw Okie still leaning over the gumball machine. Here this beautiful young woman was walking in to give him her money, and he was looking right past her as if she didn't even exist. He just stared at me, not a smile, not a frown, just a flat blank expression.

Sarah paid him and walked back out to her Jetta.

"Good luck," she said, as she opened the car door.

"Thanks."

"See you later."

"I sure hope so," I teased.

"Yeah, I bet you do," she quickly snapped back with one of her beaming smiles.

"Have fun," I said, not even knowing why I said it. "Have

fun," was something that I had picked up from an old buddy of mine. He was a flight instructor who, between helping people learn to fly and repairing airplanes, loved to chase women. Hal had helped me get my pilot's license several years ago. There was something about that "have fun" of his that stuck with me. It was Hal's have fun attitude toward life, which meant, "I hope you get laid," that was so appealing to me.

Sarah drove off, and I finished fueling the Chevy. I walked into settle up with Okie and threw another twenty down on the counter.

"That's three days in a row. You keep burnin' gas like that you might run out of money to fix that little hot rod of yours."

"I thought you were about to offer a volume discount."

"Son, I can fill a motor home with five times what that old Chevy holds and never have to see 'em again. I don't discount gas, but if I did, it'd be to one of those thirsty Winnebagos."

I wanted to ask him about the MG, but I shut up. I didn't want to give him any more power over me than he already had. Right then, I wished I was the fool driving one of those Winnebagos, because then he'd only be squeezing a single hundred out of me. He'd get it once, and I'd get the hell out of Ol' Deadeye's life without having to face him everyday, along with his smart-ass comments about my gas burning habits. I didn't say another word to him. I just turned around and walked out to the Chevy.

When I gassed the truck to get on the highway the half-ton did its normal routine of choking on the stale water from Okie's gas tank. After sputtering a couple times, it was smooth sailing towards the river. Sarah was different. She hadn't been under the spell of Flo's scrutinizing critical spirit. There was a freedom about Sarah that day. A freedom that was very appealing to me, that and the way she fit into those Levis. There was something really wholesome about Sarah, something nice.

I made a right turn, drove down to the river road, and rumbled over the cattle guard. That guard was a line of demarcation. It was where I left the asphalt world of human development and exploitation behind. It was a passageway into an older, undisturbed era where I found the permission to experience the quietness my soul longed for. I pulled up to the river and parked.

There was no sign of another fisherman, not anyone. I hopped out of the truck, walked to the tailgate, dropped it, sat down, pulled on my waders, and tied on my boots.

Struggling with the unfamiliar tie-on spikes, I finally got them mastered and attached to my boots. The spikes were set in a heavy black rubber sole. Attached to the sole were straps about an inch long with a loop on the end. The loops were like eyelets that allowed for a cord-type, shoelace to be crisscrossed over the wading boots after stepping onto the spike sole. It was a very unconventional design, but I finally got them tied on after being bent over for what seemed half a day. As I straighten upright, I almost fell. Fortunately the tailgate was still down and it caught me, rescuing me from a spill. I didn't get dizzy very often, but for some reason it had crept up on me.

I zipped up my inflatable Sterns fishing vest. It looked like a regular fishing vest for pride's sake, but inside of it was a CO_2 cartridge that, with one yank on the red handled cord that was attached, quickly transformed the vest into a fully inflated life preserver. Tom and Kent gave it to me for Christmas that same year that I had scared the shit out of all of us on my North Umpqua Cable Crossing swimming lesson. I drove fifty-thousand miles a year and flew airplanes through instrument meteorological weather conditions never questioning my mortality, but Old Man River had tamed me, and I never tempted him without my security blanket.

I pieced my fly rod together, slid the reel into the rod cradle and tightened the threaded shaft with the rounded nut that held it in place. I ran the floating line through the eyelets on the rod and after looking over my leader and finding it intact, tied on one of the decaying muddlers that Julie had gifted me. I put on the straw hat before starting my trek to the river. There was a breeze blowing from the west in the same direction that the river flowed, but not enough to keep me from throwing a fly. I looked up at the sun and calculated at least three more hours of daylight.

I walked along the river surveying it for a bit and then realized that I couldn't approach fishing like I did the rest of my life. I could keep looking for the perfect fishing hole, the perfect current, the perfect place where the perfect she-fish lie waiting to be enticed, but within three hours the sun would be down. Fishing time was limited.

The river was nowhere near as treacherous as the North Umpqua, but it didn't have to be. I entered the water feeling the Umpqua still flowing through me like the stinging memory of a lost love, a sting that was now to accompany the future of all my encounters with Old Man River.

I cast thirty degrees upstream and mended the line back to make sure the fly led the leader down river. I fished for half-an-hour with an intense and detailed attention to the fly, my line and the water. The world from the other side of the cattle guard haunted me, poking and prodding at me to be productive and to have a reason, a justified purpose for being there, for being alive. The fly rod was just an excuse. The fishing gear and attire just another mask to keep me from being branded a lunatic while I stood out in the middle of those flowing waters. After the initial intense thirty minutes of willing a fish to take my fly, I let go into the freedom of being one with the river.

I had been unconsciously casting for sometime, the breeze turning into a wind, Mother Nature's tool to rob me of my straw hat. There was a scent of fall, and the cooling wind stung my sunburned cheeks. I had goose bumps, and I even shivered a little bit. God it felt good. I tried to think of when I had last felt that cold, that alive. I had the urge to dive in, and then the image of coming up out of the river an eight year old, shivering, hungry, little boy became me.

Giving up on a fish, I walked to shore. According to the dust storm, it hadn't rained for some time in this part of the world. I sat on the tailgate and untied my wading boots, leaving the spikes strapped around them. I stepped out of my waders leaving them inside out, threw them in the back of the truck, reached for my Tonys and pulled them on.

It was cold and dusty. I didn't waste any time jumping into the cab of the Chevy. I'd forgotten the keys in my pocket and was pissed off at the inconvenience of having to dig down into my already too-tight-before-I-sat-down blue jeans. I pushed the Tonys into the floorboard, arched my back to lift myself straight enough to get my hands into the pocket with the keys. I managed to retrieve them and slipped them into the ignition to start the truck. It was still idling high from being cold and when I shifted it into gear; it died. I tried to start it again, but it wouldn't catch. I kept trying with brief interludes in case I had flooded it and for fear of running the battery down. I sat there, wind blowing and dust flying all around me as hungry as that shivering eight-year-old little boy would have been. Then another image returned to me. It was that rotten fucker leaning over the gumball machine who had sold me his cheap watered down gas.

"Fuuuuuucccccckkkkk!" I screamed, pounding the steering wheel with my fist, wishing it was his flesh. The screaming and pounding helped me feel a little better, but I knew that it wasn't going to influence the mechanical condition of the Chevy. I tried the truck to see if it had a change of heart, but nothing. I was stuck and confused. How had I so abruptly gone from being at one with the river to being one raging madman pretending that the steering wheel I was pounding on was Okie's face?

I waited a while and tried again, still no luck. I got out and popped the hood to have a look, but couldn't spot anything that appeared to be broken or out of place. I didn't like to work on cars; I was impatient as hell and usually ended up breaking something. My haste and frustration often caused the need for additional repairs, so I had learned that it was economically and emotionally cheaper to pay a mechanic. I closed the hood and climbed back inside.

The sun was setting over what I could see of the western hills. I sat trying to figure my way out of a problem that couldn't be resolved with willpower or thinking. I needed a mechanic and at the very least a ride back over the cattle guard into that world that just a few hours earlier I was dying to escape. I had tossed a medium weight coat into the cab of the Chevy earlier that morning, so I wouldn't freeze to death if I did by chance end up spending the night in the truck. The half-dozen, over-sized, wintergreen flavored Lifesavers that I had pulled from the bag before leaving in the morning would only tease me and keep my mouth watering.

I thought about the bowl of raisin bran cereal that I often times had for dinner when I was too lazy or too tired to go out for something. I'd fill a big cappuccino mug with the cereal; then pour in lots of milk so that there was no air left between any of the flakes and let it sit for ten minutes. I loved to let the cereal soak for a while because of the way the milk sweetened and the flakes turned soggy. As a kid it was the other way around, I had to have the crunch in the cereal and the milk had to be cold. I wondered what Flo might have to say about my grown-up cereal eating habits. I was sure she'd still find a way of accusing me of being a rotten, spoiled, little brat. Now that I was stranded, fighting with Flo didn't sound half bad.

I swung my legs up on the seat long ways and leaned my back up against the driver's side door. I rested the back of my head on the cold window while sliding my left elbow through the gap between the steering wheel and the steering column. My right elbow was on the top of the seat back and the lower part of my arm just hung back down over the front side of the seat back. That's when I noticed the light in the rearview mirror of the passenger door. I couldn't tell if it was getting closer, and I was afraid that it might turn off, so I hit the brakes hoping to get some attention. It worked, or at least I'd like to think that it did, but my old fisherman pal probably would have spotted me without my efforts. He circled around and pulled up next to the driver's side window of the Chevy.

"Man, am I glad to see you!" I said, without even having the window half way down. "Thought I was in for a cold and lonely night."

"What's the problem?" he shouted over the wind.

"Can't keep her running. Actually I can't even get her started now."

"Hop in. I'll haul you home."

I removed the keys from the ignition, pocketed them, took the gear from the cab and the truck bed and walked around to the back of his old Ford F-150 half-ton pick-up. The truck had a camper shell with the back window that had been left open, making it easy to dump my stuff off in haste. I climbed into the Ford and escaped the dust storm.

"Got gas?" he asked, looking at his own gauge.

"Put twenty bucks in right before I drove out. Could still be the gas though?"

"Why's that?"

"Might have some water in it."

"Where'd you get it?"

"Station cross from the diner, east of here on the highway."

"Yeah, I know the place."

"You live up that way?" I asked hopefully.

"No, 'bout half way between here and Tranquillity. How 'bout you?"

"I'm at the diner across from the station."

"Flo's place, huh?"

"Yeah, you know her?"

"Everyone knows everyone 'round here; got our own little dramas like anywhere else."

"Oh yeah?" I asked, waiting for more information.

"People get bored enough around here to the point of bein' able to tell you whose dog left the last turd along the roadside."

"Trying to tell me something, mister?"

"Take it as you will."

We zipped over the cattle guard. The speedometer read 40 miles-per-hour.

"How in the hell can you see where you're going in this crap?" I asked nervously.

"Can't."

"Can't?"

"No, but I can feel."

"Feel what?" I asked, puzzled.

"Feel the bumps and ruts of this dirt road. This Ford's been up and down this path for the last twenty-seven years. Once it catches its groove, it can practically drive itself out of here. All I got to do is give it the gas."

I closed my eyes without responding. He had the steering wheel, and I couldn't see anyway. It was quiet for a couple of minutes and then he spoke.

"Hook anything?"

"Nothing."

"I don't suppose you'd tell me if you did," he said, just to keep the conversation going.

He knew, as well as I did that when a guy hooks a fish, it's talked about. It usually grows half a foot and two pounds, especially if you're a catch and release fisherman. If you're catch and release, all you get to keep of the fish is its tale: fertilizer for a good old-fashioned story-telling session.

"It's all just one great big bullshit session anyway," I answered.

"Fishin'?" he asked.

"No. Fishing is about the only honorable thing left. I was talking about life."

"That's a mouthful," my fishing buddy said, as he pulled up to the diner.

"Thanks a lot. You saved my ass," I said, searching for the door handle in the unfamiliar dark cab.

"Not a problem. Never know; I might need a ride tomorrow."

I grabbed my stuff from under the camper shell and walked around to the driver's side door to thank him again.

"Can I buy you dinner?" I asked.

"No thanks, I'm fine."

"Coffee?"

"I'm good, thanks all the same. I'll see you around, huh. Hopefully next time you'll have a fish tale to stretch for me," he said, smiling as I walked to the front door of the diner. I turned around, raising my eyebrows and grinning. I nodded my head to acknowledge him one last time and then went into the diner. Walking into Flo's place was something like passing over the cattle guard. It was a wild frontier, and I never knew what kind of savage beast I might have to fight off in order to live to see another day.

"Well, look what the cat dragged in."

"It damn sure wasn't a Chevy," I barked back at Flo. She'd had all afternoon and evening to plot her revenge. "Thanks to old Shithead across the street and his watered down gas."

"It's not Shithead's gas," she said, sitting at the counter going through the day's receipts.

"Yeah right. I know how you locals stick together."

"Yeah that's right; we're all out to get you. Give me a break. Who's screwin' who around here?"

"Then why is it that every time I drop a twenty in his lap and pull out of his station that damn truck starts to choke up and backfire on me?"

"I've been filling up that truck for the last ten years, and it doesn't matter where I buy fuel, it still acts up."

"So you don't think it's Shithead's gas?"

"I know it's not."

"Well I don't."

"It's not Okie!" Flo shouted, slapping her hand on the coffee counter. "It's been doin' it for years. That's why the guy left it here in the first place."

"What are you talking about?"

"That truck has been leavin' people stranded long before I took it over. It's not just you! Sooner or later it happens to anyone who drives the damn thing."

"I just think about that old son-of-a-bitch, and I see red."

"It's not Okie."

"Then what is it?"

"You tell me?"

"Guess I don't like the fact that he's got so much control over me."

"You're givin' it to him."

"How?"

"You *want* someone to be pissed at."

"I want to be pissed?"

"Yeah."

"You've known me for just a few days and think you've got me all figured out, don't you?"

"You're not so unique. I've been servin' cheeseburgers to your kind for years."

"You're screwing me up here, Flo."

"You were screwed before you got here. But go ahead. Blame me like you're blamin' Okie."

"Thanks for your blessing," I said in a sarcastic tone.

"That way you can stay the victim."

"Now I'm a victim?"

"Sure are."

"I can't see how."

"You will. Well, you will or you'll run."

"Where am I gunna go?"

"If you stick around here you might learn somethin' about yourself. If you run, you probably won't."

"So sticking around here to fight with you is gunna help me. Right!"

"You just might figure out what you've been runnin' from all of these years."

"Who says I'm running?"

"What in the hell else are you doin' drivin' cross-country in that little old midlife crisis bucket of bolts?"

"I've been out buying tractors."

"Somethin's nippin' at your heels and you're runnin' from it. That's exactly why I don't want you messin' with Sarah. I don't want you using her to make yourself feel better."

"What if it makes us both feel better?"

"I'm not gunna play mom here."

"Yes you are. No one asked you to, but you are."

"You've already got a mother. And believe me, she's still runnin' you."

"Yeah, that's it," I agreed disdainfully.

I didn't get half of what Flo was talking about. Something was missing. She wasn't all glued together. She'd gone bonkers living out there in the middle of nowhere. She'd thought herself crazy. Mother, hell, we all had mothers.

"A mother who doesn't want her little boy to grow up," Flo jabbed.

"Bullshit. I left home at eighteen, and I've been supporting myself ever since," I answered.

"Yeah, you left home a long time ago, but you've still got your mother in your shirt pocket. She made you and molded you into what she believed was right for you."

I was tired of fighting Flo, so I just listened hoping for her rhetoric to end.

"You're still tryin' to be what you believe she wants you to be. She really doesn't want you with another woman."

"Flo you're high."

"Wish I was instead of beatin' my head against this stone wall."

"Quit beating it, then."

"All I'm sayin' is that what your mother taught you about woman, spoken or unspoken, isn't all gospel."

"I know that."

"Just fish and leave Sarah alone."

I couldn't see why having a mother had anything to do with me staying away from Sarah. Flo needed to learn to go with the flow. Fishing was exactly what I planned on doing, but what about my pecker? I had all the goods that came along with being a man, and they were pointing at Sarah's... well, let's just say my autopilot had locked on, captured the glide slope and was on final approach for a full stop landing on Sarah's runway.

Chapter 7
Tuesday

I fell back into my sleeping late routine, waking at eleven. After soaking in the tub, I dressed and took the stairs down for my morning cup of coffee. Sarah had the morning shift, and Jimmy was shaking the oil out of the basket of fries he'd just lifted out of the deep-fryer. Damn those fries looked and smelled inviting. My body was on breakfast time, but the fries were calling me to join the rest of the world for lunch.

"Well, well, guess he did make it back last night Jimmy," Sarah announced, loud enough to get Jimmy's attention while she smiled at me.

"Morning guys," I said, nodding my head first to acknowledge Jimmy, and then glancing up a quick smile to Sarah but just as quickly looking away. I was uncertain if I was feeling shy with Sarah or afraid of Flo. I had yet to encounter Flo that morning but for some reason felt her presence.

"Coffee?" Sarah offered.

"Please."

"Hungry?" Sarah asked, as she filled my mug from a freshly brewed pot.

"No thanks. Those fries look awfully good, but I'm still a little foggy."

"OK, let me know when you're ready."

"For what?" I asked grinning.

Sarah walked away acting as if she hadn't heard me. A few minutes later, Jimmy set a dish under the heat lamp, slapped the bell a few times and walked out from the kitchen to fill his milkshake tumbler with ice and water.

"Hey Jimmy, where's Flo?"

"Gone after that stubborn truck."

"How's she getting to it?"

"Got a stubborn mechanic to haul her out there," Jimmy answered, chuckling out loud.

"But how does she know where to find the damn thing?"

"Don't know, but there's only a few ways in to the river. I'm sure they'll find it."

"When'd she leave?"

"An hour or so ago; right after Sarah got here. The damn thing's acted up like this forever."

"Where'd she get it?"

"Some old guy friend of hers left her and the truck. Guess he must have got tired of two unreliable means of transportation," Jimmy said, belly laughing as he walked back into the kitchen.

"Catch anything yesterday?" Sarah asked, as she walked back to fill my coffee.

"Sure did."

"Let's see it," she challenged.

"Let it go."

"Sounds like a fish story to me."

"It is," I agreed, hoping to peak her curiosity.

"Well, let's hear the rest of it."

"Sometimes words ruin a story."

"Is this a trick?"

"No. It just seems wrong to put words to an experience. Kind of like talking it away, loses meaning. It becomes a wilted salad or a cold cup of coffee."

"Or the day-old remains of someone else's campfire?"

"You got it." She did get it, too, and a hell of a lot quicker than I had expected. I connected with her, so I just shut up and enjoyed it instead of pushing for more.

"When are you going out again?" Sarah asked.

"Don't know. Soon I hope. I guess it's up to that unreliable piece of transportation I've been driving around," I said, loud enough to make Jimmy start belly laughing again.

I wasn't lying to Sarah about catching something and letting it go. Sarah was talking about a fish. I was talking about the experience of being out in the middle of that river. We were both talking about something that was very elusive though, and it really wasn't something that I felt words could possibly explain. It was an experience I hoped to share with her sometime.

"OK Sarah, I better eat."

"Don't tell me, fish?"

"Well, now that you mention it, why not?"

"You don't have to."

"No, I really didn't know what I wanted. Fish sounds good."

"You want fish and chips?"

"I'd rather have a tuna melt and some hot fries just like the ones Jimmy was shaking out of the basket a little bit ago."

"What kind of bread?"

"Whole wheat."

Sarah scribbled down my order on the green pad, clipped the ticket onto the order wheel and spun it around for Jimmy. The frozen fries where already hitting the basket before the order ticket was halfway around to Jimmy's side of paradise. After dunking the basket of fries into the hot oil, Jimmy turned around to glance at my order.

He reached for the handle of the stainless steel refrigerator and after tugging it open, grabbed the container full of tuna salad and set it on the counter next to the grill. Next, Jimmy reached for the butter with a knife in his right hand and for a couple of slices of wheat bread with his left. He simultaneously brought them both together in a prayer like fashion, buttered the bread in the twinkling of an eye, laying both slices buttered side down on the grill. He dropped a slice of American cheese on to the exposed sides of the bread, daubed an ice cream scooper full of tuna salad on to one of the bread slices, and spread it around with the back of the scooper. Jimmy flipped the unencumbered bread slice over onto the tuna smeared slice with the same knife he'd used to butter the bread. Next, he flipped my melt over with a spatula, giving it a light press with its bottom side.

Jimmy flipped the melt a couple of more times while he waited for the fries to brown. When they were done, he dumped them onto a clean towel to soak off the excess oil, salted them and used tongs to drop them on my plate next to the sandwich that sat waiting expectantly for the fries, just as I was waiting for the whole plate. Sarah had been standing in front of the service window, pouring half-empty catsup bottles into the half-full bottles. As soon as Jimmy set my plate out, Sarah shuttled it to me, along with a full bottle of catsup.

I peppered the fries and pounded on the bottom of the catsup, but to no avail. I took a knife and stuck it up the catsup bottle just as Flo walked in. Sarah must have seen Flo driving up because she had already grabbed the coffee pot and had almost every customer's coffee mug refilled before Flo and whatever mood was leading her around, dragged her through the door. I had my mouth full of tuna when she walked past me and couldn't have said "hi," "bye," or "kiss my rosy red ass" if I'd wanted to. It was just as well, never knowing which way she'd swing.

"Hi Flo," naturally eased out of Sarah, as if she'd just realized that Flo had returned.

"Hi Sarah. How are things?"

"Good. Little slow, but good."

"What's with the truck?" I interrupted, after swallowing most of the bite that I'd taken when Flo walked in.

"Started right up."

"Well that damn thing wouldn't start right up last night," I said, feeling the need to justify my powerlessness over the moody Chevy.

"I'm sure it wouldn't," Flo stated, in a flat, non-judgmental tone.

"It really wouldn't," I demanded, as if she'd been calling me a liar.

"Like I said, I'm sure that it wouldn't. I believe you. This has been goin' on for years," Flo said, reassuring me before she walked off.

I finished lunch and twisted a toothpick from the clear plastic dispenser that for some reason was working that day. I wondered who else's fingertips had exploited the toothpick dispenser. Usually the damn things are plugged up with the top pulled off for half the world's population to infect with their just-been-to-the-pisser-after-eating-and-forgetting-to-wash hands. I was never sure if this was all caused by sheer laziness or lack of patience with the hot air hand dryer that usually blew cold air and took thirty minutes to do what could be done in fifteen seconds had there been a full paper towel dispenser. Damn I hated public restrooms and community toothpick dispensers. I really didn't care to share much of anything, but especially anything that could give me a cold or a good old-fashioned case of the trots.

Flo walked back up to the coffee counter as I sat picking my teeth.

"Sarah, I'll take it now. You can finish with your tables, or I'll take them if you don't want to wait around."

"I've only got two parties left. They already have their food and their checks are down."

"I don't mean to run you off. Just don't want to keep you from what's left of your day off."

"I have nothing better to do. I'll stick around."

Sarah's having nothing better to do sounded like an invitation to me. Problem was that I couldn't R.S.V.P. with my conscience standing over me. Damn I hated feeling squeezed by Flo. Sarah walked to the back for something, leaving Flo to me.

"Flo, did Okie say anything about my car?"

"No, he sure didn't," she answered from behind the counter with her back to me.

That didn't surprise me, but the "no he sure didn't" rushed down my inner ear canal, enraging every bone in my body. "That figures," I said, hesitantly, trying to hold back what was boiling inside.

"What figures?" asked Flo, in a voice that seemed to be taking on a disgusted tone.

"That he didn't mention my car. I don't think he really gives a shit if I'm stuck here or not."

"I'm gunna pretend that I didn't hear what I didn't just hear."

"That's the problem around this place."

"Excuse me?" Flo asked, as she finally turned around to do battle.

"Nobody around this place seems to know anything."

"You mean nobody around here is tellin' you what you want to hear."

"I'd just like to know what's up on with my car," I said, trying to back off a little.

"Take it easy. He'll get it fixed. What happened to that fish, anyway?" she asked, her voice softening.

"I need wheels to chase a fish."

"You got wheels."

"My wheels are broke down across the street."

"You've got the truck."

"He's still not fixing my car."

"You want your cake and you want to eat it, too."

"What good is cake if you can't eat it?"

"Your problem is that you want it all."

"So?"

"So, you're divided."

"Lady, I'm not divided, I'm stuck!"

"That's exactly right. You're stuck because you want it all."

"Maybe my life is just what it is. Maybe it's not as complicated as you've made it out to be."

"You ever get lonely?"

"Yes, and?"

"That's because the man in you wants to belong, but the scared shitless little boy in you won't let you."

"Here we go with the mom shit again."

"You want love, but you don't want to be trapped," she said, ignoring my mom comment.

"Who doesn't? I woke from that dream a long time ago."

"You just think you did. The want's still there," she said confidently.

"How do you know what I want?"

"You don't want to keep on livin' a lie. You just don't know how to stop."

"I'm not living a lie. I'm just living the best way that I know how."

"You're livin' a lie by not bein' all that you want to be," she said, sounding like a paid advertisement for the US Army.

"How exactly am I supposed to be all that I can be?" I asked sarcastically.

"Just follow your heart."

"I am."

"Is that what you're really followin'?" Flo asked, as she walked off. It was just as well because I was getting close to taking another jab at her. This dingbat was really off on one of her toots.

Was she preaching to me or trying to convince herself? I had considered some of her concepts in some way, shape or form, but I'd be damned if I was going to agree with her on much of anything. She reminded me a whole lot of Stephen, an old client of mine who turned born again Pentecostal when he was in his mid-forties after being a practicing Catholic his whole life.

Stephen became such a fanatic about preaching and saving souls that his wife of twenty years dumped his silly ass and moved her and their two boys the hell out of Stephen's heaven. When I left the area, Stephen had already lost his family, and his ranch was not far behind. Stephen had an excuse, though: persecution! He was being tested, just like Job.

Actually, it was Stephen who did the persecuting. Mail arrived at the post office every morning at ten-thirty, and most of the community was there at ten-thirty to pick it up, using it as a socializing excuse. The problem started when that goddamn Stephen began using the post office steps as his pulpit. He'd be standing right at the front door like a church greeter catching us one at a time with his friendly smile, asking us how things were going as we filed in, one by one.

Knowing that someone would respond for fear of not wanting to look bad in front of the rest of the community, he'd cornered whoever felt a duty to be nice to him. Yes, the pearly gates would swing wide open just as soon as someone looked his way. He would take them by the hand and try to lead them to the Promised Land. Stephen would get nose to nose with you breathing his locomotive bad breath into your face, arms swinging and eyes bulging with the momentum of a runaway train. A few minutes later he'd be fully engaged into whatever biblical passage had obsessed him, shaking his head up and down in a seizure-like fashion, slapping the back of his right hand into the palm of his left hand, carrying on like a raving lunatic. When he got to this point, he'd start asking questions, tapping you on the shoulder with his index finger, waiting for an answer.

Stephen waited for the answer, so he could start all over again, justifying his walk with the lord. I couldn't quite figure out if he was trying to convince his suffering audience, or himself. The moment of truth was when Stephen asked a question. It didn't matter how you answered as much as if you *did* answer. If you didn't answer, Stephen wouldn't have an argument, and he'd set you free, enabling him to pick on the next lost soul who walked up to the post office door to collect his bills and pay his dues. The others, who made it around Stephen, because he had someone else trapped, would look back out the window just after walking inside and start to make goofy faces or perform some other sacrilegious symbolic sign language behind Stephen's back. The captured soul, with his eyes dancing back between Stephen and the heathens inside the post office, would try not to erupt into a blasphemous giggling fit.

After a while, people would drive by the post office to see if Stephen's brown and white Dodge Ram pick-up was parked out front. If his truck was there, most would just keep on driving, returning later for the mail. A lot of us who still enjoyed the social content of our morning postal gathering would meet around the corner at the local auto parts store to exchange gossip. Then we'd head on over to get the mail an hour or so later.

I'm sure that in her own way, Flo had some valid questions for consideration, but I hated preachers or any other know-it-alls who thought that they had all the answers to life's problems. The real problem I had with Flo was that I needed her. I was driving her truck, renting her room, eating her food, and sniffing around her waitress, who happened to be the hottest thing two hundred miles in any direction.

I could have quit playing the game by not engaging Flo, but I was stuck there and bored. As long as I had that great big old stirring stick in my hand, I was going to entertain myself.

"I'll be right there to ring you up," Sarah announced to her last customer through Jimmy's side of the kitchen window. Less than a minute later Sarah emerged from the kitchen to cash out her last ticket.

"Thanks a lot. Hope to see you again," Sarah said, handing them their change.

Did Sarah really hope to see any of them again, knowing that with the exception of the few regulars, she never would? Before Sarah could say anything to me, Flo had walked back up to the coffee counter and tossed the truck keys down in front of me.

"It's all yours, but remember what you've got and don't blame the old fart across the street if it leaves you high and dry again," Flo said, as she turned and walked back in the same direction she'd just come from.

"Want to go for a test drive?" I asked, looking up to Sarah with a half-ass grin to hide the god-please-don't-turn-me-down look that was rumbling around behind my smile.

"Yeah, but I want to go home and change. Why don't you follow me to my place? We can go from there."

"I've got to run up to my room. I'll be right down." Yes! I screamed to myself. I got the yes from her. I ran up, brushed my teeth, grabbed a condom from my overnight bag and stuffed it into my fishing vest. After walking around in circles for a minute, I took my gear and stumbled down the steps like an excited little boy bouncing off the walls on my way down.

I didn't see Sarah when I got back down to the counter, and for a split second, I panicked.

"Hey Jimmy..." I started, and then spotted Sarah sitting in the Jetta.

"What's up kid?" Jimmy asked through the kitchen window.

"Oh, nothing; I'll catch you later."

"Have fun," Jimmy said, as he nodded his head, smiling as if he instinctively felt my panic in what I hadn't asked him.

I hustled out the front door. "I'll be right behind you," I told Sarah who was sitting in her Jetta with the window down, the engine already running. Right behind and all over her was exactly where I wanted to be with her, too.

I started Ol' Reliable and followed Sarah out of the diner's gravel parking lot, heading eastbound.

I followed Sarah to her house, which ended up being just two miles east of the diner. The house was set back off the road a good quarter-mile with a barbed wire fence to the west of the dirt road leading back to her home. It was a small, wood-sided home that was built on a foundation and had a cedar shake roof. Sarah was already out of her car when I pulled up next to it.

"I'll be right out," Sarah shouted, as she ran up the four or five steps that led to her front door.

I nodded to confirm and stayed sitting in the Chevy surveying the property. There was an old wooden barn with a corrugated metal roof that sloped down to the back of the structure. It was set back a few hundred feet east of the house and was completely corralled with a wooden fence. It was a stable-type barn, opened on the west side to accommodate livestock seeking shelter from rain or sun. When I looked back toward the house, Sarah had already walked out and was locking the front door.

After she climbed in, I did a three-point turn and headed out of her dirt driveway. As I pulled up onto the road and headed west on our test run, the image of Flo flashed to me: she was sitting in the booth of her diner watching the traffic drive by.

"Think good ol' Flo baby will see us zoom by together?" I asked.

"So what if she does?"

"She's just a pain," I said, thinking to myself: *Yeah, so what if she does?*

"How is she a pain?" Sarah asked, shifting in her seat towards me.

"I don't know. It just seems like she wants to turn me into a woman."

"A woman? I'm confused."

"That makes two of us. It's not that she wants to turn me into a woman as much as she doesn't want me to be a man."

"I still don't get it."

I took a deep breath and glanced out of the pickup gathering courage. "All right Sarah, I think that you're hotter than hell, and you drive me nuts."

"You think I don't know that? But, what's this crap about how she doesn't want you to be a man?"

"She doesn't want me to mess with you. I guess she's trying to protect you."

"How do you know that?"

"She told me so."

"She told you that?" Sarah asked in an excited, yet doubtful tone.

"Really! She told me to leave you the hell alone."

"What does she care?"

"I don't know what her trip is? The woman's half goofy."

Sarah looked away without responding. She looked out through the window almost trance-like as if she was revisiting someone or someplace that was centuries removed. I didn't interrupt her. I was hoping that Sarah would sleep with me just because of Flo's imposition. We drove for a while longer, and when she did come back, she seemed different.

"Where we headed?" Sarah asked.

"Anywhere your heart desires," I grinned, watching for her response out of the corner of my eye.

"Anywhere I want huh? How about… no, maybe… no, that won't work."

"What?"

"Never mind."

Sarah had me. She knew it and was testing me. It would be interesting to see if she abused the power I'd given her. Most of the women I had given up my power to in the past abused it. I'd been jerked around enough that I new damn good and well how to take it back. It wasn't something that I had to give up for good any longer. I had learned to live alone a long time ago. Living alone wasn't a problem, taking back my power wasn't a problem, but not having a woman in my life was. I was frustrated. I wanted a lover, wanted the companionship of a woman, but wasn't willing to sacrifice anything for her. Not like I'd done in the past anyway.

"I want to drive," Sarah decided.

"OK, I'll pull over."

"No, I mean I want to ride around with you. I just want to talk."

"About what?" I inquired.

"About anything your heart desires," Sarah replied, with one of those beaming gotcha-smart-ass smiles. What Sarah got back after her little daydream departure was her spirit that Flo was so good at crushing. "How 'bout you, what's your story?"

"Nothing special."

"I'll be the judge of that Caliboy; how 'bout your love life?"

Sarah was getting brave. Opening up my can of worms meant that she'd be opening hers, too. Maybe not so willingly, but it would still be coming.

"You sure you want to start this?" I asked.

"It can't be that bad."

"I'm not referring to good or bad. Just that I take a long time to tell a story, and you might find that you've gotten yourself into something you wished you hadn't started. I mean, being that I've got a captive audience and all."

"Sounds like an excuse, chicken. How 'bout it, you been married?"

"Once, when I was thirty and thought that life was passing me by. Everyone else around me was, and I was lonely. Guess I got caught in a weak moment."

"Did you love her?"

"Thought I did."

"So you didn't then?"

"I married her out of obligation to my religious heritage because I was sleeping with her out of wedlock, and I was scared God was gunna strike me down. Punish me, you know?"

"No, I don't know, but why else did you marry her? What attracted you to her?"

"Blonde, blue-eyed five and a half feet plus with really long legs. At first the sex was pretty good."

"That's why you married her, looks and sex?"

"That and I didn't want her to get away."

"Thought you couldn't live without her, huh?"

"The desperate insecure part of me did."

"How'd you realize you'd made a mistake?"

"Same way that all my love affairs made me realize: pain and disappointment. My ex-wife used me for financial stability, so she could live the life she never had as a child. Her mother had been married five times. She never had a home or any stability. With me she got the big house and all the dogs, cats, and birds that she could stuff into it."

"Well, just because you provided her with a dream doesn't mean that she was using you."

"All of those goddamn animals came first. I never fit in. Then she started to boast to her friends that I'd do anything for her and that she could have whatever she wanted."

"That's funny," Sarah laughed.

"It went that way for awhile, but her boastfulness got back to me."

"Maybe she was bragging about you."

"About me?"

"Yeah, flashing you at her friends; trying to make them jealous."

"Maybe, but there was no end to what she wanted. I began to tell her no on things, and that's when the bill collectors showed up at our house."

"Bill collectors?"

"Yeah, to collect on the bad checks she'd written from a closed bank account. That's when I began to open my eyes."

"So she was a little irresponsible."

"No. She was a flake."

"You couldn't see that before you married her?"

"Couldn't because I didn't want to; her lost interest in sex, bounced checks, and cussing me like I was some bastard calf from Texas helped me to see it, though."

"How long were you married?"

"Two years, but it took another two years to divorce her. That's when I realized that I had kept her with material things."

"Why's that?"

"Because in those two years of her pissing and moaning, none of it was about me."

"What do you mean?"

"It was always about how I took the house away from her. Never anything about how she missed me. She never tried to make things right. Not that I would have given her another chance, anyway. I'd rather be alone with the possibility, than stuck in that miserable hell."

"I know that all to well."

"Oh yeah?"

"Do I still get to do whatever my heart desires?" Sarah asked, changing the subject.

"What's on your mind?"

"I want you to take me fishing."

"I only have one rod."

"I don't care. I just want to go with you. I want to watch."

"OK, but I'm hungry. We're not far from Tranquillity. How 'bout a hamburger?" I asked.

"And then we'll fish?"

"And then we'll fish. I hope there's a burger joint in Tranquillity."

"There is."

"I'm glad one of us knows our way around this part of the world."

I wanted to eat and get somewhere with Sarah, and it appeared that I might be on the right road. I drove for another ten minutes and, without much effort, found the burger joint in Tranquillity. Sarah got out and ran around the back of the building to the bathroom. I studied the menu, waiting for her return. The hamburger was turning into a double cheeseburger less the mayonnaise and onions. If Sarah didn't show up soon, I'd end up with a milkshake or malt of some sort. I was already going against my doctor's orders. My bad cholesterol had been a little over the limits at my last physical, and I had received the cut-that-shit-out lecture or I'll have to put you on medication. That skinny, sawed-off, sixty something year old MD loved to tell me that I was too fat.

"There you are," I said, trying to figure out why it takes a woman four times as long to pee as a man. "What sounds good?"

"What will you have?"

"Cheeseburger and an iced tea," I answered, really wanting to say you.

"I'll have a cheeseburger and a Coke."

"Want some fries?" I asked, feeling a twinge of grease guilt.

"I'll share some with you."

"That'll work. What do you want on your burger?"

"Everything."

"You got it," I said, wanting to question her on the onions, but didn't.

"Oh, you know, I don't want onions."

"OK, hold the onions." Yes! As impatient as I was, at times I had mastered silence. It paid off that time. Is that what Flo meant by going with the flow? I ordered our lunch while Sarah grabbed some napkins and a table that was outside. I brought our drinks and joined her.

The picnic tables were long and rectangular with tops that had historical carvings from years of ass-ends that had waited for their burgers and satisfied their urges to be officially recorded in the Tranquillity's formal hall of records. The same hall of records that collected the crumbs of transients as well as the local ass-ends who drank coffee at the local hardware store/city hall where I had purchased my fishing license and gear only a day earlier.

We finished our burgers and climbed back into the Chevy. After making the sign of the cross in my imagination and silently saying a few hail Marys, the engine fired on the first spin of the starter.

"Where we headed?" I asked, already knowing the answer.

"Fishing!"

"All right, fishing it is," I replied. We left Tranquillity, eastbound for the river. After leaving the town, I figured that it was my turn to learn a little about Sarah.

"Well, Sarah, what about you?"

"What about me?"

"Oh, now Sarah, don't play dumb with me. How old are you?"

"Twenty-nine. Thirty in a few months, but that's a secret.

I'm sticking to twenty-nine for as long as I can," Sarah said, joking seriously.

"That you'll have no trouble with for another decade, I'm sure," I said, wanting to compliment her youthful appearance without sounding phony.

"Ever been married?" I asked.

"Once."

"No children?" I asked.

"No, you?" Sarah asked, looking away and staring out of the passenger side window.

"None for me either," I answered, but she was still lost somewhere.

I let her go for a while until she seemed to have returned to her seat in the Chevy. She glanced over at me.

"None for me either," I repeated as if she'd just asked the question.

"Just as well, I mean, since you didn't stay married and all."

"Thank God," I answered. "Kids would have just kept me tied to her after the divorce. At least I'm completely free of her. Now I have the chance to start from scratch."

"Yeah, if you had kids, they'd suffer as much if not more than you," Sarah reminded me.

"It's not like I don't want kids, but the idea scares the hell out of me."

"Why?"

"Hell, I'll have to give up being a kid myself."

"You men."

"But not having a child just seems so unnatural."

"I think a lot about that, too," answered Sarah. "But just having a child for the sake of having a child doesn't sound appealing to me. I guess I'll really have to love a man enough to want to carry his child. For me it's a package deal."

"How about brothers or sisters?" I asked, shifting from marriage and kids. "Got any?"

"One sister."

"Older or younger?"

"She's a year and a half older than me," Sarah answered. "How about you?"

"Three younger brothers."

"No sisters?"

"No."

"Your poor mother."

"My poor mother, hell. It's not like she didn't have a choice."

"I mean all boys."

"It wasn't bad at all. Hell, it was fun. I never knew what PMS was until I was married. If mom ever had a bout with PMS, it's news to me. She didn't have time, and even if she did go PMS on us, we wouldn't have given a shit anyway," I said grinning.

"I bet you guys were terrors."

"Nah," I answered, chuckling nostalgically. "About all I can tell you is Mom learned to say 'fuck' real good. She didn't use it much, but she learned it, and every once in a while when we'd push her past her limits, 'fuck' would pry its way through her clenched teeth."

"Like I said, terrors," Sarah laughed.

I kept driving and grinning, drifting in and out of my boyhood memories. We both seemed to have floated off into a silent time. No more words were exchanged until we crossed the cattle guard and headed for the river.

"How are you?" I asked, putting my right arm along the seat back. I relaxed and let Ol' Reliable catch the groove that led to the river.

"Good."

"Me too," I confirmed. Hanging out with Sarah was what made it good. A few minutes later we pulled up to the river.

"It won't be the same Sarah," I said, easing the Chevy to a stop in the same spot that it had given up the ghost the night before.

"What won't be the same?" Sarah asked, as we both got out of the truck to stretch.

"Watching isn't the same as being out in the river."

"I've fished before."

"I'm not talking about fishing. I'm talking about being out in the river. I'm talking about being waist high in water with the breeze hitting your face. I'm talking about the sun's reflection bouncing off the water up into your sunglasses as your arm and rod, as one, softly unfold a cast that delicately dollops your fly perfectly into the position of an intended swirl."

"It almost sounds like an art," Sarah answered, tilting her head slightly to one side, delivering a smile that made my heart growl with hunger.

"It is an art, Sarah, just like living," I said, admiring God's art in her. That's when that twinkle in her eyes that had a power beyond reasoning overcame me. I reached over the side of the truck bed to grab my waders, and after stepping into them, reached for my spiked boots.

"Some pretty dangerous looking shoes you've got there."

"Tell me about it, but it beats swimming in that cold river," I answered.

"What do you mean?"

"These goofy spiked boots are what keep me from slipping on the mossy rocks," I answered, tying that last shoelace.

"It's a guy thing. You guys just like to dress up in that crap," Sarah teased.

"I'm telling you, it's not the same unless you're out in it," I reminded her, putting on my vest. I grabbed my rod and started for the river.

"I've got an idea about something we can experience together," I yelled back to Sarah with an ornery grin as I stepped into the water.

"I bet you do, mister. I bet you do," Sarah yelled back, as she watched my entry into sanctuary.

I fished for thirty minutes before the first nibble. A nibble is all that it was, and the only one I got that day. I kept checking on Sarah. Every time I looked up she had moved with me down river and was sitting on a rock appearing to be content and at peace, gazing out toward me. It made me feel safe, not alone. In some ways it reminded me of being a little boy who was mastering a new task in life; a little boy who was ashamed of having his mother right at his side but who still welcomed her from a distance with a reassuring gaze or nodding her head with a smile.

The sun would be down before long, and I was tired of the haunting curiosity that kept luring me towards Sarah. I wanted to bridge our gap, so I gave up on a fish for the day and waded to shore.

"Ready for that experience I promised you?" I asked Sarah, as I stepped out of the water and up to her boulder.

"Yeah, right," Sarah responded in a cautious I-don't-know-or-trust-you-all-of-the-way tone.

"I'm serious."

"Serious about what?"

"Serious about dropping this tailgate, so we've got a place to sit and watch the sunset." *That was a great trial-close mister,* I thought, proud of myself as I reached for the handle. "How 'bout it?" I asked, sitting down and patting the empty slot of tailgate next to me.

"How about it?" Sarah asked, with her heart-melting smile."

"There'll never be another one like it."

"What?" Sarah asked.

"The sunset. Today's sunset; there'll be more, but this day is burnt and gone," I said, as the last sliver of the sun melted into a glow from behind the mountains.

"The moment's gone, but not its memory," Sarah said, as she slipped off the tailgate to her feet. "Come on, I need to get back home."

I didn't want to take her home, but I didn't want to lose her to my needy impatience and knew not to push her any further.

"Yeah, you're right. If I don't get back soon they'll probably come after me and this shitty excuse for a truck," I said, lifting up the tailgate and latching it.

We crossed the cattle guard back into reality, and I headed for Sarah's place. We didn't say much, but it was a comfortable silence. I walked Sarah to her door and hugged her good night.

"I'll talk to you soon, Sarah," I said, walking back to the Chevy.

"Yeah, thanks for taking me along."

"Wouldn't have had it any other way," I said, opening the truck door.

I waved as I backed out of the drive, uncertain if I should have kissed her or stuck with the hug that I had opted for. I pulled out on the road, driving in Flo's direction and contemplating my next round with Mother-may-I.

Flo was sitting in her usual booth watching "The Wheel of

Fortune" when I walked in. I didn't particularly want to see her, but I was staying in her campground and had no choice.

"Hi Flo," I said, testing her temperature.

"Hey kid, any fish?"

"None. Might need a different fly."

"Maybe you're fishin' the wrong hole."

"I guess it doesn't much matter anyway."

"Maybe you should be fishin' west of here instead of east," Flo said, with her eyes fixed on the spinning wheel. Damn, she was on to my bite.

"What happened to the last one?" Flo asked.

"The last what?" I asked, sitting down across from her in the booth.

"The last woman that you hounded?"

"Janie?"

"All right, Janie. What did you want from her?"

"Availability. I wanted her to come towards me."

"Why, so you could run away after you found somethin' wrong with her?" Flo asked, in a very peaceful voice.

"I don't know why. I guess because if she chased me, it meant I was valuable in some way."

"Ever think that maybe it's a way for you to stay stuck?"

"I thought more along the lines that it was just a way to have some fun."

"How long do you want to keep this up?" she asked, still maintaining her composure.

"What?" I asked. She still hadn't gone off on me, and it was screwing me up. Usually, my not understanding something really set her off.

"Livin' your life frustrated and lonely?"

"I've been married, and still frustrated and lonely."

"So how is it different now?"

"I can leave when they start their pissing and moaning."

"So you're just worried about gettin' laid?"

"You're damn right. I don't want to miss out on that part of my life. I'm not getting any younger, you know."

"How many women do you have right now?"

"What do you mean?"

"You know what I mean. How many you sleepin' with?"

"Couple."

"A couple as in four or five, and you damn sure wouldn't turn down another."

"Depends."

"Wouldn't depend on much," she said, shifting her gaze out the front window.

"Yes, it would."

"What's it like?"

"What?"

"Havin' all of these women? What's it like after you have your way with them?"

I didn't answer.

"How does it make you feel?" Flo asked again.

"I don't know," I finally answered, turning to look out of the window, too.

"Deep down inside of there, I think you want a woman in your life who is more than just a place to plug into," Flo said, pointing to my heart in the reflection of the window.

"Sometimes yes, sometimes no," I answered, looking into the window.

"But you don't know how."

"Maybe I just haven't found the woman that I want to be with."

"Maybe, but remember you're not gettin' any younger."

"I married on that premise. It was the most miserable time of my life. I'd rather be miserably alone than miserably married."

"Maybe you could be happily married. Maybe a woman could serve you in a way that you've never experienced."

"Maybe, maybe not."

"You'll never know the way you're goin'."

I just shrugged, thinking about how lonely Flo must have been.

"You'll never do it until you learn to let go of whatever you think it is that's givin' you security," Flo said, answering my silence. "Maybe you've missed out on somethin' in life besides sex. Maybe you've missed out on life in a way that you can't imagine."

"Maybe Flo, maybe," I answered, letting her think she'd penetrated my armor. What was Flo hanging onto? What experiences were missing in her life? I wondered if she'd ever be able to hear her own sermons. The fights we shared, perhaps they were really a displaced passion for which Flo had no other outlet.

"Flo, I've had about all I can handle for a day; time for bed."

"OK kid, pleasant dreams," she said, without looking away from the window.

I walked up the stairs to my room. Once inside, I ran the bath. Then I went over to the corner with the windows, staring across the street for a minute, and then westbound. I was hoping to feel something while staring out that west window, but didn't. I stripped off my clothes, leaving a pile on the floor in the center of the room, and took my bath. That's when the image of Lauren drifted back to me. Lauren used to haunt me, but time had passed. After having several other women after Lauren, I had come to a greater understanding of what she meant to my life. It was Janie who helped me to let go and get over my longing for Lauren.

I remember driving one time to meet Janie for dinner. Before leaving her home for the restaurant, she told me that she had been seeing someone else, and that she didn't want to expose her son to the men she was seeing unless it was something serious. We had dinner anyway. Unknowingly, I had taken the wounded little boy in me into the restaurant with her and walked out having met him. That's when I realized it wasn't me with Lauren, just as it wasn't me with Janie. It wasn't about me being enough. These women were searching the same as I had been, searching to fulfill a longing in the enchantment of another. I realized that we all suffered, not just me. The whole world seemed to be looking for something. I could see how my search for a savior out there had failed me, yet how could I be fulfilled? How could I enjoy a woman in the real physical and emotional sense without expecting her to be a goddess in charge of rescuing me? How could I let go into something ecstatic and still stay grounded?

Without knowing it, at dinner with my slighted young inner companion, Janie helped me to realize that there was nothing inherently wrong with me and that I wasn't the victim. I also learned that I had no control over others, even if at times I thought I did. As much as it was against my way of being in this world, I began to understand to let whatever was going to happen with a woman, happen. If I didn't, emotionally she'd beat my ass, and it would have nothing to do with her at all.

My bath had cooled considerably. I climbed out, toweled off, pulled on some sweats and walked back to the windows. Looking west, I realized that I'd been fighting this ever since the day I was shit-canned from my Garden of Eden. I'd been fighting life since the very day I came kicking and screaming from my mother's womb.

CHAPTER 9

Wednesday

I was restless and woke early that morning thinking about Sarah. I didn't want to think about her in that way, but the more I tried not to think about her, the harder it got. I had to find out about my car. The sooner it was repaired, the sooner I'd be out of left field. Getting out of Five Points meant missing the possible trouble that a longer stay might offer.

I didn't bathe. I brushed my teeth, slapped on my John Deere hat and buttoned on a red short sleeve cotton shirt. After slipping into my Levis and Tonys, I descended the stairs and walked right out the front door ignoring Sarah, who was waiting tables in the back, and Jimmy, who was slinging hash in his kitchen. I crossed the quiet empty highway and marched right into the garage where Okie stood under a car that had been hoisted up on the rack.

"Hello."

"Howdy, you here to give me another twenty?" Okie asked, as he was tightening the oil pan's drain plug.

"No, I want to know how things are with my MG."

"If I had some parts, I could tell you," answered Okie, as he backed out from under the car, wiping his end wrench with a faded blue shop towel.

"How about the head?"

"What about it?"

"Is it cracked?"

"How would I know?"

"You said it might be cracked."

"Might be, don't know yet."

"Don't you think that it would be a good idea to get that

checked out ahead of time?"

"Ahead of what time?"

Hell, I forgot that time stopped out there. Actually, it didn't even seem to exist. It was obvious that Okie and I weren't going to become pals, but he was downright obstinate. He didn't seem to give a damn about the fact that I was stranded. I was beginning to think he took pleasure in my misfortune. I decided to take the direct approach with the old fart.

"Why can't you just level with me?"

"About what?"

"About what you really think is wrong with my car. Look, I don't know the first thing about cracked heads. I can change a hose, a belt, or the oil and filter, but when it comes to anything major, I'm lost. Why can't you tell me what you really think is wrong? Then, at least I'll believe I have some control over my situation."

"Son, I don't know. Once the radiator is back from the repair shop and the other parts get here, I hope to have her all put back together again. It'll probably just take a couple of days once everything has arrived."

"What if I do have a cracked head?"

"If you've got a cracked head, you've got a cracked head and then we'll have to deal with it. But until we find out different, I think this is the fastest and cheapest route."

"How can we find out if I've got a cracked head?"

"By pullin' it off and sendin' it out to a machine shop to have it magna-fluxed."

"Then why don't we do that?"

"We can if that's what you want, but I'll need another two hundred up front, and you might as well trot on back across the street and reserve that room you've got for a couple more weeks."

"That's exactly why I wanted to get this moving. Hell, we're five days behind. Why didn't we send it out with the radiator?" I asked excitedly, ignoring the additional two hundred that he had hinted at.

"What if you don't need the head repaired?" he asked, cocking his head back with a disgusted look on his face. "Sounds like to me that you've got time and money to burn."

"I wouldn't be bugging you right now if I did."

"Look kid, this is how it is. Parts should be here in a few more days and as soon as they arrive, I'll start to put her back together. You had oil in your water and that tells me for certain that you've got a blown head gasket. These goddamn Limeys are known to crack heads. That's why I told you that the head might be cracked. It might be, and it might not be. I'm gunna repair it as if the head isn't cracked. If that works, you'll be out of here in less than a week. If the head is cracked, I'll tear it back down without chargin' you for any additional labor, but we'll have to find you a good head somewhere, or send yours out for repair, if it even can be repaired, that is. I've also ordered an extra head gasket just in case I've got to tear it back down. Now, do you feel better?"

"Yes and no," I answered. Yes, because I knew what his plan was. No, because I still had no idea when I was to get out of purgatory.

"Best that I can do," Okie responded, shrugging his shoulders. "I'd be lyin' to you if I told you any different."

"OK, thanks."

"Now, I need a favor from you."

"What's that Okie?"

"I need you to go pump another twenty bucks worth of my watered down gas into that worn out Chevy and go burn it wherever you've been burnin' it so that I can get back to work," Okie said grinning, appearing proud of himself for the way that he'd handled me.

Okie hadn't noticed that I'd *walked* over to check on the MG. Actually, I don't think he much gave a damn how I got there, nor did he give a shit about how I was to leave, just as long as I left. I crossed the street to the diner. Sarah was standing at the register ringing up a couple of young lovebirds.

"Morning Sarah," I said, greeting her with a directness that I had failed to leave back across the street at Okie's.

Sarah just smiled without responding, not wanting to short-change the couple. I kept on and took the stairs up to my room to finish my morning rituals.

I hadn't checked my e-mail for almost a week. Not having the conveniences of my electronically ordered life was beginning to eat at me. I dug the cellular phone out of my bag to check the voice mail. I usually carried the damn thing around like a baby with a pacifier, but for some reason I had managed to forget all about it for those past few days. I only had two messages. One was a business call from a client who had just purchased a harvester. He wanted to know when he could expect delivery. The other call was from Jenny, telling me she'd received my message about not making it back that past weekend, and that she'd talk to me when I returned to California.

I called the trucking company to check on the haul but had to leave a message for the dispatcher who was tied up on another line. It was close to noon when I finally went back downstairs to get some lunch. There was a redhead sitting at the coffee counter close to where I'd grown accustomed to sitting, because there I could see Jimmy through the window as well as visit with Sarah when she was putting her orders together.

"Hello," I said, to the redhead as I sat down at the counter.

"Hi," she responded in a flat monotone, staring into the newspaper that she had strategically unfolded in front of her. She had also strewn her purse and keys over three seats worth of the coffee counter to keep anyone else from invading her space.

"Hi there," Sarah said, greeting me with that wonderful smile of hers, bouncing up to wait on me.

"Hi Sarah. How's it going?" I asked, as the un-talkative broad looked on.

"Good. And you?"

"Feeling agitated, but in sort of a good way. I guess agitated isn't it, I'm…"

"Antsy?" Sarah answered before I could.

"Yeah, that's about right."

"What are you antsy about?"

"I don't know," I answered, as the redhead rustled in her chair.

"What can I get you?" Sarah asked.

"I don't know yet. How about a cup of hot tea and some ice water for starters."

"OK, I'll get that for you while you decide what you're antsy about and what you want for lunch."

Sarah hit me with another one of her sparkling-eyed smiles that really messed up any chance I had of deciding on a meal. Damn, she was driving me wild, and it had been a long time since I'd come across a woman who could. Why exactly she drove me so mad, I really couldn't say for certain, but she had somehow cast a spell on me.

She served a green salad that had been topped with sliced chicken breast still glistening with juices from Jimmy's grill. "Can I get you anything else?" Sarah asked the redhead, as she refilled her water glass. "Oh yeah, you wanted some bread."

Sarah looked back through the window. "Jimmy, can I have a side of garlic bread?"

Jimmy shook his head acknowledging Sarah's request as he rocked out to a Led Zeppelin tune that had something to do with finding a confounded bridge. Sarah turned around to see if I was ready to order.

"Could I have the chicken sandwich with avocado and no onions?" I asked, before she could offer to take my order.

"I don't know, could you?" she asked, penciling it onto her green order pad.

"You bet I could."

"What's he listening to back there?" the redhead asked Sarah.

Jimmy overheard Red ask the question, but before he could say anything, Sarah walked into the back and changed the music to a country station.

"Led Zeppelin," Jimmy said, peeping his head halfway out the window. "What's wrong with Led?"

"Sounds like a bad acid trip to me," said the redhead, turning to me for support.

I responded first by looking to Red, smiling reactively and then out of loyalty quickly shifting my supporting glance to Jimmy.

"Beats this pissin' and moanin' bleedin' heart country western shit. You know what, you don't know…" Jimmy started to tell her what he really thought and then his better judgment took over and he caught himself.

Red grabbed her keys as she stared back at Jimmy with an I-don't-have-to-take-this-shit-I'm-a-paying-customer glare. He walked away before he finished what the redhead had started. Red set her keys down to finish her salad, looking to me again after Jimmy walked away. She was shaking her head from side to side in disgust. I didn't say a word.

"What the heck did you change it for?" Jimmy yelled to Sarah, as she walked out of the kitchen. Ignoring Jimmy, Sarah looked to Red, smiled and then walked out into the diner to refill some drinks for her customers. He didn't expect an answer from Sarah. He had only said it for Red's sake. A few minutes later, Jimmy set my chicken sandwich up on the shelf.

"Order-up!" Jimmy barked out the window, right at Red.

Sarah came walking up behind Red looking straight at Jimmy, shaking her head with a cut-that-shit-out look. Jimmy looked at me and smiled. Red had had her fill.

"Can I have my check?" the redhead said to Sarah, as she set my lunch down in front of me. Jimmy had included a generous scoop of cottage cheese that I hadn't ordered.

"Give me a minute to total it," Sarah responded calmly, as she walked up to the calculator that sat on the stainless steel counter top below the kitchen window. Sarah tallied the bill and handed it to Red.

"Here you go," Red said, handing Sarah a twenty without looking at the total.

Sarah rang her up and brought the change back to her. "Thanks a lot," Sarah said courteously.

"Thank you," Red said, getting up to leave. She left Sarah a five-dollar tip and walked towards the door without acknowledging Jimmy or me. She stopped and looked at the bulletin board that was just inside the front door for a couple of minutes just to make it seem as if Jimmy hadn't struck a nerve and run her off.

"Change the channel back, Jimmy," I shouted, the front door still swinging from Red's exit.

"No shit!" Jimmy yelled back, going for the radio dial. After changing the station, he came up front to refill his tumbler.

Sarah came walking up to the counter. "You guys," she said, looking at me.

"What did I do?" I asked.

"Nothin'. That bitch had a chip on her shoulder when she walked in here," defended Jimmy.

"You're just lucky Flo isn't around," said Sarah.

"Fuck Flo, too!" Jimmy bellowed, walking through the kitchen door back into his own territory.

"It's not a good idea to insult the chef," I told Sarah.

"He's so edgy lately," Sarah said. "It's so unlike him."

"I guess there comes a time in a man's life when editing no longer serves him," I said, watching for Sarah's response and realizing that some of Flo had rubbed off on me.

"Editing?"

"Yeah, as in having to watch what you say."

"Yeah, but there's a time and place."

"I don't know about that. Seems to me that if you're picking the time and place you're still holding your tongue."

"Maybe so," Sarah said, unconvinced, but wanting to avoid the debate and another one of my philosophy lessons. She walked off to check on her tables. Jimmy was clanging some pots around back in the kitchen just to be making noise. Something had gotten under his skin. It was there before Red ever showed up, but something about her had tripped Jimmy's I've-got-my-belly-full-of-this-shit reaction. I was looking forward to hanging around Jimmy just to see what might happen next. Sarah walked back up and cleared the counter where Red had been sitting. After wiping it down, she poured herself a glass of water and sat down next to me.

"Whatcha doing today?" asked Sarah.

"Let me check my schedule here," I said, pulling a napkin out of the dispenser. "Says here fishing, anytime after noon 'til dusk."

"What a life. Some people have it made," answered Sarah.

"Want to join me?" I asked, grinning.

"No fishing for me today. I have to clean house and do the laundry."

"Who said I was talking about fishing?"

"Like I said, I have to clean house," answered Sarah, as she walked off to check on customers.

I finished my lunch and picked up the extra long toothpick that had held my sandwich together. With the toothpick pinched between my teeth, the red cellophane doily dangling from the opposite end, I walked upstairs to get my fishing gear. I don't know why I took the gear out of Ol' Reliable every night. It must have been my Central California programming that had taught me to bring it in at night, or run the damn good chance that it wouldn't be mine in the morning.

The Chevy fired on the first turn of the starter. I drove across the street for my ritual of burning another twenty. Okie was in the back wrenching on a car when I walked in to pay. I threw a twenty down and then picked it up and walked back into the shop.

"Okie, I'm gunna slip this twenty into the top drawer of your tool box instead of leaving it up front on the counter."

"Sounds good. Thanks."

"Thank you."

"Hey kid."

"Yeah."

"Have fun," Okie said, sensing my seriousness.

"I'll see you." I said, nodding my head back in acknowledgement as I walked out of the shop.

I hopped in the Chevy and headed for the river. I drove over the cattle guard unconscious of my passage into sanctuary. My body had made the passage, but I'd left my mind back at the diner with Sarah. I parked, slipped into my waders, and walked for the river. How in the hell was I going to catch a fish when I really didn't give a damn about catching a fish in the first place? Or did I?

Time streamed by; I was lost. For all I know I could have been wandering up and down that river for a lifetime. It would have taken something like hooking a fish to reel me out of my trance. Fortunately, or unfortunately, it didn't happen. It was the setting sun and my growling belly that woke me. I was a few hundred yards down river from where I'd started. I reeled in my line and slipped the hook into the little eyelet at the base of the rod for safekeeping until I could get back to Ol' Reliable and put my gear up. I was hungry but didn't really want to go back to the diner.

The Chevy brought me back anyway. Where else could I go? I parked, grabbed my gear and went in. I didn't see Flo, so I went up to my room to dump off the gear. I'd have to make dinner myself, so I decided to take a hot bath before going back down for a bite to eat.

When I did come down for dinner, Flo was sitting in her booth playing solitaire, ignoring the sitcom on television.

"Evening Flo."

"Hello there," she answered, flipping a card.

"I have to eat." I said cautiously.

"You never know about me, do you?" Flo asked, sensing my paranoia.

"No, guess I don't."

"Why not?"

"Just testing your mood to see what kind of a reaction I am gunna get from you."

"Isn't that kind of how you approach life?"

"Don't we all?" I asked.

"No, we all don't."

"Flo, do you mind if I make myself a sandwich before we get started here?"

"Well, that's a good start."

"What's a good start?"

"Eating, taking care of yourself, instead of listenin' to me," Flo said, smiling as she flipped another card and started making some moves.

I walked into the kitchen and found the turkey, mayo, cottage cheese and bread. I took two pieces of whole-wheat and lightly spread some mayo over them. I laid some turkey slices on the bread and scooped a gob of cottage cheese out of the container with the fork I intended to use instead of dirtying a spoon. I put the two sandwich halves on the plate next to the cottage cheese, tidied up, and left the kitchen.

On my way past the coffee counter, with my free hand, I grabbed a glass and filled it with water. I put my plate down opposite Flo, sat down, rolled up one of my sandwich halves, and took a bite.

"What's that?" Flo asked.

I frowned, pointing to my mouth, shrugging my shoulders, and thinking to give her the middle finger.

"You just put turkey on bread and roll it up?" Flo asked, with a puzzled look.

"I like it that way. There's some mayo on it," I answered,

after swallowing my first bite.

"What about lettuce or tomato?"

"What about it?" I asked, taking a bite of cottage cheese.

"You've been on your own for too long," she said, shaking her head.

"Anyway, what were you saying before I went to make my sandwich?" I asked, wanting to finish my meal.

"You're apologizin' so you can manipulate."

"I'm not apologizing for anything," I said, before taking another bite.

"It's your theme in life."

"What is?" I asked, with a mouthful, wondering why I'd opened up the door back into this conversation.

"Wantin' to be in control of your life."

"So," I frowned

"So you're run by what you believe people think, by how you expect them to react to you. You like to think you run your own life, but you don't," she said, playing another card.

"Yes I do," I said, reaching for my water and wanting to dump it over her head.

"No you don't," Flo insisted. "You still don't know how to be open and honest."

"Honest about what," I asked, unable to take another bite of my dinner.

"Honest about bein' your own man, regardless of what others think about you."

"How in the hell do you get by in this world without adapting to others?"

"By payin' attention," she said, conceding her card game and stacking the deck in one pile.

"Why pay attention if it works already."

"Because you're givin' up your power."

"I'm not giving up power by adapting."

"Yes you are. You're lettin' others run your life."

"You know what Flo. I'm damn tired of you."

"Quit it. I'd rather you be real," she said, while she slipped the playing cards back into their box.

"I should have eaten before my bath," I announced in a disgusted tone. "I'm tired of choking down your goddamn rhetoric along with my meals."

"It's bedtime for me," Flo announced in a satisfied tone, almost as if she'd accomplished something. "Good night."

"Pleasant dreams," I said, wishing her the worst nightmare of her life.

Chapter 10
Thursday

I woke and drank a glass of water to clear my hoarse throat before calling the trucker to check the haul. I got through to the dispatcher, and after confirming a delivery date, called my client and reassured him of a timely delivery on his recent purchase.

I had my business done for the day. Now it was time for a cup of coffee. I skipped my bone-warming, joint-soothing bath, dressed, hid my morning hair-do under my John Deere wig and headed downstairs for a whiff of Sarah.

"Morning," I said, greeting her.

"Don't you look cute in your Dear John hat," Sarah smart-assed, pouring my coffee.

"Pay attention now. Don't want you to get carried away and make a mess," I said, concerned that she'd overfill my cup while watching for the expression she was trying to coax out of me.

"Hey Mister, you're the one that's only been up for ten minutes. I could fill your cup in a dark room without spilling a drop."

"And I'd let you," I said, waiting for her expression.

Sarah walked off, smiling without a comeback. A few minutes later she returned with an empty coffee pot. She pulled the filter holder out of the coffee brewer and dumped the old grounds into the trashcan below the counter. She took a new filter with freshly ground coffee already in it from a stack that had been prepared earlier to save time during an unexpected rush.

"Got your skirt pressed for the river?" I asked.

"You wish," said Sarah, as she slid the filter holder into place and pushed the red button to start a fresh pot.

"Jeans will work," I said, proud of my salesman's tactic of

asking for more, so that I'd get what I wanted, considering the skirt a bonus.

"Pick me up at my house, at two."

"Two it is."

"You hungry?"

"Yeah, but I think I'll go clean up and get ready for my day. I'll grab some lunch when I come back down. OK, I'll see you at two. If not sooner."

"I won't be ready until two," Sarah reminded me.

"I mean when I come back down for lunch," I reassured her.

Now that I had my day lined up, I decided to relax in the tub and scrub up for Sarah. After the bath, I carried my gear out to Ol' Reliable. I came back into the diner and sat at the counter. Lunchtime was over, and there wasn't a soul in the place besides Jimmy and myself.

"Whatcha eatin'?" Jimmy asked through the kitchen window.

"Your call, Jimmy."

"You got it," he said, looking confident that what he was about to prepare would please me.

I walked behind the counter and poured myself a glass of iced tea. I looked for the newspaper to help me escape the silence. I had escaped the silence for years by reading. My social needs were met in the daily routines as a tractor-salesman. My evenings usually consisted of withdrawal into the silence that I found in solitude. Often the solitude would evoke a quiet terror, that, after a time, I'd escape by reading. I decided to skip the paper and honor the silence that had been offered. I wondered where Sarah had gone and I wondered which corner Flo was hiding behind. A few minutes later Jimmy backed through the swinging kitchen door with both hands full.

He placed two big bowls of soup on the counter.

"Vegetable?" I asked.

"Vegetable beef," he answered. "I'll be right back."

A minute later, Jimmy walked back out holding a pan of corn bread with one hand and a spatula in the other. He put the spatula down and reached for a couple of serving plates. Next, he cut a square out of the middle of the cornbread and halved it.

One half went on my plate and the other on his. Jimmy returned the pan to the kitchen and was back in a flash with some butter and honey.

"Let's eat," Jimmy said, proud of his creation.

"Cheers," I said, raising my iced tea glass to his tumbler.

Jimmy spread butter over the top of his cornbread and then squeezed what seemed to be half a bottle of honey over the bread.

"Looks like you won't be having desert," I said, as I sliced my cornbread in half, and buttered the freshly exposed steaming hot insides of the divided slices.

"Who says you can't have desert with dinner?" Jimmy asked, before shoveling a huge chunk of bread into his mouth.

The butter was already melting into my bread. It looked awfully inviting, but too hot, so I opted for the soup first. It was exceptional: filled with bite-sized chunks of beef as well as potatoes, carrots, green beans, and even some button mushrooms. It was a perfect meal in preparation for my day on the river. We just sat there and ate without saying a word. This time, the silence and terror was fed with Jimmy's soup, cornbread, and companionship. I ate, wondering if Jimmy ever got lonely out there in the middle of nowhere, curious when he last woke up in the morning curled up with a woman. When had he last breathed in the natural sweet scent of a lover, her head resting on his chest, his nose nestled in her hair? The curiosity evoked a longing of my own.

"Jimmy, there's a fish waiting for me out there."

"Fish, shit."

"Got to go. Thanks for lunch," I said, confirming his suspicion with a grin.

I hopped into the Chevy and headed for Sarah's place. It wasn't quite two, but I didn't want to be late. I turned down the dirt lane to her house, parked out front and waited, not wanting to be too pushy by invading the privacy of her home.

Sarah came bouncing out of her front door about five minutes after I arrived. I got out and opened the passenger door of Ol' Reliable for her.

"Thank you," Sarah said, as she climbed in.

"You look awfully nice," I said, shutting the door behind her and walking around to the driver's side of the Chevy. Sarah didn't want me at her place before two because she was busy fixing herself up for our fishing excursion. She looked and smelled so good that I wanted to slide inside of those Levis and... well, let me just say that I was grateful to God for making her so beautiful and cussing him at the same time for putting her just out of reach. We pulled onto the highway and headed for the river. Passing Okie and Flo's establishments triggered a curiosity.

"So, Sarah, what brought you to Five Points?"

"The same road that brought you," she answered.

"Maybe," I responded, and then just shut up knowing that silence, as opposed to questions, usually provoked more answers.

"I was running," she answered, after a few minutes had passed.

"From what?"

"A lot of things. Thought it was my husband."

"But it wasn't?"

"Initially, I ran because of him, but now that I've been here for a while, I can see that it wasn't just him."

"I see," I said, hoping for her to continue, but she had drifted off looking out of the passenger window down toward the shoulder of the road. Sarah was quiet for a few minutes. I left her to wherever she had slipped off.

"I lost a child," were the words that Sarah had been retrieving in her silence.

I didn't respond, except with a glance to let her know that I'd heard her.

"I carried him full term. It was congenital heart disease. He didn't even live for a whole day."

"I'm sorry, Sarah," were the only words that I could find. I wanted to hug her. I wanted to hold her for eternity. I wanted to make sure that Sarah would never have to suffer another loss for as long as she lived, but 'I'm sorry, Sarah' was all that I seemed able to offer her.

"He'd be three in about a week."

"What's his name Sarah?"

"His name was Evan."

I pulled to the side of the road, put the Chevy in park, and left it running. I turned toward Sarah leaving my left hand dangling over the wheel while my right arm rested on top of the seat back. I swung my right knee around on the seat and looked dead into Sarah's eyes. She had already turned to face me.

"His name *is* Evan. I never want to hear *was* again," I demanded, as I turned in the seat and put the truck back into drive. We crossed over the cattle guard in silence, a tribute to Evan.

I pulled up to the river, parked, and turned to Sarah before getting out of the pickup.

"I want to celebrate everything about you Sarah. I want to know all of you, even the parts that you think should be dead and buried," I said forcefully.

Sarah looked at me without saying anything. I didn't expect her to say anything. I just wanted her to have the freedom to express herself, didn't want her to think she had to hold back.

"Are you all right?" I asked, beginning to doubt my boldness. I let the tailgate down and dragged my gear out of the back of the Chevy.

"I'm fine," she answered with a fake smile.

"Do you want to go somewhere else?"

"No, I want to watch you fish."

"I guess I…"

"Please, I'm fine. I want you to fish," she interrupted, her tone more convincing.

Fish I did. I followed the same short trail into the river. I fished the waters working my way downstream, occasionally looking up to check on Sarah. Every time I looked, she had moved down the river with me and found a rock to sit on as she looked on. She seemed content in her silence, seemed to know exactly where she needed to be to regain her spirit after having shared her loss.

I looked up to check on her and then turned to spot the Chevy for reference. I'd fished downstream about two hundred yards without as much as a bite. Deciding to take a break and start over upstream, I returned to shore.

"How are you?" I asked, walking up to Sarah who was perched on a huge boulder that sat halfway in the water. "I brought you along for luck, you know," I teased.

"The problem is all that wrong living you've done."

"I wish."

"Well, if you haven't lived wrong, then you better start holding your mouth different," Sarah giggled.

"Come on, walk back upstream with me. You can give me some pointers on my mouth."

"Well, all right. But I don't see how we're gunna cure years of habit in less than ten minutes."

"Come on," I said, starting back upstream. "Sarah, did I ever tell you that my mom and dad still live in the same house that they brought me home to when I was born?"

"No you didn't," she said, looking down again as she had in the truck when she was looking for the courage to talk about Evan.

"They've been there for forty years."

"My parents just sold our home after twenty-eight years. It was a horse ranch. It had everything. They sold it and moved to the Keys," Sarah said, her eyes wide with tears.

"You know what's one of the most screwed up things about being human?" I asked.

"What's that?"

"We can't be in more than one place at a time."

"God, I miss that place. Now they're fly-fishing in Florida. I mean that's what they wanted. They're happy and all, but..."

"We never really leave home completely," I whispered, to validate the nostalgic tug that was pulling her back to the innocence of youth.

"I just never thought I'd be somewhere like here. I always imagined..." she stopped.

"Imagined what?" I asked.

"Imagined that it would be like... like where I came from. Like mom and dad and our family. You know, home and the security it brings. Belonging."

"It's hard to do, isn't it Sarah?"

"What's that?"

"I don't know. Like, do you ever... I guess I don't feel like an adult. I'm almost forty, no kids. I do what I damn well please. At forty my mother and father had four boys to care for. I can hardly imagine what it would be like to have a child, the responsibility.

I still feel too much like a kid, myself."

"It's sad to think about how it used to be. I mean, how it's gone and all," Sarah replied.

"It just pisses me off, but... but just about anything pisses me off these days. I never know when the pissed off breeze is gunna hit me."

"Typical guy-response. You guys aren't allowed to be sad, so you have to be pissed."

"Sarah, I'd trade pissed for that bucket of tears that's hidden away in me any day. I'll take them, just help me find them." All that I could ever find was a silent longing deep down in the hollow canyon of my soul. It was an emptiness, a dry freezing cold emptiness that was praying for a warm tropical storm.

The typical guy-response wasn't going to work for Sarah. She just looked at me and listened to the silence. It wasn't an uncomfortable silence. I didn't want any words. I just wanted to walk with her in this sacred place.

I'd spent most of my life alone in that hallowedness. It was nice to know that she had the capacity to share it with me. It was also nice to know that I could share it with a woman and not some fleeting image out of my dream world, always gone when I woke up.

"Sarah, I've had enough for one day."

"What's the matter?"

"Not a thing."

"You don't want to fish?"

"Don't feel like it right now."

"Is it me?"

"Yeah, but in a good way."

"You can take me back if I'm bothering you."

"NO! Hell no! I want to be right here with you. I don't want to wander back out into that river alone and miss out on time that I can spend with you."

"That's sweet of you."

"Well, I wasn't tryin' to be sweet."

Sarah turned to face me, looked up into my eyes, wrapped her arms around my waist, and pulled me to her. She turned her head to one side and rested it against me as she squeezed me closer to her.

"You're sweet," she whispered, as I felt her breath on my chest.

"Come on let me get out of these waders."

I let the tailgate down and sat down to shed my gear. Sarah sat down to the right of me. I stripped the waders off and threw them behind me. I slipped back into my Tonys and slid off the tailgate. Sarah followed right behind me, took my hand and pulled me to her.

"That's how you hold your mouth," Sarah whispered, when she had finished kissing me.

"I'll try to remember that."

"You better."

Little was said on our drive out. I savored the silence until we rumbled over the cattle guard back into the other world.

"Where're we headed?" I asked, anticipating her proposal.

"I should probably get home. I have an early start, you know."

"Yeah, I guess you do. Besides, you hang around me much more tonight you'll find yourself in a whole lot of trouble."

"That's exactly what I'm afraid of," Sarah said, smiling.

"Home it is."

"I just don't want to start what can't be stopped."

"I wish you would," I said, feeling a fire burning in me. *Damn I wish you would*, I thought silently.

Sarah didn't respond except with a confident smile. She knew she had me right where she wanted me. She was in control of everything, even if I did believe myself to be the seducer.

I parked; then walked her to the door. We climbed the steps and I waited while she fished around in her purse for the house key. I kissed her while her hand was still in the bag.

"What do you think you're..." she stopped, flustered.

"Just helping you find your keys."

"I can find my own keys, thank you."

"That's obvious," I said, her hand still digging around in her purse. I kissed her again and she pulled out the keys before I finished.

"Time for bed," she said, after she finished giving me another mouth-holding lesson.

"You bet it is."

"Go," Sarah said, as she slipped the key into the lock.

"But…"

"Good night," Sarah said, before kissing my cheek.

"All right, good night," I said, skipping down the steps back to Ol' Reliable. "I hope this damn truck won't start."

"You'll get awfully cold tonight if it doesn't," she said, before closing the door.

I drove out the dirt drive toward the highway. With every fence post that went by, I felt a deeper tug back towards Sarah. I didn't want to go. I didn't want to go back to that damn diner, and I didn't want to sleep alone that night. I didn't want to sleep alone ever again. By the time I got back to Flo's, I was twisted.

It was dark when I walked in. Flo was sitting in her booth without the television on or the radio.

"Hi Flo. What's up?"

"Enjoyin' the quiet; watchin' the cars pass by. What's up with you?" Flo asked, changing the subject.

"Not much."

"No luck?"

"Just another fruitless day on the river. I'm beat, headed for the bath. I'll see you in the morning."

"Good night kid."

I wasn't in the mood to deal with Flo. For some reason, I felt a twinge of guilt when I walked in, and I didn't particularly want to dissect it over dinner.

Chapter 11

Friday

It felt like a hangover. I was anxious but didn't know why. I hated feeling that way, but on some mornings I had no choice. I didn't drink, didn't smoke, and rarely over-ate, but felt trembly, queasy and a little out of focus.

I ran a bath hoping that it would help me out of my waking state, but I knew better than to expect any relief. Coffee would only add to my agitation, and I didn't feel hungry. I would have liked the convenience of remedying my altered state with ten milligrams worth of mother's little blue helper but knew that the chemical compounds of a Valium couldn't remedy my condition.

I dressed and descended from my lofty bungalow to the waking world below, hoping to be charmed from my trance by a real world drama at the coffee counter.

"Watch out, Sarah's pissed," Jimmy told me, walking back into the kitchen.

I grabbed the weekly rural newspaper whose publisher actually printed daily, but for five different communities, all of which had weekly distribution. The benefit to placing a classified ad in the Five Points Tribune was that it ran in all five of the publisher's weeklies. It was nice for the advertiser because of the broader coverage, and it was nice for the publisher because he only made changes once a week. It also made the classified section look a hell of a lot more impressive than it really was. I sat back and stared blindly at the want ads as Sarah walked up to the counter. Hoping to soon learn why she was pissed, I feigned innocence over a survey.

"Hi there, coffee?"

"Please. A glass of water, too."

"You hungry?" Sarah asked, filling my coffee cup with her left hand and delivering the water with her right.

"This is good for now. Thanks."

"Whatcha looking for?" Sarah asked, noticing my make-believe attention to the classifieds.

"Nothing really, just snooping. How's your day?" I asked, changing the subject.

"OK," Sarah answered in an unconvincing tone.

"Just OK huh?"

"Actually it's not OK, but it is what it is," Sarah answered, as she left to tend her tables.

Jimmy walked out to fill his tumbler with water and looked at me with a half-assed grin as if he might be guilty of something. He filled his glass and nodded his head to me as he backed through the swinging door into the kitchen. I put the paper down and took another sip of coffee. It was still too hot to drink, so I added some cream to cool it and doctored it with a quick stream of sugar from the glass dispenser that had a Saltine cracker in it to soak up the moisture. Sarah returned with the coffee pot and set it on the warmer. Jimmy came back out front and sat down next to me.

"Ever been in love Jimmy?" I asked, as Sarah walked off with a glass of milk for one of her tables.

"Oh yeah."

"What happened?"

"Misery."

"Misery?"

"All misery."

"Come on, there's usually some ecstasy before the misery."

"It was all misery," Jimmy maintained. "How 'bout you?"

"Marriage was all misery for me, too."

"That bad?" he asked.

"Jimmy, all I can tell you is that when I was twenty-five, I checked myself into an alcohol rehab and shaking the booze wasn't shit compared to my marriage."

Jimmy took another swig from his tumbler without responding.

"Fell in love when I was getting divorced, though," I

announced, uncomfortable with his silence.

"What happened?" Jimmy asked, as Sarah returned from her milk delivery and walked behind the counter.

"Left. I loved her, and I left."

"Why?"

"I couldn't handle it."

"Love?"

"Yeah, and the conditions."

"Love and conditions, huh?" Jimmy asked, with a perplexed look.

"Conditions. You know, timing. Lauren was a couple of years older than me. She was getting divorced, too. She also had a couple of young boys. Got tired of all her distractions: couldn't stand not being the center of her life."

"Is that why you really left?" interrupted Sarah, curiosity getting the best of her.

"Left because I was too raw, too exposed. Felt too vulnerable."

"For love?" Sarah interrupted again.

"To be hurt," I answered.

"Then it was just bad timing. It wasn't meant to be, but you learned," Sarah reasoned.

"Learned a lot," I answered, as Sarah walked off to seat a new party.

"Mine was married," Jimmy said, turning away to the right and looking down towards the floor. "She left her husband for me."

"What happened?"

"I thought she wanted me."

"How old was she?"

"Thirty-four. Ten years older than I was. I was just back from Nam," Jimmy answered, shifting in his seat.

"Sounds like you were just an excuse."

"An excuse?"

"Yeah, to help her leave her husband."

"I don't know what I was. All I know is that I was miserable. Thought she wanted me, but I thought wrong."

Sarah returned, slipped an order ticket into the wheel, and spun it around, summoning Jimmy away from the inquisition and back into his harbor of safety. Admiring her finer qualities, I watched Sarah scoop cups of ice just like I had the first day we met. Over that past week, I had begun to know Sarah a bit better, but that still hadn't taken away my admiration for her ass-end. If anything had changed, it was my wanting her all the more. Sarah filled two glasses with soda and delivered them. She then returned adding another ticket to the order wheel.

"What happened to you Sarah?"

"About what?"

"Why'd you leave him?" I asked, wanting to tell her to quit playing dumb.

"I don't know," Sarah replied, acting a little put off that I asked.

"What's the big deal?"

"You guys always need a reason. You need it to be simple, so you think you can understand it. It makes you feel better that way."

"Be nice now," I said, as Sarah walked off with the coffee pot.

I was curious why she was pissed and curious about her marriage. Sarah came back a few minutes later and started a fresh pot of coffee.

"Sarah, what are you so pissed off about?" I asked, figuring that at least one of my curiosities would get satisfied.

"Who says I'm pissed?" Sarah asked, glaring back at Jimmy.

"Nobody; I just thought…"

"He was just a jerk, all right?"

Jimmy flipped a couple of plates up into the window. Sarah slipped the catsup bottle into her apron pocket before she grabbed the plates and rushed off to deliver them. I left her alone when she returned. She took the coffee pot and filled my cup.

"He just wanted me around, when he wanted me around."

I didn't respond.

"He thought he could just turn me on and off like a light switch."

"So, he wanted you at his beck and call. Wanted you when it was convenient for him, but when he didn't, you were left out in the cold?"

"Exactly."

"He needed you until it was time to chase Bonefish," I said, hoping to rub salt in her wound.

"How'd you know he Bonefishes?"

"Lucky guess," I answered, and guessing was all that I had done. I remembered that her parents were living in Florida fly-fishing and decided to take a run at it. I accidentally ended up hitting the Bonefish on the head.

"That's all that he could think about," Sarah said, staring at me, wondering how I had nailed her husband. "I think my parents care about him more than me. He's like the son they never had," she added as Jimmy placed another order up into the window.

I hadn't learned what she was mad about, but I was beginning to get a clearer picture as to why Sarah was in Five Points. I just couldn't figure out why she picked Five Points of all places. Flo walked in through the back door and up to the counter as Sarah went to deliver her order.

"Whatcha got goin' today kid?" Flo asked.

"Don't know, why?"

"Thought maybe I could enlist your help," she said, without really describing the task-at-hand.

I wanted to know what the hell I was getting into, but also knew I didn't have much of a choice as I had been driving her truck, eating her food, sleeping at her diner, and chasing her waitress for the last week without as much as paying her a dime.

"What do you need Flo?"

"I need you to take a run to the hardware store in Tranquillity to pick up some supplies."

"No problem."

"It isn't much. We keep blowin' electrical fuses and can't afford to be without them over the weekend."

"Like I said, no problem. I'll run up to my room to get my watch and wallet. Then I'll head out."

I went up to my room, unloaded some coffee and grabbed my things. I walked out the back door and fired up Ol' Reliable. I had just started rolling out of the parking lot when Flo walked out waving her arms for me to stop. I pulled back in and rolled down the window to see what she wanted.

"Wait up for a minute," Flo said, as she stepped back into the diner. A few minutes later she returned with her purse and hopped in on the passenger's side. "I need to get out of this place for a while. Mind if I ride along?"

"Not at all." What in the hell else was I going to say? Now she had me cornered for at least the next couple of hours.

We pulled across the highway to fill up the Chevy. Flo walked in to see Okie while I pumped the gas. I decided to check the oil, finding it just below the full mark on the dipstick. I topped off the gas tank and started in to pay.

"Where you headed?" Flo asked as she stepped out of the station.

"To settle up with Okie."

"I took care of it already," Flo said in her boss-lady tone.

"OK," I said, feeling the need to pay for the gas, but not wanting to start an argument that early in our journey.

I fired up Ol' Reliable and pulled out onto the highway waiting for it to backfire, but the damn Chevy proved me wrong. It reminded me of taking a sick car to a mechanic and having it miraculously recover about a block from the shop. Flo was quiet, not in one of her inquisitive moods.

"When was the last time you got away, Flo?" I asked, breaking the silence.

"Depends on your definition of away. Probably been a month since I made a run to the hardware."

"Been anywhere else?"

"It's been about five years since I've traveled any distance."

"Where'd you go?"

"Funeral," she answered, looking out the passenger side window.

"Hell of a reason to travel."

"Funerals are a hell of a reason for anything," Flo said, without revealing whose funeral she'd attended.

"Where was it?"

"Southern California."

"Family?"

"My mother."

"I'm sorry," I said, not knowing how else to respond.

"Part of life," Flo said, as she shifted in her seat.

"Your father still alive?"

"No. He died ten years ago. Left me the diner."

"What about your mother?"

"What about her?"

"Why didn't she take over?"

"Mom left Dad years ago; ran off with some guy who came through one summer. Guess the solitude finally got to her."

I waited to hear more from Flo, but she remained silent. I wanted to ask more, but knew that I was already treading on ground that was sacred to her. I started thinking about my mom and dad; I was fortunate to still have my parents.

I recalled our summer vacations and how my three brothers and I were loaded into the back of that old camper. It not only transported us to our vacation destination, but doubled as sleeping quarters as well. Four boys in the back of that camper with no crawl space up into the front of the truck meant, at minimum, a two-hour non-stop ass-kicking free-for-all that the younger brothers always had to endure.

The only intercom was one of the younger boy's fists pounding on the back window of the pickup while the rest of us anxiously awaited the reply of our creators. Dad never turned around; he couldn't because he was driving, and I'm sure that he had designed it that way. Mother, on the other hand, always responded, pointing her finger at us with the rage of Kali painted all over her face, mouthing the words: "If you guys don't shape up you're going to get your asses beat at the next stop." We'd point at each other, blaming one another for our aggressiveness: it was the territorial imperative in action. After mom had bestowed her benediction of threats upon us, and realizing she still loved us, we'd crawl back up onto the top bunk of the camper to repeat our rituals.

If we had to pee, it was in a Folgers coffee can. If we had to take a dump, we waited. We spent most of the time on the top bunk of the camper beating the shit out of each other or sharing our brotherly love giving the peace sign and forgetting to include the use of our index finger and shooting brown eyes to our audience of oncoming traffic through the camper's Plexiglas front window.

A semi blew by in the opposite direction and woke me from

my trance. I looked at my watch and realized that half-an-hour had disappeared.

"She ever complain?" I asked, as if no time had gone by.

"Who?"

"Your mom."

"'Bout what?"

"About living out here, her life?"

"All the time, but dad wasn't about to leave this place. He loved it."

"How old were you when your mom left?"

"Fifteen," Flo answered, without thought.

"Could you have gone with her?"

"Oh yeah, but I couldn't leave my father behind. I'd go spend time with my mom once in awhile, but she had somebody; dad didn't."

"So you've spent your whole life out here?"

"Yeah."

"I was gunna ask you if you liked it, but that would be a pretty damn dumb question. If you hadn't, you'd have left."

"Not necessarily. A lot of why I'm here is duty. I couldn't leave my father while he was alive, and I couldn't leave what was dearest to him after he died."

"You're still holding on?"

"Maybe, but what's wrong with that?" she asked in a defensive tone.

"I guess not a thing if you're happy."

"Happy's an illusion. Besides, what else could I do at my age?"

"What do you dream about?"

"I don't know."

"Well, what do you miss in your life?"

"Don't know if I miss anything."

"So your life is just fine right here? You're fulfilled and nothing else excites you?" I asked, realizing that we had reversed roles.

"Sure, why not," she answered, as we pulled up to the hardware store.

I watched Flo walk through the same huddle of ass-ends that I had parted a few days earlier. Flo, too, had become an ass-end in her own diner; watching the world, as well as her own life, drive by. Was she living the miserable existence that her father had handed down to her or was Flo genuinely content with her lot in life? Was she aware that she had other options, or were the unseen powers of her past generations creating the illusion of contentment?

I watched Flo visit with Julie at the back counter. What were they talking about? Did the two women both share the same life of quiet desperation? A desolate life that neither was able to share with the other for fear their mutual discontentment would be discovered. Hell, they had to be talking about the weather, or about how unpredictable the arrival time of the UPS driver was.

A few minutes later, Flo emerged from between the ass-ends and out the front doors.

"What about you?" Flo asked, after she had climbed back into the Chevy.

"What about me?"

"What about your dreams?" she asked, relieved to shift the questions in my direction.

"Ever been to San Francisco, Flo?"

"Twenty or more years ago."

"There's something about that place. I fantasize about living downtown in the city. I want to be a writer. I want to hang out by day in the city, write until the early hours of morning, and sleep 'til noon. That would be my routine, everyday. That's my dream."

"Do it!"

"How?"

"How did you get to where you are today?"

"Worked real hard, but that was tractors. A tractor-salesman is a far cry from a writer. Hell, I don't even have a college education let alone know how to write."

"Like I asked, how did you get to where you are today?"

"By not compromising and not making excuses."

"You believed in yourself."

"My friends ask me if I've started my book. I've never hinted to them once about my dream. In the last few months I've had at least six people ask me if I was a writer or suggested I write. It's almost like... well, like I'm supposed to write."

"See, there you are," Flo encouraged.

"I really don't know what I have to say or where to start."

"I don't think that's the problem."

"What is it then?"

"Do you ever get tired of talkin' about somethin' and just do it?"

"Yeah, my old job. I pissed and moaned for a few years. Got pissed off at people just to have a reason to quit."

"What happened?"

"I stopped making excuses and quit."

"One of these days you'll stop. You won't talk, you'll write. You'll know when it's time. Just like when you knew it was time to quit your job."

"You think so?"

"I know so. But I think you left your job for more reasons than just bein' fed up."

"Yeah?"

"Yeah, you wanted your freedom to become whatever you're becomin'."

"What do you mean?"

"You're your own man with your own life to live. You don't need anything or anyone to hold you back."

I listened.

"You needed to prove to yourself that you could make it on your own."

I just grinned. I didn't know what to say. Flo's encouragement caught me off guard. She actually seemed to believe in me more than I believed in myself.

The remainder of our trip back to the diner was quiet. Sarah's image flashed before me. The harder I tried to push her away the more she became reality. I couldn't quit thinking about her and it began to scare me. Falling in love always scared me. Actually, it scared and excited me. The excitement had once overwhelmed any fear that accompanied this falling, but having lost my innocence, fear now ruled me. The same fear that had robbed me of a good part of my life.

What would I do with Sarah? How could I live the nomadic life that I had designed for myself and fall in love with any woman? I had no business falling for this woman, no business whatsoever. Falling in love meant forgetting everything. It meant no more girlfriends, no more fucking around. It meant commitment, having to take care of another. It meant the work of a relationship, a life filled with duty; or did it?

CHAPTER 12

Friday Evening

Sarah was still working when Flo and I came back from our Tranquillity run. I went over to the coffee counter, and Flo disappeared into the back.

"What can I get for you?" Sarah asked.

"How 'bout some water?"

"That's it?"

"Yeah, I'm feeling antsy. Don't need anything with caffeine."

"You're always antsy," Sarah said, setting a glass of water down in front of me.

"No, I'm not."

"You're always something."

"So are you. You want to fight?" I teased with a grin.

"Sure, let's go."

"When and where?"

"Right here."

"The kind of fight I have in mind can't be fought here," I said.

"Oh, so you're chicken?"

"No, you are."

"You think you're so sly," Sarah said.

"No, you just drive me wild."

"Well, what do you plan to do about that wild man?"

"All that I can get away with."

"You know what I think?" Sarah asked.

"What?"

"You're chicken."

"I'll show you chicken."

"Come on."

"You can't handle it," I told her.

"You'll never know."

"Your loss," I said, as Jimmy dinged the order-up bell.

"Chicken." Sarah whispered at me, as she reached for the order in the window. She turned around, order in hand, with all the intention in the world of having one more jab at me when she spotted Flo, who was less than ten feet in front of her, walking towards the register having just taken in Sarah's whole act. First Sarah's face turned red and then faded to a pale white as she jostled off to shake off her embarrassment and deliver the order.

It was getting closer, the bantering a dance, my favorite kind of dance. I loved the pursuit, the foreplay, but I knew it was always the woman who came to the man. Man chases, pisses on tires, jumps up and down like a baboon drooling all over his red-assed self, but if the woman doesn't come to him and open herself to him, he might as well take his shriveled up hard-on back upstairs to the bathtub. I was getting impatient. I wanted Sarah, but I knew that I still had to wait for her to invite me in.

"Sarah, can I have some more water please?" I asked, as she returned from her delivery. Flo was walking off with a now-I got-your-ass look and a fist full of money from the day's trade.

"So how was your ride?" Sarah asked sarcastically while she filled my cup.

"Not bad."

"Tell the truth," she said, fishing for another response.

"Really, not bad at all," I said, wondering what she was jigging for. Maybe she was worried that Flo had spoiled something for her. That's when I figured that I'd use her curiosity to my advantage.

"That's nice." Sarah said.

"I can't really talk about it right now, anyway," I said, as she started to walk off to refill water glasses. My response stopped her in mid-stride, but she quickly recovered and continued on with her intended mission and soon returned with the empty pitcher.

"You drink much more water you'll be up all night," Sarah poked at me on her return.

"It'll take a hell of a lot more than that to keep me up all night. It's been a long damn time since I've found a woman worthy of my sleepless attention," I said, grinning at Sarah.

"Well, I wouldn't count on any drastic changes in your sleeping habits out here in the middle of nowhere."

"Oh, not to worry, my dear. I don't count on anything."

I loved it. Sarah was stammered inside. She covered it quite well, but her Flo-induced color change and the impulsive tug had jerked her from her usual confident and graceful dance through the diner. If I had my way, she would slip one more time before the night was over.

"So what do you think?" I asked, as she walked behind the coffee counter.

"'Bout what?"

"About later?"

"What did you have in mind?"

"I really didn't have anything in mind. Just thought that maybe we could hang out a while."

"OK. I'll see you at my place at seven-thirty."

"Seven-thirty," I confirmed, as I swiveled to the right and slid off the stool. I landed on the heels of my Tonys and rolled up onto the balls of my feet in a proud-of-myself gesture and started for the stairs. I still had a few hours to kill and decided to spend them in the solitude of my room. I'd talked most of the day and was quite certain that the evening would bring more of the same.

I kicked off my Tonys and dragged the desk chair over to the corner with the windows. I sat down in the chair and lifted my feet up onto the west window ledge, pushing off with my arches and teetering onto the back two legs of the chair. I glanced to the right through the north window and realized that I'd forgotten all about the broken down MG. It stirred me up for a minute or two, but I caught myself and decided to accept my fate, at least for the evening.

I was stuck in Five Points and there really wasn't a damn thing I could do about it, or at least if there was, I'd chosen not to pursue it for some reason. The sun was about an hour from setting as I looked to the western horizon anticipating the brilliance of another passing day. I started thinking about Lauren and felt a wringing in my guts.

I'd never fallen for anyone like I had for Lauren. It had been over four years since I'd last made love to her or even spoken to her. It hurt too much just thinking about not having her, and I wasn't about to subject myself to the futile hope of reclaiming a lost love. Her voice alone would send me back into a spiraled tailspin.

Why Lauren? Was it because she was in many ways unavailable to me? Was it because she was the mother of two young boys whom I had to compete with for her love, just as I once did with my own mother and brothers? I needed her to love me like a young boy and a man. She had two little boys, and a husband who she was trying to change by threatening divorce. He'd called her bluff and left before I had come into the picture. Lauren was looking for someone who stood for everything that her husband wasn't when I came along. I became everything he wasn't, alright, but got lost in the process.

I'd been letting people make me into what they needed me to be for my entire life. Becoming what people needed sold a lot of tractors, it allowed me to gather material possessions and build up a fair retirement at an early age. It gave me the security of an identity, but it had also robbed me of some things.

I almost tipped too far in the chair and lunged forward trying to recover my balance; it worked. I was still feeling the panicky rush that the impending fall had provoked when I looked out of the north window to see the blue Jetta pulling across the street and into the gas station. Okie walked out as Sarah pulled up to the pumps.

She got out to fuel the Jetta, but Okie beat her to the punch and started filling her car. After he had started the pump, he reached inside the driver's side window and pulled the hood release. He checked under the hood and walked off, returning shortly after with a quart of oil and a red funnel. After dropping the hood of the Jetta and pressing down where the latch was to make sure it had caught, Okie tossed the empty container into an old thirty-three gallon oil barrel that served as a trash can.

Sarah had been standing by Okie the whole time while he attended to her car. What could they be talking about? Okie pulled the nozzle from the gas tank and slipped it back into the holder on the pump. I watched him wash her windshield, and watched her give him a warm hug when he had finished. After that, she got into her Jetta and headed home. I wondered why she didn't pay him and then wrote it off to her being a local who probably settled up on payday.

I shifted my gaze back to the west to watch the sun melt. It was a beautiful sunset. There was a string of gapped cirrostratus clouds that resembled the lace on the pillowcase I had as a child. The line of clouds seemed to have no beginning or end, extending from west to east. The clouds made the sunset that evening. I dreamed of skidding along this puffy highway in the sky as if it were an endless slip-n-slide tendering my eternal enchantment with youth.

I was called away from my youthful joy ride by an inner voice, reminding me to brush my teeth. I ran the tub figuring that I better get the rest of me scrubbed up, just in case the goddess of love would be enchanting the evening's breeze.

I was late getting to Sarah's. She was sitting outside on her front steps, waiting for me. Sarah had her hair held up in a clip and was wearing a red cotton tank top under a long sleeve, unbuttoned denim blue shirt. The legs of her faded Levis dangled in simple elegance from her perfectly defined ass and hung down an inch from her white tennis shoes. She didn't have socks on, and her tan ankles were inviting me to climb up into her from the opening between the bottom of her pant legs and the tops of her tennies.

"Thought maybe you got lost."

"Kind of did," I answered, ruminating how lost in thought I had been, reflecting on Lauren and the sunset.

"Well, more importantly, you made it," Sarah said, standing up to hug me.

"Nice to see you," I said, noticing how differently she treated me when we weren't at the diner. The diner often provoked in Sarah a mask of toughness and of being in charge of her environment, which left little room for the girlish spontaneity and sweetness that I experienced with her while driving around or at the river.

"Have a seat," Sarah said, patting the step next to where she'd just sat down.

I sat without saying a word.

"Are you hungry?" she asked.

"A little bit," I answered, hungrier than a horse that had been ridden all day because I'd lost track of time and didn't get anything to eat before leaving the diner.

"Well, I've got something in the oven for us. It'll be ready in about twenty minutes."

"What's that?" I asked.

"A surprise. Besides you're just a little bit hungry," Sarah smiled. "Would you like a drink?"

"How 'bout an iced tea?" I asked, swatting a mosquito that had started to drill into my neck.

"How 'bout it," Sarah answered, with another one of those smiles that had already melted the ice in my glass. "Come on in."

I followed Sarah through the front door and into the kitchen where she poured my tea and set it down on the table.

"Have a seat," she said, pointing to the chair.

"Thanks," I said, sensing a fear in my partially arrested breath. Sarah was treating me like a real live person, someone who she might actually have even cared for. She was treating me with respect, something that I wasn't used to and didn't trust.

"I hope you like lasagna," she said, as she bent over to open the oven for a peek.

"Love it," I said, staring at her ass, trying to balance the fear I'd discovered in my breath only moments before with the hard-on that overtook me from the scent that flowed from that just-opened oven door. Damn, she was a tease even if she wasn't trying to be. It was that just-out-of-reach shit that always drove me mad, but it also kept me going. I stood up and walked over to Sarah.

"Smells awfully inviting," I said, reaching around Sarah from behind and pulling her to me. I nestled my zipper into the curve of her ass, kissing her on the back of her neck

"Wait 'til you see what's for dessert," Sarah said, just before turning around to kiss me.

"Don't know if I can wait."

"If you've waited this long..."

I started to kiss Sarah, robbing her of words and breath, and

I didn't stop. Damn, I wanted to suck every last drop of juice out of this woman. She was open to me, and I wasn't going to let this chance slip away. Dinner or no dinner, I was having dessert. I pushed her up against the refrigerator and started kissing down her neck, tonguing down her top as far as the collar allowed, but not far enough. I started rubbing her breast.

"Time out," Sarah said, as she slid out from between me and the fridge. She walked to the oven, turned it off, and grabbed a potholder to take out the lasagna. She opened the oven and retrieved her dish while I was still standing next to the refrigerator, trying to cool off.

"Dammit!" Sarah yelled, as she pulled back the hand she had failed to cover.

"To hot to handle?" I asked, walking over to attend to her wound. "Let me see."

"I'm all right. It scared me more than it hurt."

"Let me see anyway," I demanded, as Sarah held up her hand with an innocent hurt-little-girl look. She had burned the side of her left hand just below the pinkie.

"Really, it scared me more than anything."

"It doesn't look bad, but burns can be deceiving. Maybe we should ice it?" I suggested.

"No, I'll be fine," Sarah reassured.

"You already are," I said, as I pulled her to me. I kissed her on the forehead again rubbing her temples and then I went for her mouth. She tasted so good that I couldn't help myself. My hands went for her breast, and this time she didn't stop me.

"Come on. The lasagna has to cool," she said, leading me to the couch in the living room.

She pushed me down onto the couch and straddled me. She was in charge of things now, and I wasn't going to fight it. She started kissing me and I just kept swallowing her juices. I started rubbing her breast again and a few minutes later slipped the denim button-up off her. Sarah kept kissing me and started to grind on me until I was feeling raw under the Levis. I pulled her top off and started to suck on her nipples. From there I left a tongue trail down to her belly button and then back up to her breast.

Sarah reached for my crotch and started rubbing me. A few

seconds later she went for my belt and unzipped me. I considered this an invitation to do the same for her, and within minutes we were shed of our denims. She straddled me again and this time without cotton barriers. Her touch pulsed through my body, exciting every nerve ending that I had. I was massaging her; waiting for her to take me in, but for some reason Sarah didn't seem rushed.

A few minutes later, she rose up to take me, but as she did I went limp. She settled back down and started rubbing me until I became hard again. She raised herself up again to take me, and again I went limp. This had never happened before and was producing an unbearable anxiety in me. Sarah just stayed close to me without pushing.

"I'm scared," I confessed, surprising myself with my own words. I'd never been scared before, or if I had, I was never aware of it.

"What are you afraid of?" Sarah asked softly.

"Not being in control."

Sarah just listened.

"You remind me of a woman who I fell in love with once."

"You don't want to be hurt again," Sarah responded.

"I left because I wasn't in control. Because I was scared."

"I'm not gunna hurt you."

"I'm different than I was then. I was so needy. I was just divorced, and starving to be loved like a motherless little boy," I said, surprised again at what had just slipped out of my mouth.

Sarah just listened.

"I don't think you'll hurt me because I'm not the same person I was four years ago. But damn, something old is getting stirred up."

What was throwing me was the potential of falling in love again. I'd had several women in my life since Lauren, but none who could provoke what I once felt for this old love. Yet, for some unknown reason, Sarah was dancing around on the fringes of my heart.

She slid off me and lay down on the couch with her head resting against its arm. She slid one of her legs behind me, the other over my waist. As Sarah slipped her leg around me, her calf caressed my foreskin and my hard-on returned.

"Come here," Sarah said, as she scissored her legs around my waist and pulled me on top of her. I reached for her hands that were lying on both sides of her head and grasped them. Using my elbows, I pulled the rest of my body up onto her and just like that, I had entered Sarah. We melted into one another. Now we were making love, and we continued for what seemed to be hours, if not eternity. I watched her on top of me as she bore the ecstasy and agony of orgasms. Watching her and pleasing her was all that mattered to me. My hard-on had been earned that night and I wasn't done. I'd be damned if I was going to blow it by letting go into Sarah, not yet anyway.

Sarah finally rolled off me, lying by my side with her arm around my chest and her face nestled into my breast. My chest hairs waved back and forth with her breathing, causing a chill that hardened my nipples. Making love to Sarah had only awakened an insatiable urge for more, a longing to be lost in an orgasmic oblivion. We dozed off, and when Sarah woke me, I had lost all track of space and time.

"Come on, I'm hungry," Sarah whispered, nudging me.

"I'm hungry for you," I said, thinking about our just shared communion.

"You have to eat your dinner before you can have dessert," Sarah explained, just before she kissed me.

She got up and slipped her panties on. I wanted to push her down and tongue her until the windows shattered from her screams. She slipped her tank top on and then her denim shirt before walking into the kitchen. I lay there proud of myself, but hidden behind my pride was the fear of my own inadequacy. I had yet to give everything I had to Sarah; I still had to prove myself a worthy, virile lover.

She returned with two plates and placed them on the coffee table in front of the couch. My mouth began to water as she went back into the kitchen. A few minutes later she came out with an iced tea and her own glass of water. I had cuddled up under a blanket and was leaning against the arm of the couch. Sarah handed me a plate and set my drink on the table. She sat down opposite me, leaned against the other couch arm and slid her legs under the blanket touching her toes to mine.

"How is it?" she asked, reaching for her water.

"It was great."

"The lasagna," Sarah smiled.

"Wonderful," I said. Hell, it could have been cardboard. All that I could taste when I swallowed was Sarah.

I had just finished and set my plate on the table when Sarah slid up on top of me as if she'd been waiting for me to take the last bite.

"Come on, let's go to bed," she said, tapping me on the chest.

"What am I gunna tell Flo when she finds out that I didn't make it back?"

"Screw Flo, come on," Sarah said, as she grabbed my hand and led me to her room.

We didn't sleep much that night, but we got a lot of other things accomplished. I finished what I had started with Sarah or what she had started with me. Sarah was right: Fuck Flo!

Chapter 13
Saturday

It was still dark when I woke to Sarah's scent. I pulled myself close and cuddled up behind her like a spoon. My hard-on swelled into the flesh of her ass. After another round of trying to outdo each other, we hopped into the shower.

"What are you gunna tell mom when you get home?" Sarah asked.

"Gone fishing."

"What?"

"Got up early to go fishing."

"You're a pretty good liar, aren't you?"

"I don't know, am I?"

"I suppose you want me to cover for you at the diner?"

"Well, the way I see it, you'll be covering for yourself," I said with a smart-ass grin before stepping into the living room to find my discarded wardrobe. I dressed, slid into my Tonys and walked back into Sarah's bedroom to say goodbye.

"What time are you supposed to be at work? I asked.

"Seven."

"OK, well I'm gunna hit it," I said, as I grabbed Sarah softly behind her head and drew her to me for a kiss.

"I hope you catch a big one," Sarah said, with a sparkle in her eye.

"For some reason, I think this might just be my lucky day," I said, as I held her and kissed the top of her head, breathing in her scent one last time before returning to reality.

"Guess I'll see you at the diner," Sarah said, as she walked me to the door.

"Thanks Sarah," I said, before kissing her one last time

and then skipping down the steps. Hitting the ground, I felt complete, like a man in charge of his universe. I turned around to find Sarah still watching me walk away and another surge of confidence shot through me. "Thanks for everything," I shouted to her, stepping backward in long gaits towards the Chevy.

I fired up Ol' Reliable but didn't feel the tug until the fence posts began to stream by as I made my way down the dirt road to the highway. I thought about stopping at the diner, but sense guided me right on by and drove me towards the river. I crossed over the cattle guard hoping that my entry into sanctuary would sever the thread that had been tugging at my heart ever since I'd left Sarah's. When the tug didn't go away, I knew that I'd tapped into a deeper longing than I ever believed possible.

The fishing gear was back in my room. I knew I'd left it behind but kept driving to the river anyway. I didn't know why, but I had to. Something other than reason was dragging me out there. I drove up to my usual parking spot, got out, and walked up to the bank. I walked downstream until I found a rock that protruded halfway out into the water. It was the same rock Sarah had sat on when I stepped out of the river to join her a few days earlier.

I sat down on the rock wanting to scream but held back. There was no breeze, and the sun had been up for less than thirty minutes. I gazed across the river, soaking up the sound of the water rippling over rocks, silently falling back into the endless current, drifting toward an unknown destination. I looked at the sun rising in the east and then to the west, gauging the remainder of time left for the day and all the possibilities it might or might not afford.

I turned my head and looked up. Twenty feet straight out from the rock I was sitting on, the fish leaped. The trout was airborne for what seemed minutes. I watched her tail dance across the water like a ballerina. The sun glimmered on her shimmering body as the water drops pearled off her. Then just like that, she was gone.

I stood up and walked back to the Chevy, now knowing what had been calling me out to the river. Now there were two tugs pulling me in opposite directions. I rolled over the cattle guard and headed for the middle ground of the diner where I could endure the discontent of both forces equally.

I parked the Chevy and walked in through the back door, trying to sneak up the stairs. Jimmy caught me as I rounded the corner.

"Where the hell you been?"

"River."

"You're not fuckin' 'round with that fish anymore, are you?" Jimmy asked, grinning as if he knew where I'd been the previous evening.

"You got that right Jimmy," I said, just to go along with him and to cut the conversation as short as possible. I had to; I was incapable of talking to anyone at that moment.

"Jimmy, I've got to get. I'm gunna pee my pants," I said, excusing myself and starting up the stairs.

"Better hurry then," Jimmy said, excusing me even though I had already started my ascent.

I didn't bother bathing but did shed my pecker-stained boxers, trading them for a clean pair. I rolled on some deodorant, brushed my teeth and changed into a cotton T-shirt. I wore the same jeans just for luck, but exchanged my odorous ankle cut white socks for fresh ones before slipping back into the identity of my Tonys. I dragged us, me and my booze-less hangover, down to the coffee counter.

"Good morning," Sarah said, smiling as if this was our first encounter of the day. She poured my coffee without asking if I wanted any.

"Morning," I said, feeling the tug.

"Any luck?" Sarah asked, with an I-got-your-number look.

"None," I said, feeling like a disappointed little boy.

"Never give up," She said in a pep-talk-like fashion.

I smiled a half-assed grin. Pissed off at her and half starving for another slice of pie. I hated the feeling of being out of control. I had bedded countless women in my life, always walking away as if I'd just conquered Napoleon, but for some reason, usually once every decade, I left feeling empty, like a hurt, disappointed little boy whose mother forgot to pick him up after little league practice. I sipped my coffee as Sarah tended to the more meaningful demands of the Saturday morning breakfast patrons.

Jimmy walked out to fill his tumbler with ice and water. It was early for ice water, I thought, recalling the numerous mornings, winter or summer, when I woke with a hangover whose only hope for temporary relief was ice water, lots of ice water. Jimmy just nodded his head at me and returned to the breakfast heat. Sarah returned with an empty pot of coffee and started a fresh one. Slices of toast popped out of the toaster and after buttering them, Sarah took them to a waiting table.

Jimmy placed a couple of omelets up into the window and rang the bell. After Sarah had returned to pick up her order, Jimmy came out and sat down next to me.

"Fishin' my ass," were the first words to part Jimmy's lips.

"What?"

"You look like you've just been weaned."

"What are you talking about?"

"Kid, you've got blood-shot eyes and a chin that's draggin' this coffee counter like a wash rag. Don't give me that *what* shit."

I just stared straight ahead saying nothing.

"You caught a fish you thought you could throw back and forget about."

I still sat there quiet.

"Problem is, you can't shake the scent," Jimmy said, before taking a swig from his tumbler.

"Who says it's a problem?"

"Your face," Jimmy said, setting the tumbler down on the counter.

"Fuck, I don't know Jimmy. I'm just all fucked up over this deal."

"Slow down now. How are you fucked up?"

"I don't know. Guess... I... I don't know."

"Well if you don't know how you're fucked up, maybe you're not," Jimmy said, as his eyes swung up to the right sensing Sarah's return.

She walked up, grabbed a pot of coffee, and turned to look at us as she returned to the room full of empty cups.

"I mean, I couldn't even get a hard-on at first."

"Big deal."

"Big deal, hell!"

"Well, you got one didn't you?"

"Yeah, but I had to bare my soul to get it," I said, looking behind me to make sure Sarah wasn't on her way back and to see if Flo had decided to grace us with her presence.

"If you bared your soul, it was about more than a hard-on."

"I was desperate Jimmy. I was already fucked in my head about not being able to be enough of a man for her. The fucker would get hard and then when she was ready for me, I'd just lose it. It would go limp. I mean, I felt that was all I had to offer her, and I couldn't even offer her that."

Sarah came back up with an order and slipped it up into the wheel. She dropped a couple more slices of bread in the toaster and walked off with the water pitcher.

"What do you mean that was all you had to offer her?"

"Well fuck. I'm hardly working and don't really want to have to work hard enough to keep a woman interested in me."

"So?"

"So how can I keep a woman without a job?"

"You've got a job, but how do you know you want to keep her?"

"I went half the night unable to be in her. It only got hard after I told her how scared of her I was."

Jimmy let me carry on.

"I had to tell her I was afraid because she reminded me of an old girlfriend that I'd fallen in love with and that something about her scared the hell out of me."

"You not havin' control scares the hell out of you," Jimmy said, turning around to affirm our privacy.

"Yeah, no shit. Even after making love to her I felt like a fucked up weakling. I mean, once I got it up, I did OK, but I still walked away from the whole experience like a shamed little boy who popped a foul ball straight up over the plate and into the catcher's mitt."

"You'll be all right."

"I don't feel all right. I feel beat up and helpless. I want to run back to her to prove what a real man I am."

"The only place you're goin' is the river."

"What?"

"You heard me. It's time for you to fish, alone. You've got to get your head cleared out kid."

"But if I could just talk..."

"Kid. Did you hear me? I said it's time to fish, alone. You're minds goin' way to fast. Go to the river and get your head cleared out. If you run back to her right now you're gunna fuck things up real good."

Sarah returned, slipped another order into the wheel, then turned around and looked at Jimmy without saying a word. Jimmy stood up without looking at her and went back into his little world.

Jimmy was right; I needed to fish. I hadn't been that fucked up over a woman since Lauren. The control thing was eating me up. How could I make her like me? How could I make her want me? How could I make her fall in love with me so damn hard that she'd never be able to leave? It boiled down to a timeless primal urge: my need to possess.

I went upstairs for the gear and lay down on the bed. I was tired, but restless. So I got up to search for a book to quiet my mind. I went back to bed with the book and woke a couple of hours later sensing an obligation to follow Jimmy's prescription. I didn't feel like fishing, but I had to go through the motions.

I looked out of the window across to Okie's garage and found that the normal rage the old man stirred up in me was gone. That's when I knew how jacked up I really was. I looked out of the window to the west, longing for the normal existential anxiety that my routine life back at home had to offer. Living with a longing had a way of protecting me from the vulnerability that really loving someone had to offer. Why in holy hell did it have to happen there in Five Points? It was just supposed to have been a blown radiator hose or a stuck thermostat. The MG had just been completely gone through from one end to the other. There simply was nothing left to go wrong with the little sport.

I walked down with my fishing gear. When I stepped off the bottom stair, Flo was standing at the register having just rung up an older couple in their early seventies.

"Hey Flo, how's it going?" I asked, just then remembering that I'd parked the Chevy out back.

"Not bad, you?"

"I'm headed out for the river," I said, avoiding an answer.

"You sound so enthused," Flo responded sarcastically.

"Yeah, guess my mind's somewhere else."

"I see," Flo said, as if she was waiting for me to come clean.

"I'll see you later," I said, taking the back door that led to Ol' Reliable. I threw my things in the front seat and followed them into the truck. After starting it up, I drove across the street for twenty bucks worth of Okie.

I put the nozzle into the tank opening and slipped the gas cap under the handle so that I could wash the windshield while the tank filled. I'd collected quite a few bugs over the last few days and after going twice over the windshield, all was cleaned off with the exception of some stubborn baked on honey bee remnants who refused to accept their newly appointed detritus state; I left them as a memorial to my current emotional state. I'd forgotten the pump and the overflow valve tripped it off at twenty-two bucks plus some change. I topped it to twenty-three dollars and walked in to settle up with the old fart.

"Howdy," Okie said, as I walked in.

"Hello Okie," I said, putting down a twenty and still sifting through my wallet for some ones.

"What else you need?" Okie asked, assuming that I'd only got twenty bucks worth of gas and that my searching for ones was for an additional purchase.

"I still owe you three bucks. I let the pump run past twenty."

"Must be plannin' on an extra long trip today."

"No, nothing besides a run to the river. I was washing the windows on the old Chevy and overfilled her. Here're the three more that I owe you."

"Thank you, son."

"Thank you Okie. We'll catch you later."

I walked back toward the Chevy, fired it up, and drove out onto the highway. I gave it the gas, and after backfiring a couple of times, Ol' Reliable and I were river bound. Okie seemed so friendly, but maybe my point of view was all that had changed. Perhaps he was still the same person I'd met just a few days earlier.

When I passed over the cattle guard, it hit me. I'd let her in. I had let Sarah into my sanctuary and was now paying the price of suffering for the spiritual expectations that I'd imposed on her. I wanted to make her into more than the woman she was. I wanted to make her into something divine. I wanted Sarah to save me from the existential pains of life, and it wasn't her job.

I pulled up to the river and parked in the usual place with the front of the truck facing west. I got out and slipped into the spiked waders for my encounter with Old Man River. I threaded the line through the guides and tied the tippet to the same old muddler that I had started fishing with a few days earlier, minus some hackling. It looked as poor of an excuse for a fly as I felt a man, but I wasn't giving up on that old fly.

I entered the water at the same familiar spot that I had on previous occasions. I waded across three-fourths of the river and found myself in chest-high water, but able to cast to the opposite bank, something I'd yet to risk until that day. If I wanted a real chance at that fish, my routine had to be altered but not compromised. I almost always fished muddlers and even if I tried something else out of discouragement, it was short lived. I had also fished the same length of river and didn't want to give it up. The only way to alter my routine was to take on deeper waters in order to fish the shelf just off the opposite bank.

The water was cold as it crept in over the top of my waders and oozed past the safety belt that cinched them to my T-shirt covered chest. I tiptoed to avoid taking on water, fearing washouts on the river bottom and slipping off into one of them. I finally came across a tree trunk at the bottom of a washout. I stepped up onto it to gain another six inches of chest out of the water, enabling me to improve my casting technique. I'd swing my rod back and forth until I laid the fly five feet or less from the bank and then let the current pull it downriver. I held my arms up to keep them out of the water, but I got tired and my elbows always ended up cold and dripping.

After five casts, I thought I had a taker for the muddler, but she was just a teaser and missed the hook. I now knew where a fish was holding and wasn't giving up to any other parts of the river. If a fish was to be caught, it would probably be right there. I just didn't know how the hell I'd keep my balance on that log if I did hook her.

My cast fell into a rhythm and the rest of me into a trance-like state. If I had fallen much deeper into the dream, I'd have either ended up drooling on myself or swimming. A light breeze started, and a pair of Mallards flew directly overhead and landed on the river a couple of hundred feet west of me. The ducks were flying very low, and it was only the whispering of their flapping wings that drew my attention to them. Following their flight over to the west, I noticed the descending sun that had less than an hour's life left for the day.

The fish hit when I was still looking west, and she hit me hard. There was no rat-a-tat-tat warning. It was a slam-dunk, and she was giving up no ground. She started peeling off line because I always fished with a loose drag setting, the optimist that I was. The spikes came in handy as I turned and balanced on the underwater log. This fish would only be taken if I tired her out, not from horsing her in. A part of me wanted to horse her just to say that I caught her, but a wiser part of me knew the need to play her until she was tired enough to come to me.

I worked her for a good half-hour as I spun around on the log, sometimes gaining line until her mood swung, and she'd take it all back. Was she a Rainbow or German Brown? How many times had she been hooked and gotten away? She was a big fish, no less than five pounds, but most likely bigger. I caught myself getting excited again and wanting to horse her, but backed off. There was as much art in landing a fish as there was in hooking a fish, the second had been mastered, but the first was still a work in progress.

She came dancing out of the water about twenty-five feet downstream, and I just knew that she was going to throw the hook. She didn't, but she managed to throw me from my perch. I was in water up to my armpits but quickly started tiptoeing backwards to shallower waters and then to shore where I had entered the river.

That dance was her last hurrah, thank God. Between balancing myself unsuccessfully on a log in the middle of a chest-high flowing river and the ice-cold water seeping around my balls, I'd just about had all the finessing I could stand for one day.

Chapter 14

Sunday

My maternal Grandfather's funeral was held in the same church where we both had been raised and which had instilled in us the unattainable goal of perfection that I was still trying to realize. I remember the feelings I had for my Papa and how, at his funeral, I at last understood that I loved my Grandfather exactly for who he was: an imperfect human being.

I remember him sneaking the drinks behind Grama's back, the vodka bottle hidden in the top part of the toilet. The toilet worked as a great hiding place until the bottle somehow got lodged under the float, flooding the bathroom and leading Grama to his secret hiding place. He used to host parties in the back room or the basement of his appliance store. Grama never did find those empty vodka bottles.

There was an old lady who had a kink in her neck and would rest her chin on her left shoulder. She rode around town on her bike with a cage strapped to the back rack where she carried stray cats. She'd often show up to bum some money from Papa. When he'd see her coming, he would run to the back and send me out to tell her that he wasn't around. Papa was always lending money to people like the cat lady, if they caught up with him that was. I'm sure that even with his big heart, there were some days that he just didn't want to deal with her kind. Running to hide in the back room also gave him the chance to swig from his vodka bottle that he didn't particularly want us kids to know about, for his sake more than our own.

When I was just a few years old, my grandfather was the county coroner. In order to help himself out of a bind, Papa had used some funds that had been placed in his care. He had already repaid the money when his misconduct was discovered, but he made the headlines and lost his job because of his lost integrity. Mom told me that I walked over and kicked the console stereo cabinet telling it not to talk about my Papa that way.

I cried out loud for my grandfather at his funeral, realizing how much I loved him and was like him. I realized the stinging loss of not having had him for those past twelve years when he lay curled up in a rest home before actually passing. I didn't know how much I missed him until his physical death made my loss a reality.

I was also crying for a lost part of myself at his funeral. My weeping in church that day was the loss I felt for the discarded parts of my own humanity. As a child, I learned from my rigid Calvinistic heritage to be a tough stoic without emotion. The loss of my grandfather allowed me to begin shedding what had been imposed upon us both in the innocence of our youth.

My grandfather's death taught me how very important it was to live my own life, regardless of what any church, woman, job, employer, teacher, or any one person or institution might expect of me. I'd never forget that day in church, weeping those bittersweet tears, mourning for my Grandfather, as well as my own soul. They were tears of liberation that I cried out loud in that very same sanctuary that had so long ago taught me not to honor my feelings and not to trust myself. The day we buried Papa, I began to reclaim my own position and place of reference in this world.

His death made me quit giving a shit about what others thought of me and to stop calculating every single item's impact on my present and future life. I began to recognize that critical voice within that haunted me so, and it was then that I decided it would no longer run me and rob me of life. It had kept me from becoming my own man. It had robbed me of any potential of living my own authentic life. It had robbed me of sharing my life with a woman. I had been burdening myself with the arrows of self-doubt and defeat and was tired of this illegitimate bastard robbing me of life. That was when the little Hitler's reign began to crumble.

That was also when I began to realize that the people I encountered who had the ability to upset me were often reflections of unacceptable parts of myself. It was my own voice that I heard coming from them, the people out there. I was blaming 'them' out there for what I was in here. Sure, I still fell prey to these inner demons, but... well, hell, I was only human.

I crawled out of bed and into the bath before I walked down for Sunday morning breakfast with Jimmy. When I finally made it downstairs, Jimmy was sitting at the counter reading the Sunday funnies.

"Morning Jimmy," I said, helping myself to a cup of coffee before sitting down next to him at the counter.

"Mornin'. Hungry?"

"Not yet. Still goda wake up."

"How was the fishin'?"

"Same as always," I said, not wanting to brag of my good fortune for fear of losing it.

"How's your head?" Jimmy asked, continuing his gaze into the comics.

"Same as always."

"Still fucked up, huh?"

"Yep."

"All over a piece of ass to boot."

"What?"

"You don't even know her," he said, as he got up.

"I know her a little."

"You know her too little," he said, walking to refill his tumbler.

"What are you saying?"

"She's still married."

I was silent. It wasn't that I was above sleeping with her because she was legally still a married woman. It was about falling for Sarah and the pain and suffering that went along with it. I'd been there before and knew better than to get involved with a woman who was dressed in an available skirt, but whose heart was clad in remnants of the past.

"How do you know that?" I asked, as he sat back down next to me.

"If she wasn't, do you think she'd be stuck up here in Five Points?"

"Maybe."

"Maybe hell, and just to relieve you of walking around in a maybe funk for a few more days, I know she's married."

"How?"

"Okie."

"How would that old fart know?"

"She's Okie's niece."

"No shit," I said, realizing why she had been so affectionate toward the old fart for filling her gas tank. "That's why she didn't pay for gas."

"No shit kid. Okie's her father's brother."

"How'd you find this out?"

"Sarah told me. The brothers haven't talked for years, but Sarah has always gotten along with her uncle. That's why she's here. Nobody knows and Okie would be the last to tell even if her father called lookin' for her."

"Makes sense why she's here," I said. She was close to family just in case some sort of trouble came up or if there was an emergency with her parents. Okie would find out, and Sarah could get back to them if she had to.

"You hungry yet?" Jimmy asked.

"No, but I should probably eat anyway."

"What'll it be?"

"How 'bout some toast and oatmeal."

"You got it," Jimmy said, as he slid out of his chair and walked back to the kitchen.

I got up, poured another coffee, and sat back down. I had assumed that Sarah was divorced by now. Then I remembered what she said about her husband being like a son to her parents. She didn't want to disappoint any of them. She'd just stuck her head in the sand and left them all, traveled halfway across the country, but they were still running her life.

Toast popped up just as Jimmy came out with my oatmeal. He put the bowl down in front of me.

"Want butter on your toast?" Jimmy asked.

"No. Dry's fine," I answered, spooning brown sugar from the dish that he had set down next to my oatmeal and crowning the cereal with some milk. I didn't need the butter and liked to dip the bread into the oatmeal's sweetened milk.

"Dry it is," Jimmy said, setting the toast next to my bowl of oats.

"They at church?" I asked, already knowing the answer.

"Every Sunday."

"Why?"

"Who cares," Jimmy said, content with the mystery of it all and the quiet time he had to himself on Sunday mornings.

"Guess it doesn't matter, does it?"

Jimmy didn't answer.

"Well, this sheds a different light on my situation," I said, after having thought about it over my bowl of cereal.

"Go slow kid. Don't get too fucked up over her. Remember what you're dealin' with. You've been through it before."

"Yeah, how could I forget," I said, staring out the front window and reflecting back on my affair with Lauren.

The blue Jetta pulled up to the front of the diner. Jimmy stood up and walked back into the kitchen. Flo and Sarah got out of the Jetta and walked in.

"Hello ladies," I said, greeting them as they passed through the front door.

"Good mornin'," Flo said, walking by on her way to shed her Sunday duds.

"Hey there," Sarah said, sitting down next to me at the counter.

"How was church?" I asked.

"Nice—a very nice service."

"Good," I said, not wanting to know more.

"Whatcha got going today?" Sarah asked, perking up my hopes of sharing it with her.

"Not sure yet," I answered, restraining an impatient urge to invite her to join me, partly out of fear of rejection and partly not wanting to appear too eager.

"Well I've got the next two days off. Unless somebody takes the Chevy out to the river and gets stranded that is," Sarah said, smiling.

"If you came along we could get stranded together, and you wouldn't have to worry about my rescue."

"That's not exactly how I want to spend my days off."

"What is?"

"Wouldn't you like to know?" Sarah knew she had me and was enjoying every bit of her power.

"You're damn right I'd like to know, and that's not all that I'd like."

"I'm sure you'll figure things out in time."

"Haven't got that much time."

"Sounds like you have a problem then."

"Wouldn't be a problem if I could get a little help," I hinted.

"Wish I could help, but I've got chores to do around the house. You know, domestic stuff, or are you one of those guys who hires it all out?"

I smiled, not wanting to admit that I had taken my laundry in for years. I sold farm machinery, piloted airplanes, and drove fifty thousand miles a year, but didn't know the first thing about running a washer and dryer.

"That's what I figured. An easy chair boy," Sarah said. "Live your life kicked back in your recliner with the remote control."

"Well, it isn't quite that cushy."

"Yes it is," Sarah said, sure of herself. "I'm afraid to ask anymore."

"Why don't you come with me this afternoon?" I invited in a more direct fashion.

"Why don't you come out to my place?" Sarah suggested as she stood.

"What time?"

"Around two?" Sarah said, on her way to the front door.

"Two it is," I confirmed, just before she left.

I was glad she was willing to see me again. There always seemed to be a silent terror that overtook me after I'd slept with certain women, women who I wanted to be with again, that was. My mind started wandering, first if I was going to get laid again and secondly if I could rise to the occasion without suffering the fear of possible failure.

Sarah was sitting on the porch enjoying the September afternoon. It was sunny with a breeze and a few clouds floated overhead, occasionally blocking out the sun. The darkness of Good Friday resurfaced, the product of my childhood Sunday school lessons. Revealing its radiant presence, the sun came out again from behind the vapory formations, and like ghosts, the cloud shadows hauntingly danced away over the dry rolling hills.

The imminence of the changing season had stirred something within me, and it was competing with the direction finder that was leading me toward Sarah's zipper. I was still confident that my mood wouldn't interfere with all of the blood that was rushing to the backside of my fly.

"Hello," I said, greeting Sarah as I stepped from Ol' Reliable.

"Hey there," Sarah said with a warm smile, standing as I climbed the steps.

"Nice to see you." I hugged her and kissed the top of her head, inhaling her scent.

"Nice to see you," She said, hugging me. She felt so solid and grounded as she squeezed her arms around my chest.

We were silent as we embraced. Time seemed to take on another dimension as I stood on the porch, hugging and smelling her, the clouds floating by. Sarah looked up and kissed me, waking me from my flighty trance and bringing me back down to earth.

"Come with me," she said, grabbing my hand and dragging me inside.

I followed without a grunt of hesitation. She led me to her room, pushed me down onto her bed and hopped on top of me, legs straddling my lower rib cage. She started kissing me, and in less than five minutes our clothes inhabited every corner of her bedroom. Thank God my anxiety had floated away with one of the clouds before I had crossed over Sarah's threshold.

After our encounter, we both drifted off to sleep. I woke just as it was getting dark. Sarah was spooned up in front of me, her ass in my groin and the back of her head just below my chin. I reached around and pulled her closer to me.

"Good morning," I said, teasing.

"Who's that?" Sarah asked, playing along.

"Thought it was a dream, huh?"

"I wish my dreams were that good."

"Let them be."

"I'd never wake up."

"I wouldn't want to either. Maybe we should drift back into

another one right now," I said, pressing up against her.

"That would be nice, but I've got things to do," she said, waking me out of my wistful state.

"So how long do you plan to stay in Five Points?" I asked, swaying away from more sex.

"No plan, really."

"Why are you even here?"

"Just seems like a safe place."

"Safe from what?"

"I don't know."

"You still married, Sarah?"

"No," she answered hesitantly. "Why?"

"Just thought that this might be a safe place to hide from a husband or anyone for that matter."

Sarah rolled over and kissed me. Then she crawled out of bed, in search of her panties and the rest of her misplaced attire.

"You thirsty?" Sarah asked, walking out of the bedroom as she dressed herself.

"Yeah, I sure am," I answered, as I stumbled around looking for my pants. I pulled on my Levis and Tonys and strutted into the kitchen where Sarah was pouring an iced tea.

"Here you go," she said, handing me the glass.

"If we weren't stuck out here in the middle of nowhere I'd take you out for dinner."

"Sounds nice, but its probably just as well. I've got things to do," she said, as she nervously started moving stuff around as if the kitchen needed to be straightened. "Besides, I don't need any more trouble from Flo."

"More trouble?"

"She knows something's up."

"What happened to screw Flo?" I reminded her.

"That was when I was lost in one of those dreams we were just in."

Sarah's house seemed far from needing attention. Flo's influence had some bearing on Sarah's relationship with me, but not enough to keep her from sleeping with me. Sarah had something else that needed straightening out, and instead of taking care of that mess, she'd run off to Five Points and started a new life of her own that she believed could be kept nice and tidy. Sarah had let me in as close as she wanted or was able. I could sense her need to be alone.

I finished the iced tea and walked up behind her to set the glass on the counter, giving her one more thing to straighten out.

"Time for me to get," I said, hugging her from behind after having set the glass down. Sarah turned around and kissed me. We hugged for a few minutes, then, without words, she led me to the door.

"I'll talk to you soon," I said, after having kissed her one last time. I wanted to make plans with her for the next day but knew better.

"I'll see you," Sarah said, as I descended the steps.

The tugs started long before the fence post passed me on my drive out to the main road. This time the tug had started when she climbed out of bed. Married or not, there was something about this woman that had gotten under my skin.

I pulled onto the highway and headed for the diner, wondering what was really running Sarah: her family, her husband? They were physically several hundred miles away in the Florida Keys, but these images were still commanding her life. She was running from herself, and the only way that she'd stop was by returning to where she'd come from. My being in love with her, or not, had little bearing on her ability to accept me into her life. But why had she lied about being married?

CHAPTER 15
Monday

I woke at eleven that Monday morning. If my bladder hadn't been close to bursting, I'd have slept on into the afternoon. I was slightly congested, and my head throbbed because of dry inflamed sinuses. My throat was tight. It felt as if there was something stuck in it, something that I couldn't quite seem to swallow away.

I drank a glass of water to smooth out my graveled waking voice. Most of my clients and business constituents knew that I was a late riser and loved to tease me, mostly out of friendly jealousy because they believed I was living the lifestyle they dreamed about. I seldom talked to them about my private life, which seemed to fuel their imagination all the more. They made me into what they needed me to be, and I didn't mind as long as the money kept coming in.

I made some calls and then bathed. I spread on some shaving cream and noticed how shaggy my hair had grown. I got lost in the crow's feet that were cawing out to me on my tanned face. I'd been shaving every day for the last twenty-five years, but for some reason I appeared to have aged ten of them in one day.

I had been able to stretch wearing my Levis into three-day intervals. I was out of clean underwear and had made do without. I pulled on my last clean shirt and had only one more pair of socks, so washing clothes had become a priority. I also had business with Okie, business I'd have rather done without, but it had to be addressed.

I walked downstairs thinking about how lucky I had been to avoid Flo when I had returned from Sarah's the evening before. Actually, I had managed to avoid her for the last few days, or she had avoided me, just as Sarah had when I started prodding into her past life. Flo and Jimmy were winding down from lunch, so I postponed eating and walked across to visit Okie.

Okie was sitting Buddha style on a stool behind the cash register, boot heels wedged on the lower ring that held the stool legs in place, knees bent and spread apart with an opened and no more than half-full twelve ounce can of Mountain Dew in his hand. I knew that it had to be half finished because he was swishing the can around in a counterclockwise motion in front of the knee that supported his forearm.

"You grounded today?" Okie asked.

"What do you mean?"

"Thought maybe you fucked up and Flo took the Chevy away," he said with a proud-of-himself grin.

"No such luck," I said smiling back. "At least I don't think so. Haven't really talked to her for a couple of days."

"Whatcha been doin' to keep her out of your hair, son?"

"Not much. Fishing," I answered, halfway wanting to say fucking your niece every chance I get.

"Hook anything yet?" Okie asked, before he took the last swig of his soda, tipping his head back and completely inverting the can to get every last drop.

"Few little ones. No keepers though."

"I've never heard a fish of any size come out of that river."

"I don't doubt it, but it keeps me from going insane while I wait for this little hot rod of mine to get put back together."

"Sounds like your fish hunt might be in service to us both, then," Okie said, as he tossed the aluminum can over his shoulder into another one of his converted thirty-three gallon oil barrel trashcans that sat behind him in the corner of the room.

"Speaking of insa…"

"Talked to the radiator man this mornin'. It was shipped out Friday," Okie interrupted. "Should be here in a day or two. I've already got your water pump and the other parts I ordered."

"Sounds good. I'll check back in a few days."

"Good luck with that big one, son."

"Thanks, I'll catch you later."

"Stay out of trouble now," Okie said, as if he knew where I'd really been fishing.

"I just won't get caught," I said, walking out the door with a good idea that I already had been.

Crossing the highway, I became aware of how hauntingly quiet the day was. There was no natural breeze, nor the wind of passing traffic, but there was something else that I couldn't quite make out.

When I walked through the front door I found Flo and Jimmy sitting next to each other at the coffee counter of an otherwise deserted diner.

"Well, I don't see any black eyes," Flo said smiling.

Jimmy was without words, and I wasn't quite certain how to respond to Flo, so I hesitated before saying: "Can't afford any right now. I need my wheels back on the road."

"Don't you hate that?" Flo asked.

"Hate what?"

"Playin' nice to get your way."

"I guess it depends on what I want and who I'm wanting it from," I answered ambiguously, avoiding either of us being right or wrong.

Flo appeared uncertain of how to respond this time.

"Speaking of wants, where does a stranded transient find a place to wash his clothes?"

"Most likely where he has found everything else since sufferin' his misfortune," Flo answered sarcastically.

"I'll do them. Just need to be directed to the washroom."

"I think God has showed me what I've missed with no kids," Flo said, turning to Jimmy and rolling her eyes. "Bring 'em down. I've got some wash to do myself," she volunteered.

I scurried up the stairs like a little boy who had just been relieved of his chores and gathered my goods. I ran across my pecker stained boxers as I collected my clothes and wondered if Flo would discover me, then I wrote it off just like I had with the turned inside out T-shirts that I foolishly believed to have slipped past my own mother when I had learned that my pecker allowed for much more pleasure than just peeing. I rolled my loot up in a couple of towels and stumbled back downstairs.

"Where you want these, Flo?"

"I'll take 'em," she answered, relieving me of my excess baggage.

"Thanks," I said, as she walked off with my dirty laundry.

"What's up on with you?" I asked Jimmy, sitting down in the seat that Flo had just vacated.

"I was about to ask you the same thing."

"How about some lunch?" I asked, wanting to change the subject.

"What's your pleasure?"

"A cheeseburger and fries sounds good."

"Easy enough," Jimmy said, as he stood up and headed back to the grill.

I poured myself an iced tea as Jimmy cooked my cholesterol infested lunch. While I was behind the counter, I took a bottle of catsup and mustard. I waited for my burger, anticipating what my afternoon might bring. I thought about Sarah, wondering what her day would consist of. I was willing her to include me and fighting my intuition that told me it wasn't going to happen. Jimmy walked up with the cheeseburger, interrupting the daydream.

"Now, what the fuck?" Jimmy asked, as he sat back down on the same stool he'd left to cook my lunch.

"Same old shit."

"Thought I smelled that mackerel."

"What mackerel?"

"Same one you've been draggin' around for the last few days," he said, without turning to look at me.

"I asked her if she was married."

"And?"

"She told me no," I answered, walking around the counter to pour a glass of water.

"Why'd you ask her when you already knew?"

"I just wanted to see how she'd respond."

"You baited her?"

"I guess," I answered, sitting back down.

"Did you get the response you wanted?"

"I didn't want a lie."

"Then what did you want?"

"Truth."

"Why, when you already knew it?"

"I don't know," I said, dipping a fry into the catsup.

"What were you really lookin' for?"

"Doesn't matter. She lied. Now I know she's a liar."

"So."

"So how could I ever trust her?"

"Weren't you a little dishonest with that question in the first place?"

"No," I answered self-righteously.

"You sure?"

"No," I repeated.

"Would you have still chased her if you knew she was married?"

"No. I wouldn't have."

"Even if you knew they were separated?"

"No."

"You're full of shit. You'd have done her even if she was still with the guy."

"No. I wouldn't have," I said smiling, trying to hold in my bite of burger.

"Yes, you would have you little fucker," he laughed.

"So what?"

"So everybody lies, even you."

"How do you figure?"

"Fear."

"What?"

"Fear of losin' or not gettin' what we think we need."

"So I should expect her to lie?"

"You should expect everyone to lie."

"What happened to the truth?"

"Truth's an illusion. It's a bill of goods that we've been sold."

"How do you figure?"

"Think about it. Everybody wants to be told the truth. Everyone wants to believe in the truth. That right there is your first clue."

"What do you mean first clue?"

"It's a set-up. The truth's been created to control and manipulate. It has been pounded into our minds from the day we were born."

"So I should have been taught to lie?"

"Don't need to be taught. It's natural."

"Bullshit."

"If you think you need somethin' bad enough, you'll lie to get it. It's primal."

"Where'd you get this bullshit from?"

"Didn't get it from anywhere. Let's say you lived before agriculture when people had to hunt and gather their food. You don't suppose that they hunted animals with the truth do you?"

"You've lost me."

"They tricked the furry fuckers. You know, snares, traps, bait, blinds... I mean hell, they didn't exactly invite their prey over for a cocktail party, you know."

"So to survive is to lie."

"Yeah, it's primal. Tellin' the truth's bullshit."

"So I should just accept her lie?"

"I don't give a damn what you do with it. I'm just sayin' that what we've been told about the truth is an illusion," Jimmy said, standing. "I don't think you should punish Sarah for bein' human," he said, right before walking back into the kitchen.

I finished my burger. Jimmy had said a mouthful that I now had to digest. He spoke with the conviction of experience, quite possibly from having been sold the noble bill of goods of protecting his country. Only to find on his return that he'd fought a thankless war.

So there I sat with a belly full of burger, waiting for my Tonys to take me somewhere. I wanted to be with Sarah, but was afraid to pursue her any further than I already had, fearing any move on my part would be counter productive. I could have gone to my room and read or slept. I could have fished. I could have gone for a ride to Tranquillity. For what, I didn't know, but it was somewhere to go. Then I realized that I had limited myself to the confines of which I had become accustomed. It was time to explore new territory out there in the vastness of which Five Points was only a molecule.

Leaving Five Points reminded me of leaving my own hometown.

I drove east, and after a short-lived tug from the first fence post that led to Sarah's place, I broke free. I'd fallen in love before and left; I could certainly do it again. Besides, Sarah wasn't a free woman: no freer than I was of my own personal history.

Driving, I began to experience the sense of freedom I had missed. I drove without a destination, without cause or purpose. That was what I longed for in my life, the freedom to float and experience whatever fell into my path, no attachments to yesterdays or tomorrows, just living in the present moment, going wherever the here and now took me.

After traveling several miles east, I turned south onto a paved road that, according to the potholes, had been abandoned to maintenance years earlier. I sat in Ol' Reliable as it guided me along the S-shaped curves of the old road. I rode the waves of hills; ascending and descending through them like a roller coaster that had been set to a slower, less violent, peaceful and dreamy ride.

I continued my excursion, expecting to stumble upon something of significance if not magnificence, but found neither. As I crested the curve at the top of a rolling hill I decided to stop to relieve myself. I unzipped and let it hang in the expansive freedom that my heart and soul were breathing in. I breathed deeply and sighed, noticing the tension in my jaw and neck that extended down my back and out to my arms. I had been carrying this tension for ages, long before I'd put on the mask of the tractor man. The deep breathing brought relief. It also brought the awareness that there were tears bottled up in those tense muscles, tears that weren't ready to express themselves; tears that for some reason didn't feel safe enough to be exposed.

I stepped up onto the back bumper and climbed into the bed of the Chevy and walked towards the back of the cab. I turned and slid my own ass-end up on top of the truck's cab and let my legs dangle in front of the rear window, my Tony clad feet a couple of inches from resting on the formed rail of the truck bed. I just breathed deeply in and out with a steady rhythm. I closed my eyes and listened to my breath and the occasional rumbling in my belly. I listened to whatever wanted to be heard.

Returning to Five Points that afternoon reminded me of returning to the Central Valley. A depression almost always overtook me as I descended the hill into the vast wasteland that had been converted to an agricultural Mecca, a result of the

Central Valley Project that brought northern California waters to a previously dry, barren valley.

The Valley was my birthplace and still the home of most of my family and friends. The landscape of my parents' faces always appeared to be as youthful as they were when I was three years old. The Valley never seemed to change much with the exception of new industry, which fueled increased populations, which fueled cycles of home construction to satisfy the demands of the growing communities.

The population had probably tripled in my hometown since my birth thirty-eight years earlier, but the vastness of the Central Valley seemed to have consumed what little expansion the town had seen, along with any potential shifts in consciousness. I'm sure this was why my parents, as well as the rest of the community, always appeared as youthful as they had been nearly forty years earlier.

Many of the kids who I grew up with followed in their parents' steps. After high school and their short-lived youthful follies, they took jobs, married, and had children. Twenty years later they'd become clones of their parents, repeating the routine existence of living flat mundane lives, which to me a few years earlier seemed perfectly acceptable, if not desirable.

Now this lifestyle incited the bellyaching cringe I felt when I used to watch the herdsman castrate the bull calves at the dairy where I once worked part-time during high school. They had these mechanical devices that would allow them to stretch a thick rubber band wide enough to slip over the baby bull's balls, sliding the device away, but leaving the band to do its deed. A few weeks later the sack and all of its goods would just drop off.

There was really nothing wrong with the lives that my family and friends lived. I had been living the same sort of life, quite unaware of my discontent, but for some unknown reason, I found myself feeling suffocated and discovered an urgency to make a change. Only nine months earlier, I had found the courage to leave the security of a conventional life. I stepped out into the unknown to escape the rubber band that I feared was to be my own fate.

The Chevy and I coasted up to the backside of the diner. It had been treating me well for some odd reason. It was as if it sensed my state of unrest and felt compelled to grant our relationship a time of peace and harmony. I walked through the back door and tried to sneak up the stairs before anyone had a chance to corner me. It didn't work. Flo was at the register.

"Hey there kid. How was your day?" she asked.

"OK. Been out exploring new territory," I said, sliding into the end seat of the counter.

"What were you searchin' for?"

"I don't know if I was really searching for anything. Just satisfying a wanderlust was all."

"So you weren't in search of anything?"

"Like what?"

"Contentment."

"Aren't we all looking for that?" I asked.

"No."

"Maybe I want too much."

"When you quit lookin', you got nothin' to lose or gain."

"So quit?"

"You can't find what isn't lost, kid."

"What's wrong with wanting to be fulfilled?"

"Nothin', but find it now. It's about livin' your life right here and right now."

"So I'm supposed to be fulfilled right now, stuck out here in Five Points while life passes me by?"

"It only passes you by if you aren't livin' it."

It was time to be silent for a while. I needed a break from Flo. She seemed to have some valid advice, but... well, I'd found what I needed out on the road that afternoon, and I didn't need anyone to rob me of my new found gold.

"Excuse me, Flo. I need to clean up. I'll see you after a while," I said to excuse myself.

First thing that I did when I got to my room was to check my voice mail. There was only one call from a client looking for a used cotton picker. I called him back and got his voice mail. Cell phones, voice mail, e-mail, we'd been reduced to machines talking to machines. I left a message to say that I'd get a few machines rounded up for him to choose from.

Jimmy was still in the kitchen when I walked back downstairs.

"Jimmy is it too late to get a bite?" I asked through the portal between the kitchen and the diner.

"What's your pleasure?"

"Whatever's easy," I answered, grateful that he was still there. I scooped a glass of ice, filled it with tea, and walked over to the booth that Flo was sitting in.

"What's goin' on?" Flo asked, as she shuffled through some old order tickets.

"Not much. Took care of a little business is all. How 'bout you?"

"Just tryin' to keep track of what we've sold the most of lately. Changes all of the time."

"Sounds like my life."

"Your life doesn't sound bad."

"Discontentment doesn't sound bad?" I questioned.

"Maybe you're supposed to be."

"Discontented?"

"Maybe this is just how it is for you right now. I mean, sometimes it's how it has to be."

"So I should just accept it?"

"Just let go of whatever, or whoever it is you're wantin' to manipulate."

"I don't want to manipulate anything."

"Then you're tryin' to protect somethin'."

"Whatever?"

"Just sit back and let things work for you instead of tryin' to control everything."

"I don't know what you think I'm trying to control."

"It doesn't matter what I think."

Jimmy came out of the kitchen and delivered my dinner to the table. Two, grilled center cut pork chops, a baked potato, green beans, and a steak knife.

"Looks great. Thanks Jimmy." He nodded and walked off without a word. Flo was making up for Jimmy in the word department.

"You goda give up on all of your planned outcomes."

"How can you get by in life like that?"

"It's not just gettin' by."

I picked up my steak knife and sliced into one of the center cuts, pretending that it was Flo's tongue.

"It just sets you free. That's all," Flo said, as I chewed on my chop.

"What does?"

"Seein' things differently."

"What?"

"The way that you see yourself in the world."

"The way I see myself in the world?" I asked, reaching for my tea.

"Maybe you have to learn to be in the world and relate to people from a different perspective."

"How do I get a different perspective when mine is all that I've got?"

"That I can't answer. You've got to find that on your own."

"So you think you know what I need, but you can't tell me how to get it."

"That's right."

The light in the kitchen went out, and a few seconds later Jimmy walked out into the dining room.

"I'll see you tomorrow, Flo," Jimmy said, approaching the back door.

"Thanks Jimmy. See you in the mornin'."

"Good night, Kid."

"Night, Jimmy. Thanks for the dinner."

Flo got up and locked the back door behind Jimmy. She went over to the front door, locked it, and flipped the closed sign to the front side of the window. Back at the table, she took the tickets and went over to the register, giving me a chance to finish dinner. Flo was right about me having to figure things out on my own. Along with my anger and frustration, I'd felt twisted and unfulfilled for quite some time. I wanted some relief, just wanted things to be easy for a while.

Flo poured herself a cup of coffee and walked back to join me. She was making up for the last few days we'd missed each other.

"Why the hell am I here, Flo? I mean, I'm traipsing around the country in search of who knows what, when I should be home with a wife and kids, a normal life."

"The guy at home with the wife and kids wants what you

have. Everybody suffers one way or another," she said, turning and staring out of the front window.

"Yeah, you're probably right about that."

"That's why you're alone," she said, looking back to me.

"Why?"

"You lack compassion. You can't stand your own sufferin', let alone anyone else's."

I was alone and tired of being alone. I wasn't sure that I lacked compassion, but I listened to her anyway. "How do I lack compassion?"

"Well, your little car for example, and the man who's fixin' it for you, too. You need to be more compassionate with that little red bullet of yours. You have a few problems with it, but I'm sure you'll get it fixed. That car is a lot like you, not a whole lot wrong with it, just has a few bugs to be smoked out."

I didn't know how she expected me to be compassionate with that damn little old red bomb that had a habit of leaving me stranded in the most inopportune places. Seemed that the longer I was there the more trouble I found.

"Flo, I've had it for the night. I'll see you tomorrow."

"Good night, kid," she said, as I slid out of the booth. I bussed the table and climbed the stairs back up to my room. It had been one hell of a long day, week...

CHAPTER 16
Tuesday

Economics weighed on me. I had a broken down car and over a week's worth of food, lodging, and transportation tickets adding up at Flo's. I no longer had the comforts of my old life and the financial security that it brought me. I had traded my job and my identity for freedom or for what I believed was freedom. I was tired of the people, the responsibilities.

I was tired of Art Farmer telling me that he wanted to see me at the tire shop at six-thirty every morning to drink coffee with the rest of the early birds who gathered to insult each other. I was tired of having to go by and bless every little squeaky nut and bolt on the equipment that I had sold over the years. I was present every single day in a sense, reselling what had already been sold, coddling and feeding my clientele heaping spoonfuls of reassurance.

I wasn't ready to bathe, so I dressed and pulled on my John Deere hat while descending from my lofty hide-a-way in search of a cup of coffee. Sarah was walking around refilling empty cups when I walked up to the counter. I flipped a coffee cup over when she walked back behind the counter, and she turned to fill it.

"Good morning," Sarah said, in a detached tone.

"Morning," I responded, disappointed in the sound of her response.

"Want to order?"

"Not yet," I answered, wanting to order her into reacting like a love-struck woman who was unable to resist me.

"Let me know if you change your mind," Sarah said, walking off to tend her flock.

"Will do," I answered, out of a sense of respectful duty. The same duty, that for most my life, I had assumed, when someone had something that I wanted. Sarah was turning into a great big pain in my ass.

Jimmy came out of the kitchen. "Go easy now," he reminded as he sat down next to me.

"I'm more fucked up over money today than I am with that little trout," I said with a slight grin.

Jimmy didn't say anything. He just sipped the coffee he had poured for himself before pulling up next to me.

"I mean... I've been fucking around out here, stuck in the middle of nowhere. I need to move on. I need to make a buck. Sometimes I think I fucked up leaving that old job behind."

"Why'd you leave?"

"So I didn't have to listen to Joe tell me about how his wife wouldn't blow him."

"Who in the hell is Joe?"

"One of the guys who bought tractors from me."

"Well, that's a hell of a reason to leave a job," Jimmy said, smiling.

"I left because I was tired of being Peter's shrink. I walked him in and out of three marriages."

"Yeah?"

"I was tired of the farmers bitching about their foremen who wouldn't follow orders, and I was tired of the foremen bitching about their bosses, about how they really should have been doing things differently."

"Why'd you do all of that shit?"

"Had to; part of the job."

"I don't get it."

"Jimmy, when a guy's giving you a hundred thousand dollar check for a tractor, you'd listen to just about anything that he wants to tell you."

"No. You did," Jimmy said, as he got up and walked back into the kitchen to start on an order that Sarah had just spun around to him.

I sat there thinking about all of the pissing and moaning I'd listened to over the years. I listened to the mechanics that wrenched on my clients' tractors piss and moan about being underpaid. I listened to the owner of the company, who spent two hours a week in his office, plead poverty all of the way to the bank. I quit because if I hadn't, I'd be dead.

I quit at thirty-eight with no bills and some money in a retirement plan that would probably be all that I would need to provide comfort in my old age. When I left, I had twenty-five thousand in cash, three homes that were all rented out and paying their way, and the Bonanza that I owned free and clear.

The Bonanza was my airplane that I'd purchased a few years back from the widow of a deceased friend. It was a single engine, retractable gear, high-performance airplane that cruised at two hundred miles-per-hour. Bonanza 1MC was more than an airplane and served me in several ways. She was a savior when it came to shagging parts for the farmers with broken down cotton pickers in the middle of the harvest season. A day or two was the difference in harvesting a crop before it was destroyed by rain. 1MC was also my ego bolster so that everyone could see how successful I'd become. She was also a toy that occasionally took a few of my close friends and me fishing, but most importantly N1MC was my symbol of freedom.

The Bonanza might not have left the hangar for a month or two at times when I was busy, wrapped up in all of the duties of my life, but she was always there ready for me; waiting to whisk me away from it all if things got unbearable. N1MC made the unbearable, bearable, knowing that at any given minute I could escape my reality. I hardly ever flew anymore and wrestled with selling the plane. Selling her would have been an amputation of sorts; Bonanza 1MC was a bigger part of me than I could really understand.

All in all, I was worth a little less than half a million dollars, but it was all tied up in fixed assets. After nine months, the twenty-five thousand bucks were gone, and I didn't want to start selling things off. That was why I was out on the road. I was kicking up rocks trying to find a buck to pay my way without being shackled to a job. I was just trying to find a way to keep fuel in the Bonanza.

Jimmy returned from the kitchen. Why'd ya really quit?" he asked, as he sat back down next to me.

"Freedom."

"What did you want to be free from?"

"Other people's problems."

"I can see how that might grind on a guy who was in your slot, but what else?"

"Demands."

"What demands?"

"I just wanted to sleep as late as I damn well pleased."

"So you don't want to be bothered."

"What I want is to sleep as late as I please. I want to get up when I feel rested and do what I damn well please until I am tired and ready to sleep again."

"Do it then."

"I am," I said, walking back to refill my coffee and looking around for Sarah.

"Well, then what's the problem?"

"They..."

"They are you!"

"What?" I asked, sitting back down at the counter.

"They aren't out there anymore. Remember, you quit."

"But they..."

"I'm tellin' you, *they* are *you*," Jimmy said, looking straight ahead.

"What do you mean?"

"OK, you quit. You have no job or clients to bitch about."

"Well, they're still my clients."

"Only if you choose them; remember you left them. You moved away. You continue to make them your clients, and your problems."

"Well, what am I supposed to do?"

"I don't know."

"You know all of this other shit, but you don't know what I'm supposed to do?"

"You're the only one who knows what you need to do," Jimmy answered.

"Well, I don't."

"Good."

"Why good?"

"It's OK not to know, just quit blamin' your past and the people from it for your problems."

"I know what I need."

"What's that?" he asked, walking around and dumping his coffee cup in the dirty dish tub below the counter.

"To do exactly what I have been doing," I answered, as he picked up his water tumbler and walked to the ice machine.

"Which is?" he asked, scooping his cup full of ice.

"I'll sleep as late as I damn well please. I'll spend the day as I damn well please. And, I'll go to bed when I damn well please," I answered, as he filled the tumbler with water.

"How you gunna do that?"

"Just like I have been."

"What about *they*?" he asked, turning to face me and leaning against the counter below the kitchen service window.

"I'm the only who can give myself permission to do it. I mean, I'm doing it, but I'm punishing myself at the same time."

"That's right kid."

"I've got to give myself permission to live my own life."

"Yes you do. And you're the only one who can."

"You want freedom from somethin' else, too."

"Like what?"

"You'll figure it out."

"God damn it, Jimmy!" I shouted at him, as he walked off taking a swig from his tumbler.

It was time to clean up, so I climbed back upstairs for my morning soak and shave. Jimmy was beginning to remind me of Flo a little bit. He was full of questions but not able to provide me with any concrete answers. I tried to figure out what Jimmy knew I needed to figure out, but all that I could come up with was a headache. I was ready for some food to cure the pain, so I walked back down to place an order.

Lunch was winding down and Sarah had only two tables when I slid into my seat at the counter.

"This must be a sign," Sarah said, walking up from behind.

"What's that?" I asked, hoping that her comment had something to do with her and me.

"That you're finally ready to eat."

"Oh, I'm more than ready to eat, but I can't find her on the menu," I answered with grinning frustration.

"How 'bout the special?" She asked.

"How 'bout it?" I asked back.

"Soup or salad?"

"I don't care."

"OK," Sarah said, turning around to slip my ticket into the wheel. A few minutes later she set a salad with Thousand Island dressing down in front of me.

"Who said I wanted Thousand?"

"You didn't care, remember?"

"Can I have some crackers, please?"

"Want something else to drink?" Sarah asked, as she set a basket of crackers and a glass of water in front of me.

"Nah, this is fine," I answered, reaching for a packet of Saltines. The salad was good and crisp. Thousand Island dressing wouldn't have been my first choice, but for some odd reason it fit. We were both edgy. We had come together and were now trying to find a way to be in the world without getting lost in the entangled attachments of a potential love affair.

I was dancing toward Sarah, and she was dancing away from me. I'd done this before and promised myself that I'd never do it again. I believed myself to be above these childish maneuvers, but somehow the little boy in me managed to take over and was drawing me back in.

Sarah slid my lunch down in front of me. It was meatloaf, mashed potatoes, and green beans, this time with some sliced mushrooms.

"Looks great."

"Need anything else?" she asked, setting a dinner roll next to my entree.

"Catsup and more water, please."

"Happy now?" Sarah asked, fulfilling my last request.

"No, but this will do for now," I answered, just before I shoveled in my first bite, and just before I burned my tongue. I couldn't get to the water fast enough as I juggled the incinerating chunk of meatloaf on my tongue. Sarah just looked at me, chuckled, turned and walked off, shaking her head. She came back a few minutes later and refilled my water glass.

"You gunna be around later?"

"Yeah, why?"

"Thought maybe we could get together."

"Today's not good," she answered, after hesitating.

"What's the matter, Sarah?"

"Nothing! It's just not a good day, all right?" she snapped back.

"Yeah, sure. No problem," I answered calmly, as she walked away, but I was feeling a rush that accompanies the relief of having just avoided a head on collision. I knew I needed to back off, but the more I knew it, the closer I was drawn to her.

Sarah came back up to the counter and sat down next to me.

"Look, I'm just in a shitty place right now."

"That's all right."

"It's not that I don't want to see you, it's just me."

"OK, just as long as you know that I want to see you. Just let me know when you're ready."

"Thanks," Sarah said, in a somewhat relieved, yet disappointed, tone.

I had a lot of energy pumping through me and Sarah wasn't allowing me to direct it her way, so after finishing lunch I decided to take a ride. First stop was the routine for fuel across the street; fuel in the form of gas for the Chevy and in the form of one of Okie's smart-ass remarks that would spark the ignition of my mercurial rage. On this encounter, only the truck was fueled and it was just as well considering my previous lunchtime agitation. After Okie, I headed for the river without retrieving the fishing gear from my loft.

I had very few outlets in Five Points. If I had been at home, working out on my eighty pound heavy bag would have been my choice. I used to have to deal with a man a lot like Okie when I was in the machinery business. He was the service manager, and his ego was as big as mine. I wanted things my way or my customer's way, and he wanted things his way. It was a constant negotiation over power, and it usually had very little to do with our clients' best interest. He had mechanics Johnny-on-the-spot for the customers he liked, but the ones that he despised he'd punish by dragging his feet and making them wait.

I was the one that took the farmers' money when they bought the tractors, and I was the one they called when the damn things broke down after having been insulted and given the run around by this egotistical service manager. After swallowing years of this crap and wanting to go and beat the living shit out of this guy, I went out and bought the heavy bag to save myself the impending jail sentence.

When I rumbled over the cattle guard, the vibration seemed to shift me out of the trance that had driven me there. It wasn't Okie that I was feeling frustrated over. I'm sure that my dislike and intolerance of Okie was a lot more about the remnants of my relationship with the old service manager from the tractor days of my past. I was frustrated about something else.

I was tired of hiding. I was tired of hiding Sarah and myself from Flo. I was tired of hiding and protecting myself from how I believed others saw me. I was tired of hiding from me, and I was tired of living my life driving around in the same great big old circle. I turned the Chevy around when I got to the river and drove back to the diner. The Jetta was gone when I returned.

"Where's Sarah?" I asked Flo, as I walked in through the back door. She was standing up from the booth she often sat in when things were quiet.

"Just missed her."

"Damn!"

"Is it that bad?" she asked, putting her glasses on.

"I just wish that she'd let me into her life," I answered, and then wished that I'd kept my mouth shut.

"Looks to me like you're already in it and against my better judgment at that," she said, walking up to the cash register.

"Not the way I wanna be in it," I replied, ignoring her better judgment and going up to the coffee counter.

"Well, just exactly what *do* you want?" she asked, before reaching under the register for something.

"A hell of a lot more than I have right now," I answered, sitting down at the counter.

"So that you can find out that she is just another woman that you've grown tired of," she said, rising from behind the counter with her clear Tupperware container.

"So that I can gobble her up," I said, as she set the Tupperware down in front of me.

"And spit her out when you've grown tired of her aftertaste," she said, leaning directly in front of me with both hands on the counter and staring down at me like a preacher from the pulpit.

"So that I can love her."

"So that you can feel complete."

"Yeah, complete," I answered, feeling uncomfortable with the lack of space between us.

"Completely devastated when you find that your hunger can never be filled," she said, pulling back from the counter and crossing her arms.

"I don't want to die alone," I said, swiveling from side to side on the counter's bar stool-type chair.

"Then don't."

"Then what should I do?"

"Love her anyway."

"How?"

"Let go."

"Of what?"

"Everything," she said, leaving the Tupperware in front of me on the counter and backing up to lean on the service counter below the kitchen window.

"How?"

"By bein' still and lettin' her love you back, her way."

"How can she love me?" I asked, thinking of all the baggage she had back in the Keys.

"How can she not?"

"I don't get it," I said, putting both elbows up on the counter and folding my hands together.

"You're not supposed to get it."

"What, love?"

"That and not being in control."

"Fuck, this pisses me off. So in order to have what I think I want, I can't try?"

"Tryin' and not tryin' are opposite sides of the same coin. Not tryin' is just another way of tryin'."

"Don't tell me. I just have to give up?"

"You know what you have to do."

"Fuck, I want to be God."

"You what?"

"I want to be God. I want to control everything," I answered, wanting to make real what I was constantly trying to do in my mind.

"Doesn't work that way."

"No shit."

"What do you really want?"

"I want it all. I want whatever I want, and I want it now. I want to be five places at one time. I want to live forever, no more pain, no more suffering. I never want to be in want again."

"Sounds to me like you want to be dead. Wake up, kid. You're dreamin'," Flo said, taking off her glasses and letting them hang down around her neck from her fake strand of pearls.

"What?"

"No wonder you can't enjoy what you have right here in front of you."

"I could enjoy Sarah if she'd let me."

"No you can't."

"Yes I can."

"Then do it."

"She won't let me get close."

"You won't let yourself get close. Don't go hangin' the blame on Sarah," she said, walking around to my side of the counter.

"I don't blame her."

"Yes, you do. Simply because she doesn't fit your image of what you need her to be," she said, sitting down next to me.

"Why can't she just say yes to me?"

"Maybe she is, but you can't hear her."

"If she was, I'd hear her."

"She just doesn't fit your mold," she said, pulling the Tupperware in front of her.

"My mold?"

"Yeah, she doesn't fit into the fantasy mold that you have of her."

"So what if I want her? What's wrong with that?"

"Havin' Sarah and holdin' on to her are two completely different things. You can't have her because you're tryin' to hold on to her."

"You're damn right I want to hold on to her," I said, pulling my elbows from the counter, leaning back into the seat and crossing my arms over my chest.

"You want power."

"I want Sarah."

"You want to make her want you," she said, popping open the top of the Tupperware.

"So?"

"Damn! Can't you see what you lose when you try to force someone to love you?" she asked, slipping her glasses back on.

"So what if I want to be loved?"

"As long as you try to force love, you'll never get it. You've used every muscle you have to get love, except for the right one."

"Like what?"

"Your heart, kid. Your heart."

CHAPTER 17

Wednesday

Having slept with her, all I wanted was more. Sarah's husband still ran her life, in spite of her proclaimed freedom from him. She wasn't available to me because of all the power she'd given up to this captivating image. Time would reveal if we both could step out from the excuses we hid behind.

Sarah appeared to be a strong woman, but it might not be the time for her to expose her heart, let alone let go of the other attachments that she was tied to. If we were to be together, she'd have to give up her whole way of seeing and being in the world, as well as her way of relating to man. In spite of all the energy I expended in willing her transformation, this would be no easy task, and it would not happen overnight, if it happened at all.

I woke up that morning thinking of Sarah, longing for her. I made love to her image. I had to because of all the energy that this woman had ignited within me. She'd touched me somewhere that no other woman had ever touched me, and now I boiled.

I lay there with a belly button full of cum wishing that she was lying next to me, finger painting the yin yang symbol in my hopeful progeny, her legs tangled up in mine, her head just under my chin. Sarah's scent came to me and I drifted off to an image. A door opened and led into a chamber. A chamber whose depth I could not sense. It was dry and dusty. It was wide and deep, and it looked as if it had been uninhabited for centuries. My heart; Sarah had led me to and opened the door to a chamber of my heart, to a place that I never knew existed.

I didn't know if she could ever let herself love me. I didn't know if she had it in her, but I had her in me. I might never again physically make love to Sarah, but I had her spirit within to make love to for the rest of my life and lifetimes to come. But God I wanted her physically as well. I wanted to kiss her, I wanted to lick her, I wanted to gobble her up and bask in the delight of realizing my greatest desire. Problem was, my greatest desire was always fleeting and changed from day to day. I wanted Sarah today, and tomorrow I might want her second cousin. It wasn't that I didn't care about her; I was just afraid of being pinned in. I didn't want to get swallowed up by life and all those attachments that seemed to accompany relationships. I didn't want to get tied to anything with permanence. In most of my liaisons, I had been able to move on, but occasionally there was a woman who wandered into my life who somehow had a way of torturing me. Actually, the woman didn't torture me; it was the part of me that wanted attachment fighting the part of me that longed for freedom. This was the source of my suffering.

I dressed after my morning rituals and descended the stairs into my other reality. Jimmy came out of the kitchen as I walked up to the counter. I poured a coffee before sitting down.

"Hungry?" Jimmy asked.

"Fuck no, I'm pissed."

"At who?" he asked, sitting down next to me at the counter.

"Where's everybody?" I asked, looking around before spouting off anymore.

"They went to Sarah's."

"For what?"

"Hell, I don't know. Does it matter?"

"Guess not."

"So, who ya pissed at?"

"Myself."

"Why?"

"Because I got a taste of that stuff and it wasn't enough."

"Go back for more."

"Won't help."

"What will?"

"Death."

"What?"

"It'll be with me until I die. It'll probably live on long after my bones are a dusty dry heap."

"What are you talkin' about?"

"This longing; it's insatiable, and it runs me."

"What do you want?"

"I want it all. I want Sarah to say yes to me so that I can devour her, to satisfy my hungry heart."

"If you know you're that way, why can't you stop?"

"That's a damn good question. Why do any of us do the crazy things we do?"

"Maybe you don't want to stop."

"Maybe."

"Maybe you shouldn't try."

"Seems the harder I try, the hungrier I get."

"So, what do you want?"

"Not to want."

"You're fucked up, alright."

"No shit!"

"I don't mean that you're nuts or anything like that. I mean that you're torn," Jimmy explained

"Yeah, I wish I could just figure out how to get un-torn."

"Once you're torn you never get back together like you once were. I don't know if it's gunna be that easy."

"It hasn't been so far. Why should I expect anything to be different?"

"You've got to give somethin' up."

"What do you mean?"

"You've got to give somethin' up. You've got to make a sacrifice."

"Like what?"

"I don't know. That you've got to figure out on your own."

"Thanks a lot." I answered sarcastically.

"I really don't know, but even if I did, I wouldn't say."

"Why."

"You've got to do this on your own, or it won't be real."

"So what do I do?"

"Wait."

"That's the story of my life," I said, as Sarah and Flo pulled up to the front of the diner.

How could a woman make love to me as passionately as Sarah had and then pull away? How could she not want more? I'd been pulling away from women for years, but now that it was happening to me, I didn't like it. I didn't like the power I'd given Sarah. I didn't like caring for someone who didn't want to be cared for. I didn't like not calling the shots, and I didn't like being held away.

"Morning," I said, as the two skirts walked into the diner.

"Good mornin'," they both said in unison, seeming almost too happy for the occasion. Flo walked on to the back and Sarah stepped behind the counter resuming her duties.

"More coffee?" Sarah asked.

"No thanks, I've got to go up and make some phone calls."

"Did you eat?" Sarah asked, in what appeared a concerned manner.

"Not yet. I've got to get some business taken care of first," I said, walking for the stairs.

Once in my room, I phoned the dispatcher to check on a haul of a harvester and found that there were complications. I hadn't communicated clearly that the combine was a wide load and would take permits. After renegotiating the haul and committing to another five hundred dollars in freight charges, the dispatcher assured me that the harvester would be picked up and delivered within a week's time. This problem wouldn't have been my first choice, but considering the uncertainty I had with the direction of my life and with Sarah, it was probably a healthy outlet as opposed to torturing myself.

I decided to pay Okie a visit and spy on the progress of my little red get-away. I walked through the diner without saying anything and crossed the highway.

"Hey kid, how goes it?" Okie asked, as I walked into the station.

"Not bad, you?"

"I'll have her done by Saturday," Okie said, sensing the agenda of my visit.

"Great."

"One problem."

"What's that?" I asked, as a jolt of anxiety burst through me.

"You can't leave until Monday."

"Why?"

"Because I want to make sure it's right."

"You mean the head?"

"I mean everything."

"OK."

"I want to have a couple hundred miles on her before she leaves here for good."

"Fair enough," I responded, having gained a little more respect for the old fart because of his concern.

"The way you cover ground, I figured you won't have any trouble gettin' the miles over the weekend," Okie said, as I was leaving.

"Yeah, yeah," I cawed back at him, unable to hold back my big grin, knowing that he couldn't let our encounter go without getting in the last jab.

If everything worked out, I'd soon be leaving my little paradise. This changed things for me because the dream of my escape had become reality. This meant I'd soon be moving on and getting back to my normal life. It also meant leaving Sarah and letting go of my quest for the mystical union with her that had been torturing me since arriving in Five Points. Actually, I'd been pursuing that mystical union my entire life, and as much as I didn't like admitting it, I knew that if it hadn't been Sarah, it would have been another Sarah, or Sara, or countless other hers.

As I crossed the highway for the diner, I looked up and saw the blue Jetta backing out. Sarah waved to me as she drove by. I wanted to be able to love a woman the way that I dreamed of, but I had yet to find a way, and was becoming angry and frustrated with myself. Why did I find this task so difficult? Why couldn't I fall into the convention of the modern-day romance? How had I avoided falling in love and living happily ever after with a house full of kids, a wife who would suddenly discover that sex had become nasty, a mortgage and a job to support such a glorious existence? Most of my life had been spent trying not to be caught by that great big lie.

"Where'd Sarah run off to?" I asked Flo, who was standing behind the register.

"She had a letter that had to be mailed today. Why?"

"Just curious," I answered. "Can I order some lunch?"

"What'll it be?"

"The special with an iced tea," I answered, not knowing what the special was. Flo scribbled my order, clipped it to the wheel, and spun it around for Jimmy. Then she scooped ice into a glass for my tea as I drifted off to the memory of Sarah scooping ice the day that I'd met her.

I was lying to myself thinking that I had to have Sarah. A part of me wanted to have her and a part of me wanted to run. I wanted to make it her fault for not being able to let me into her life, but it was more mine. Yeah, it would be something wonderful for a while, but I knew how I got when the novelty wore off, and I started getting pissed over not having my space. Falling in love usually meant falling out of love, and usually after I'd made some silly-assed promise about never leaving and having bargained away my freedom to roam.

I was torturing myself, dreaming of Sarah, of having to have her. I was torturing myself with the illusion that making love to her one more time would set me free of her spell. I was frustrated. I wanted to believe that I could let myself have her and simply love her for the rest of my life, but I didn't believe in myself, didn't believe that I could.

I remember learning to ride my first bicycle without the training wheels. Mom would hold the bike up and steady it as I started peddling, eventually letting go. I'd look back and fall when I realized that she wasn't holding me up anymore. Mom ran up and down that sidewalk at my side for days and my frustration grew. All the other kids in the neighborhood, except me, were zipping around on two wheels, and I didn't like not measuring up.

"I think I can, I think I can, I think I can. Say it to yourself. I think I can," was mom's way of getting me to believe in myself. "OK, lets try it again and remember, just keep saying I think I can."

"I think I can, I think I can, I think I can," I'd say, as I peddled off riding an extra twenty feet the next time before taking another spill. Mom would be right there to help me up and dust me off, readying me to try it all over again.

"I think I can, I think I can, I think I can." I turned around and mom was fifty feet behind me. I looked back ahead of me and kept on going, waiting to fall, but somehow keeping my balance. "I think I can, I think I can, I think I can," I repeated, then turning around to find mom half a block away. Looking ahead a huge euphoric smile overcame me, "I can! I did it!" resonated up out of my racing heart.

Flo plopped a plate of spaghetti with a side of peas down in front of me; I hated peas.

Chapter 18

Wednesday Afternoon

I was picking the peas out of the last few strands of spaghetti before twirling the last bite onto my fork when Sarah walked into the diner.

"Aren't we a busy bee today," I said greeting Sarah.

"Queen bee and don't you forget it," Sarah said with her mesmerizing smile.

"Are you accepting any worker bee applications?" I asked.

"Depends."

"On what?"

"On how many other hives you've been hovering around."

"Hell, I'm a virgin worker bee."

"Inexperienced, huh?"

"Yeah, but I catch on real quick."

"You ever stung anyone?" Sarah asked, leaving me without a comeback. "That's what I thought. Just like all the other young inexperienced ones. Don't know how to keep your stinger in your pants."

"Now I didn't say..."

"That's OK, I won't hold it against you. You can't help that you were born with a hair trigger. Maybe after you get a few more years of experience under your belt that stinger of yours won't get you into so much trouble."

"This mean you're gunna give me a chance?" I smiled, proud of all the trouble my stinger had already rewarded.

"Maybe, if you're lucky."

"Well, you'll have to leave a message for me here at the diner, because I'll be at the river this afternoon."

"OK," Sarah said, as she picked up my plate. "Hum,

inexperienced and doesn't like peas."

"Always save my peas for the queen bee," I said, standing.

"How gracious," she said, sliding the dirty plate into the tub under the counter.

"I don't always think with my stinger," I said, walking off to get the fishing gear.

I fired up Ol' Reliable and scooted across the street for fuel. After pitching Okie another twenty and getting jerked around by the old Chevy as she huffed and puffed out onto the highway, I was river bound. Driving west, I noticed how clear and cloudless the sky was. I looked at the trees and the grass along the roadside for evidence of a breeze, but couldn't detect one.

The rumble over the cattle guard seemed to shake me into a new dimension. A few hundred yards later, I slowed down and pulled up next to the Ford F-150 and my fisherman buddy.

"How's it going?" I asked, greeting my friend.

"Not bad. You?"

"Thought I'd try my luck again."

"See you got the old Chevy purrin'."

"Hiccupping is more like it," I said cynically.

"Long as it gets you here and back is all that really matters."

"Yeah, guess you're right. Only have a couple more days. Car should be fixed by Saturday."

"That your last day?"

"I'll leave Monday. You do any good today?"

"Want the truth or a lie?" he asked, firing up the F-150.

"Never mind," I answered, dropping Ol' Reliable back into gear. We nodded to one another and drove off, each in our own direction without the formality of wasted words. I wondered how many fish the old boy had hooked out there over the years. Would the groove lead him out of sanctuary once again? Was he married; did he have anyone at home to listen to his fish tales?

The spikes were the last of my gear that had to be tied on before entering the water. I broke the cord as I cinched the right one to my wading boots. I yelled "shit" a couple of times as I knotted it back into one piece. I then reached for the fly rod and was river bound. I walked into the river at the same spot I'd hooked up before and found the downed tree trunk to stand on as I fished the opposite bank. My body fell into the rhythm of casting while my mind drifted off with the river.

I dreamed myself back in my studio in Carmel: coming home from class, slopping down a bowl of generic Safeway raisin bran, bathing and then downing a couple of glasses of orange juice. I'd sit around, wishing I had something good to write about, but the only thing that would come out of me would be bran farts and OJ belches.

I'd be somewhat upset about the state of my life, frustrated with the discontentment that I thought I'd left back in the Central Valley. Then I'd ask myself, "What the hell are you doing this school shit for, anyway? What the hell are you doing this work shit for, anyway?" Then I'd fire up the iMac so that I could try to type away my discomfort. I'd write for sanity, as much sanity as my physical genetics and social heredity would allow.

I got my first strike of the day, but the fish had been fated with good fortune and evaded the hook hidden inside the feathery muddler. I fell back into the cadence of my daydreaming.

What would it have been like having been born into another time and era? Would I still have been suffering my discontent? Would inherited wealth have molded me differently? I liked to believe that if I had been born with a silver spoon, I would have already died from living life to excess, but that was just another lie I told myself to sweep away an uncomfortable jealousy. There could have been a trillion other variables that I had been born into, but fortunately or unfortunately, I had to live my reality as I continued trying to escape it.

Why did the others all have nicer cars than I, and why did they always seem to have the beautiful wife driving the goddamn nicer car to boot? They'd beaten me to the punch. The bastards all had a jump start on me. They had parents who sent them off to college, bought them the car and put up the down payment on their homes. Hell, no wonder they'd gotten the good-looking wives. Good-looking wives came along with high paying jobs, nice cars and big houses.

I never really had these things because I chose not to. I didn't want the obligations that went along with having parents supporting me as they dictated the run of my life. I didn't want the obligations that were attached to the ass-end of one of those good-looking wives. They would demand security for themselves; after having three of my children, they would have their fangs nestled deep in my jugular with a clench that lasted a lifetime. Yeah, I was rebelling against the world into which I had been born.

There were a lot of fucks out there who tried to tell me how to live my life, but the problem wasn't the fucks out there. The fucks out there were just phantoms wandering around with their back-sides painted black like mirrors reflecting the images of my own inner demons who stared me down with eyes of intimidation, shaking their pointed index fingers at me, their other fists pounding pulpits, lips thundering echoes of thou-shalt-nots reverberating in elevated canonical tones that bounced off of the walls of my empty Wednesday afternoon sanctuary-like hollow soul.

I knew why I wept so hard the day we buried my Grandfather. Papa got to quit seeing and hearing the phantoms. I knew how relieved he must have been when that first shovel full of dirt landed on the top of his casket. I cried because I wouldn't have him anymore, but I also cried because I feared the phantoms that he had willed to me. I wanted to believe that another grandchild would be the beneficiary of this inheritance, but I was his firstborn. At Papa's burial, it was time to assume the birthright that had been assigned to me the day I had been cast out of Eden.

The fish didn't hit as viciously as my Saturday hook-up. It felt like a damn big fish, but it wasn't as wild as my first. Maintaining my balance on the log took little effort. I decided to step back from the trunk and started my retreat for shallower waters, this time by my own decision instead of being forced off my insecure perch and taking on the chilly water.

I back-stepped my way to shore where I had entered the river, never taking my eyes off the rod tip and line. I knew that if I eased up on the tension, she'd throw the hook and be gone. I let the trout tire as I stood in the knee-deep current of the river and within a few minutes I slowly reeled in the line, raising the rod to ease the fish in to me.

I tucked the rod under my armpit and gently pulled the line, easing the fish into my cupped hands. I had her out of the water just long enough to admire all twenty plus inches of her broad shimmering body and to relieve her of the barbless muddler she'd mistaken for dinner. I set the Rainbow back down into the water, holding her until she started to flutter with energy, then releasing and watching her fade back into the river.

I was proud of my catch, grateful to have held her, feeling reverent and empowered as I returned her to her element. I called it a day and turned to the shore looking up towards Ol' Reliable and was surprised to see the blue Jetta parked by its side. Sarah had found a quiet place to sit on the shore and had been looking on.

"How long you been here?" I asked, without a formal hello.

"A while," she smiled. "That was something else."

"She was beautiful."

"What happened?"

"What do you mean?"

"How'd you lose her?"

"Didn't; I let her go."

"You let her go?"

"Catch an' release. I let them all go."

"Why?" Sarah asked with a puzzled expression.

"Wouldn't be right."

"Guess you're right about that."

"What are you doing out here?"

"Nothing really."

"I see," I said, walking up to Sarah and hugging her with my free arm.

"Guess I just wanted to see you," she said, as I let her go.

"About what?" I asked, feeling a bit nervous.

"Nothing really, I just wanted to see you," she said, like a little girl wanting something from her father but afraid to ask.

"OK, walk with me to the Chevy so I can shed this gear," I said, starting for Ol' Reliable, impatiently wanting to know what Sarah had in mind but holding my tongue.

I dropped the tailgate of the Chevy and climbed on after putting my fly rod and vest in the truck bed. Sarah didn't sit down; instead she stood watching me take off my waders with her hands in her front jean pockets, shrugging her shoulders.

"I just wanted to check on you," she said, finally breaking

her silent spell.

"Check on me?"

"Yeah, I just wanted to see how you were."

"Doing pretty damn good considering that trout I just set free."

"I mean how do you feel?"

"Empty."

"Where?"

"In my guts." I answered, feeling like a wet towel being rung out.

"From what?"

"Don't know."

"A longing?" she asked.

"I used to think so, but I don't know anymore."

"What do you think it is then?"

"Don't know. Guess if it was a longing I'd have filled it up by now."

"How?"

"That's my problem. Haven't found anything that'll work."

"What do you mean?"

"I mean as in booze, food, money, or women. Anything tangible."

"Well, then what do you do?"

"I don't know. Just feel fucked up I guess. What else can I do?"

"I don't know."

"I guess I could be mad at you for not loving me enough, but if it wasn't you it would be another woman."

"What does that make me?" she asked, still standing with her hands in her pockets.

"I'm not saying you're not significant. I mean that if I had never met you, I'm sure that I'd have fallen in love with another woman."

"What's so bad about falling in love with me?" she asked, her face shifting to a look of disappointment.

"You're not available."

"According to you."

"Yeah, according to me. Hell, you're not even divorced."

"So…"

"So that's the problem."

"Because I'm not divorced?"

"Hell yeah. I want to invest my heart in you, but I'll be damned if I'm gunna if you aren't open to me."

"You aren't open to me," Sarah countered.

"Yes, I am."

"No, you're not."

"Bullshit, you've got me. All that you've got to do is say the word."

"Yeah, right. I say the word and you'd be on your way back to California with or without that damn little car. You'd run so fast that I wouldn't even be able to find your trail," she said, shifting her hands from her pockets to her hips.

"I'm not running anywhere."

"You're running right now."

"I'm right here in front of you making a complete ass of myself. If that's what you call running, then I guess I am."

"You're running with the excuse of my being unavailable."

"No, I'm not."

"Yes, you are. If you really loved me, you'd wait."

"Wait for you not to let me in," I said, imagining how a few more years would slip through my fingers. "I'm tired of waiting. I want you now."

"You've got me now," she said, crossing her arms.

"All that I've got right now is a dream, a desire."

"You'd rather have the dream than the real thing anyway. It's safe for you that way."

"Maybe that's why you're living out here, to hide," I suggested.

"Maybe."

"More than maybe."

"You don't know…"

"Maybe I do and you don't want to hear it."

"Maybe you're wrong!" she said, taking a few steps backwards.

"Sarah, it's all up to you."

"What's up to me?"

"Us."

"You want to shove it all off onto me."

"I just told you that I want you. What else do you want?"

"More than words."

"Me too, Sarah. Me too."

"So how does this happen?"

"We quit talking and just let it happen."

"How?"

"You have to risk too, Sarah. You've got to open yourself up to me."

"So you can run?"

"Or love you."

"Or run."

"Game's over Sarah. I quit. I love you, I want you and I'm here. Now all that you have to do is move toward me. If you want it, you've got to come and get it."

"So do you," she said, back-stepping for the Jetta.

"Sarah! I just told you that I quit, no more games. Here I am. If you want me, clean house. Go back to him and your parents and clean it up."

"How?"

"I don't know, but you've got to do it if you want to be with me."

"They'll just freak out like they always do."

"Then let them continue to run your life from halfway across the continent."

"They don't run my life."

"You're hiding, Sarah. You're hiding from the woman that you are. Your parents aren't gunna run my life. They might run yours, but not mine. If you want to be with me you have to grow up and take back the power you've given them."

I hated women who argued with me. I hated women who wouldn't fall into my ideas of how things should be. My biggest problem was that these women who I hated were the only women that I ever truly fell in love with. I'd heard that if you went to the drugstore for power and love, you had to carry them out in separate bags because mixing the two caused a devastating chemical reaction.

CHAPTER 19

Thursday Morning

I woke to a wind whistling through a gap in the window. It was still dark when I got up to shut the damn thing. I figured that it must have been predawn, but when I turned on the light and found my watch, it read six-thirty. I pulled back the curtains to observe the storm that had descended upon Five Points and its inhabitants as they escaped their mundane lives at the carnival of their nocturnal Mardi Gras.

Heavy rain drops began to pound the window pane as I peered out of the west window searching for some sign of the storm's clearing, none of which I found. I remembered days like those as a child, the doldrums of not being able to go outside and play. It was stormy days that caused Mom to introduce the routine of construction paper, Elmer's white glue and Magic Marker felt pens, all of which never really allowed us to paint the real sky bright and sunny again, returning us to our true calling of being at one with nature in the outside world.

It was days like this day that my brothers and I would beat the living shit out of each other just as soon as Mom was two steps down the hallway. It was usually about the territorial rights to her pinking shears or her good sharp sewing scissors. We never had those safety scissors like the ones at school; besides, those rounded off kiddy scissors were for kids whose parents were afraid their children would actually get hurt. We had no interest in actually offing a worthy opponent or inflicting any permanent bodily harm to each other with Mom's sewing paraphernalia. We enjoyed the pleasures of our sibling rivalries and looked forward to future chivalrous encounters.

I lay back down in bed allowing my body to decide whether

to continue with sleep or honor the accusing voice that haunted me whenever I slept past the time that the normal world would allow. I was still tired, and wrestled with the voices that were bargaining for my attention. The resonating echoes of duty prevailed over my rebellion. I think that duty won out just so it could torture me like on those stormy childhood-construction-paper days that left me waiting for a clearing in which I'd find real meaning and purpose for the day. All I needed to complete the reenactment was a little brother holding a pair of scissors to be robbed.

Without underwear, I pulled on the previous day's Levis and stepped into my Tonys without socks, pulled on a clean T-shirt, and slapped on my cap. My toes, arches and heels stuck to the leathery insoles of my boots as I descended the stairs for a cup of my morning eye-opener.

"Good day," I said, greeting Flo who was standing behind the counter.

"Good mornin'. Coffee?" Flo asked, before I had a chance to flip the cup over in request.

"Please," I answered, already finding my cup poured half full. "What's with the weather?" I asked.

"Nothin' out of the ordinary," she answered. "Normal to get a storm this time of the year."

"What do you do?" I asked, as if I'd never been in a thunderstorm before.

"What do you mean?"

"I mean what do you do when it storms around here?"

"Same as I do any other day around here," she answered, seeming put off with the question. "What do you do when it storms?"

"I don't know," I answered, never having really given much thought to how I did alter my adult life for weather. "The same as any other day I guess."

"Do you eat when it storms?" she asked in a insulting way to see if I wanted to order anything else.

"Only when I'm hungry," I slapped back.

"Are you hungry?" she asked in a toned-down fashion, sensing my agitation.

"A short stack sounds good."

"Comin' up."

Flo scribbled down the order and spun it to Jimmy's side. I sipped the coffee wondering what my day might bring. I looked around the diner and then out the front window toward Okie's place. I started thinking about my impending departure from Five Points, the experiences I'd had, and the discontentment that had been reawakened there.

Jimmy walked through the kitchen door with my pancakes.

"Blueberry or Maple?" Jimmy asked.

"Maple sounds good."

"Maple it is," he said, setting the syrup down in front of me. He topped off my coffee and filled the empty cup on the counter to my right. He put the pot back on the burner before sitting down.

"What do ya think of this storm?"

"OK, I guess."

"It'll settle the dust."

"That'll be nice." I answered just to answer.

"Now, if we could only get your dust settled."

Uncertain how to respond, I turned to my right, smiled at Jimmy and returned to my short stack. "Don't think this storm's gunna settle my dust, huh?" I asked, after a bite.

"No."

"Car'll be ready Saturday."

"Oh yeah."

"Leaving Monday."

"Sounds like you're all set."

"We'll see."

"You still have a few days to pack your bag."

"Problem is my bag's not big enough for what I want to stuff in it."

"Yeah, I know how that goes."

"I want to…"

"You sure that's what you want?" Jimmy questioned.

"Yeah, well no… I… I don't know. I've just got to let go of this whole thing."

"What whole thing?"

"Me."

"How you gunna do that?"

"Hell, I don't know. It just now came to me. I don't even know why I said it."

"I see," Jimmy said, before taking another swig of coffee.

"I'm still figuring it out."

"Hmm," Jimmy grunted.

"A new mask."

"What?"

"I need a new mask."

"What kind a mask?"

"One that fits. One that lets me live without duty."

"You got me kid," Jimmy said, shaking his head, trying to clear his confusion.

"I used to love selling tractors. It wasn't a duty, but I lived for it."

"You hate what you used to love?"

"Oh yeah, just like an ex-wife," I said, smiling and looking around for Flo.

"You are a mess," Jimmy laughed.

"Speaking of wives, it is my ex's birthday today."

"Gunna call her?"

"Hell no. I had her served with divorce papers on her birthday."

"You're a rotten little fucker aren't you?"

"Top that, the judge stamped it official on the same date the following year. It's the five year anniversary of my divorce today," I answered. "Fuck marriage anyway."

"Still tryin' to get rid of that mask, too, huh?"

"What's that?"

"The fool's mask."

"What?"

"For bein' foolish enough to marry her in the first place," he said, turning to the back door that was opening.

"I see what you're getting at," I said, chuckling from embarrassment.

Flo walked in and climbed the stairs.

"Hard to get rid of what's comfortable sometimes."

"You mean my pissing and moaning?"

"It can still be comfortable, even if it doesn't serve you any more."

"Comfortably uncomfortable."

"You got it," Jimmy said. "Got any ideas what you wanna do?"

"I'm not sure," I answered, feeling depressed.

"Good," he said, and took another sip of coffee.

"Whatever," I said, pushing away my empty plate.

"It's part of it."

"Part of what?" I asked.

"Of dyin' and bein' reborn."

"I hope you're right."

"I'm right," he answered without hesitation. "Ever wonder how you fit into this world?"

"Don't feel that I do right now."

"That's a good thing to know, too."

"What's so good about not fitting in?"

"It's good to know, so you don't try to."

"Why's that?"

"Because you're not supposed to."

"I'm not supposed to fit in?"

"Yeah, just let it happen. Whatever it is, let the world make room for you."

"That's what I'm trying to force into my bag."

"That's right," he said, as he walked back into his kitchen.

Maybe Jimmy was right. All of the construction paper and Magic Markers in the world wouldn't let me color away the storm outside or the one that was raging inside me.

I dragged myself back upstairs to call and check on the hauling status of the harvester and to ready myself for the remainder of the day. I did a few crunches trying to eliminate some of the collected tension in my muscles, but my attempt was futile. I ran the bath hoping to find relief there, but my agitated state wouldn't permit me to soak for any lengthy period. It was one of those days where I was going to be volatile. On this particular day, I had to watch and guard against life's surprises, things that normally passed by silently.

After dressing and slipping into my Tonys, I phoned the truck dispatcher and was informed that the harvester would be delivered a week late. I then informed him that if the goddamn rig wasn't delivered by our contract date that he could shit-can the haul and forget about doing any future business with me. He said that he'd get back to me. I told him not to bother and to just get the fucker there like he'd promised. He said that he still had to get back to me. It was a good thing I had no need to talk to Okie about the MG.

I went downstairs expecting to see Sarah, but found Flo trading change at the register. She accompanied her patrons to the door and long after they'd left, hands inside of her apron pockets, continued her gaze outside.

"Looks like it's gunna be one of those days," Flo said, as she walked back towards the counter.

"Where's Sarah?" I asked.

Flo ducked down to look for something under the counter, not bothering to answer. She rustled around in whatever had collected in the cubby below the register.

"She'll be in later," Flo responded in a half-pissed-off tone as she stood up. "Why?"

"Because I want to know, that's why." I was tired of pretending around Flo. She knew damn well what was going on.

"I told you to leave her alone."

"So what."

"So now you've made a fucked up mess around here."

"What do you care?"

"Fuck you, you self-absorbed little bastard."

"No, fuck you, Miss Fuckin' Know-It-All."

"If you'd have left her alone..."

"If I'd have left her alone what?"

"I wouldn't have to be cleanin' shit up around this place."

"It's your place," I reminded her.

"I mean yours and Sarah's shit."

"What's to clean up?"

"You haven't got a clue have you?"

"Help me out here."

"You're such a fuckin' man it's pitiful."

"Wow, from a boy to a man in less than two weeks," I said, reminding her of our first encounter.

"I wish," she said, going back into the kitchen.

I considered myself the victor of that spar with Flo, as well as my earlier round with the dispatcher. I decided it best to retreat to the corner of my room before I bit off more than I could chew. With my luck, I'd stumble into some cranked out trucker who stopped to stretch and use the diner's pisser, finding myself like a Poodle taking on a Great Dane.

Chapter 20
Thursday Afternoon

Deciding that a nap might rescue me from myself, I kicked off my Tonys and plopped onto the bed. Lying there, I started to fantasize about Sarah knocking on my door, but that only excited my agitated state. I got up and walked to the windows, looking first to the north at Okie's station and then to the west into the darkness of the embedded squall line of thunderstorms that showed no signs of breaking up.

I picked up my cell phone and tried to phone my buddy Lewis, to shoot the shit with him and pawn off as much of my frustration as he'd take, but got no answer. I walked over to the bookshelf and rummaged through the books that had been laid to rest and forgotten in the recesses of my cell. I paged through several of them searching for an interest to rescue me from my reality, but my unhappiness was too strong to be overcome by someone else's scribbling. Had I been at home, the heavy bag would have suffered the brunt of my turmoil.

I lay back down on the bed. The image of Lauren came to me along with the uncomfortable twinge her memory always seemed to stir. I slipped off into the memory of falling in love and losing myself in her. I had finally settled into something that delivered me from the realm of physical agitation and into one of mental aggravation by torturing myself with "what ifs."

I fell for Lauren because she had been safe. She lived two hundred miles away, the distance and the complications of our lives kept us from getting too close and imposing demands on each other. Lauren had kids and didn't want more, didn't want more obligations; she already had more than she could handle. Lauren just wanted a lover when she had time for him. Lauren was a lot like me; I just wanted an on-call love, but business took priority. The frustrating thing about the Lauren type of woman was that it was hard to match the limited time of her freedom to mine. It was hard for me not to take her unavailability personally. It poked the needy-little-boy part of me right in his hungry belly, his tender heart.

My cell phone rang. It was the dispatcher informing me that things had been worked out and that my client would take delivery as we had originally agreed. I thanked the dispatcher for straightening things out, feeling a slight remorse before justification neutralized the guilt of my earlier outburst. One battle had been won, the precursor, I hoped, to the inner conflict still being waged. I took a few deep breaths and drifted off to sleep.

I woke to explosive thunder, trembling with a bellyache, a backache, a muscle spasm in my right calf, and a fluttering heart. Why didn't I just get a gun and put myself out of my misery? I wanted to crawl back up into the womb. I wanted security. I wanted to go back to what I knew, prison. Returning to the womb and death were one and the same.

I didn't want the responsibilities of supporting a woman and a potential family. I didn't want to be or feel as vulnerable with Sarah as I had in the past. I was afraid of repeating the same pattern with her as I had with Lauren and my mother, silently whispering that someday-they'll-be-able-to-love-me mantra. All I had to do was get them to listen, to convince them to follow my path and everything would fall into order. I'd show them the way, and we'd all live that happily-ever-after fairytale.

I might as well have been high. I was angry. I wanted to live in my old illusion, but no longer could. I was still fighting but knew it was a lie. I was hoping for a big old case of the shits to flush the fear from my system once and for all.

I wanted to hop off of the soapbox and put an end to my pissing and moaning. I didn't want to live that old life of being the wounded little boy who had been displaced by his younger siblings and countless other obstacles that life had dealt. I didn't want to continue suffering the disappointment of being unable to realize the unattainable, illusive perfect love of my mother, or any other woman that I encountered, for that matter.

I could no longer stand myself, being upstairs alone with my inner conflict. Although, it didn't seem to matter where I was, alone or in company, the battle was in me and was waged wherever I went. I planted myself into my Tonys and went downstairs. "How's it going?" I asked Sarah, as I pulled up to the counter.

"Hey, I wondered about you."

"About what?" I asked recalling our confrontation at the river the previous day.

"'Bout how you are."

"OK. Actually, I think I'm depressed," I confessed.

"Me, too."

"I've been this way for a few days."

"Three for me."

"I feel like I want to kill something."

"I did for the first few days."

"Actually, I go in and out of it. One minute I want to kill, the next I want to crawl into a hole."

"I just want to crawl into a hole. I cried for forty-five minutes when I woke up. Now it feels like I'm skidding downhill out of control."

"We got to go there."

"What?" she asked looking relieved.

"We got to go down there. It's the only way out."

"You're so right."

"It's that or Prozac, and I don't do any of that shit," I said.

"Me either, but sometimes I wish I did."

"It's our souls asking for attention."

"It's a mind thing," Sarah said.

"No, it's a heart thing."

"You're right, but the mind gets in the way," she said, walking around and sitting down next to me.

"Yeah, because we've been taught not to let ourselves get this way."

"Isn't that terrible," Sarah said, shaking her head in disgust.

"Part of life."

"I think we're supposed to be this way sometimes."

"It's our souls calling out for attention, I'm telling you."

"Yes, but sometimes I don't have time to listen," she said, turning to see my expression.

"If I let it go long enough, she just beats me."

Sarah nodded her head.

"I mean... I've got this huge ego that thinks it can fight it. That's when she really kicks the shit out of me," I said, looking at Sarah.

"When you don't listen," Sarah answered, looking distant. "I used to really dump this shit off onto Mark. I mean, I was a real bitch at times."

"I had a wife like that once."

"Well, I wasn't always like that."

"It had to be more than that."

"I guess so, but I'm alone now. I mean, an hour after I went off on him, I knew it wasn't him."

"Usually isn't," I said, as she stood and walked behind the counter.

"Funny how we dump on the person we're supposed to love."

"It's too bad. We all do it though," I answered, thinking about my ex-wife and how I was unable to understand or tolerate her mood-swinging bitchiness. I couldn't stand her because I couldn't stand myself. I had spent a good portion of my life unconsciously in that moody state. If I couldn't stand myself, how in the hell could I have tolerated her, or anyone else for that matter? "What are your parents like?" I asked Sarah.

"A mess."

"What do you mean?"

"Dad's an alcoholic. Mom bitches about him but protects him."

"Like she can't stand him, but doesn't want him to change?" I asked.

"He quit drinking when I was thirteen, but he started again."

"Does he still drink?"

"Well, no, but he was... oh you don't want to hear this stuff," she said hesitantly.

"Maybe I do."

"He quit for years and then he started to bother my mom for

just one glass of wine with dinner."

"That you knew about," I interjected.

"Mom said that he was OK for the first year."

"Yeah, but you've been gone. He was probably sneaking more than a glass the whole time."

"Mom said that he went to two glasses, but they were probably like Jimmy's water tumbler."

"How long has this been?"

"Three years. My sister told him that if he didn't stop she never wanted to see him again."

"What did he say?"

"He said OK."

"OK what?"

"He stopped. He never went to AA or anything. He just stopped like he did when I was thirteen."

"How old is he?"

"Fifty-four."

"What does he do?"

"Works at a fishing tackle store."

"What did he do before that?"

"He never worked when he was younger."

"What did he do?"

"We had a big swimming pool. He'd invite all of his old high school buddies over. They'd hang out at the pool and drink all day."

"Hell of a life! How'd he support you?"

"Mom worked," she said, rolling her eyes.

A retired couple walked into the diner and Sarah went to seat them.

I was actually connecting with Sarah again, and the nicest thing about it was that it was helping me out of my depression. Sarah knew how important it was to let depression take its course instead of trying to deny or get rid of it. She was letting me be depressed without trying to talk me out of it. Actually, she was honoring my depression, honoring me.

"Why don't you come for dinner?" Sarah asked, as she walked back up to the counter.

"When?" I asked, feeling surprised, excited, and afraid all at once.

"Saturday."

"You sure?"

"Of course!"

"OK."

"Good," she said, walking off with the coffee pot.

Dinner would be fine. Dessert would be better, but for some reason I felt awkward and hesitant. I was afraid of the price tag. Jimmy walked out of the kitchen, filled his cup with ice water and sat next to me.

"What's up?"

"She just asked me to come for dinner on Saturday."

"Good."

"I guess."

"Had any better invitations?" Jimmy asked, sliding his tumbler from hand to hand on the counter.

I looked at Jimmy and grinned. "What do you think?"

"It's a good thing."

"I feel like a five-year-old little boy lost in a department store."

"You what?"

"I'm scared," I said, turning around to look for Sarah.

"Of what?"

"Fuck, I don't know. Getting lost."

"Kid, you're lost already."

"No shit."

"So why do you give a shit?"

"I don't know."

"Kid, when you die, you're found."

"What?"

"You're fuckin' lost until you die."

"What are you saying?"

"What I'm sayin' is that you've got a choice."

"About being lost?"

"No, but you got a choice of who's lost."

"How?"

"You can be two feet tall lost between the racks of women's dresses shittin' your britches like a little boy who's lost his mama, or you can be a grown man sittin' in one of those nice chairs they have for the gentlemen to relax in while they admire the different skirts droopin' off the backside of the woman who's modelin' for you."

Chapter 21

Friday

I lathered my hair with shampoo and dunked myself under water like a full submersion baptism. "Why do I have to choose," is what I spit out, making room for a breath of fresh air. I dunked a second time to rinse the shampoo again and exhaled a: "Why do I have to do anything?" Then I sat there and looked down at my hairy chest and aging sagging belly. Sarah was going to make me into whatever she needed me to be, so why didn't I just let her?

To feel secure, I always wanted to have things in their place, but deep down inside I knew that it was false. Maybe I wasn't supposed to be in control, sounded a lot simpler than trying to force myself to be anything. I could then allow the process of my life to unfold, as fate would have it. My need to fix things in order to find security was an illusion that had failed me time and time again. I wanted and desperately needed to develop the art of living and being what was real and true for me in the present moment.

I went downstairs. Part of me believed that a she would never pacify my discontent, or anything else out there on the corporeal level, and that it could only be mastered within, on an ethereal plane. Unknowingly, I wanted neither one of these alternatives to be realized. I didn't want to figure it out; I wanted to keep chasing whatever it was that I was chasing. I wanted to keep living with this purpose even if it was futile. Chasing an illusion somehow served me.

"Coffee?" Jimmy asked.

Lost in thought, I didn't hear him.

"Coffee, kid?" Jimmy rumbled in a deeper and sharper tone, waking me from my trance.

"Yeah, thanks," I answered, as he filled my cup.

"Where you at this mornin'?" Jimmy asked, standing behind the counter.

"Pissedville," I answered, frustrated with being frustrated.

"What's new?"

"Not a damn thing," I answered, as he put the pot back on the warmer.

"What's goin' on?"

"I'm pissed at myself for getting stuck on the image of a woman."

"You mean Sarah?" he asked, as he leaned on the service counter below the kitchen window.

"I get stuck on the idea of a woman, but I never actually seem to let a real live woman into my life."

"Who, Sarah?" Jimmy asked again.

"Like, I'll find a woman who I really think I could be with, and if she's open to me I run, but if she's out of my reach, I've got to have her," I answered without addressing Jimmy's reference to Sarah.

"Sounds like you want more than a woman."

"I don't think so."

"I think so, or you'd already be with one."

"What do I want then?"

"I'm not sure, but it sounds like what you want is more than human," he said, looking up and over me.

Sarah came gliding up, ticket in hand, heading for the order wheel.

"Morning, Sarah," I said, greeting her as she slipped the ticket into the wheel.

"Good morning," she replied, grabbing a coffee pot and scampering off to fill the empty mugs. It was as if she sensed the privacy of my conversation with Jimmy.

"I don't know what I want Jimmy, but I know I don't have it."

"Don't know what to tell you, kid"

"I don't think anyone does."

"How long have you been like this?" he asked, standing.

"Forever," I answered, frustrated with my age-old discontent. It was days like this that I wanted to break something. I felt like shattering something, a window maybe. Yes, the panes of the glass prison in which I felt captive.

"Forever's an awful long time."

"You're telling me. I feel so stuck right now. I mean... I can hardly stand myself."

"Yeah."

"Yeah, what?"

"I mean, yeah I hear you, but I need to get back there to fill that order. I'll be back in a while," Jimmy said and went to carry out his job.

I drank my coffee and made small talk with Sarah between her counter runs. The place was busy enough to keep her hopping that morning. It was busy enough that I wasn't able to demand either Sarah's or Jimmy's attention at will. Ten minutes later Jimmy resurfaced from the kitchen.

"What am I supposed to do?" I asked as he pulled in next to me at the counter.

"Don't know. Wish I did, but I don't."

"I know what I have to do."

"What?"

"Same thing I've done most of my life. Wait!"

"Wait for what?"

"I wish I knew."

"Maybe your answer isn't in waitin'."

"Where is it then?" I asked.

"If you're in wait, you're expectin'. If you're expectin', good chance you'll end up disappointed."

"Yeah, but if..." I stopped, as Sarah walked up with another order. She took the coffee pot and walked off again.

"No *but if*. Your life is as it is."

"But if I could only figure out how to..."

"Don't figure. Just let your life happen."

"I'm fight..."

"If she was only this, if he was only that, if they could just understand, if I could just get this one more thing, then," Jimmy added.

"No wonder I'm so pissed and frustrated."

"Yeah, no wonder," he said, getting up and walking back to start another order.

Finding the right woman would never happen because she was not of this realm. The perfect woman was impossible because I wanted her to be impossible. I needed her to be impossible because my quest for her gave meaning and reason to continued pursuit. Chasing her gave me purpose. I needed her to be unattainable so that I could continue to live. That was why I chased the unattainable instead of the attainable. The attainable ultimately was recognized and the challenge lost. The unattainable was never realized, but the pursuit to fulfill the insatiable longing gave meaning to my life.

"I just want to turn around and drive somewhere that I've never been before," I said, as Jimmy sat down next to me again.

"Do it."

"You don't understand. I mean for good."

"Why?"

"Start over."

"What?"

"My life. I want to erase the blackboard and start over, clean slate."

"What about your life?"

"What about it?"

"What about your family and friends?"

"I want a break from them, too. I can start over somewhere. Then after I've got my life in order I can visit them."

"Hmm," Jimmy grunted.

"I'm tired of the obligations that are tied to my relationships."

"You'll just make new friends and new obligations."

"Maybe, maybe not."

"What will you do that's different?"

"I'll choose who I get close to."

"You mean withdraw?"

"No, I mean have fewer people in my life; a life that will let me have my space, where people aren't always in want or need of me."

"Good luck. Sounds like you want to step out of life."

"I am: stepping out of the life I've been living and into a new one that serves me better."

"What will help you is findin' out what you feel obligated to, findin' out what haunts you."

"What do you mean?"

"I mean, wherever you go, your own sense of obligation will follow."

"It just seems that my life is so messy and complicated."

"That's life."

"That's fucked."

"Sometimes it is and sometimes it isn't."

"I just want it to be easier."

"You're runnin' from yourself. If you want to start over, that's fine, but just make sure you know why you're doin' it."

"Self-containment."

"What?"

"Self-containment: being responsible for myself. That's what I want."

"What do you mean?"

"I mean that I don't want the responsibilities that people shuffle off on to me."

"Don't take 'em."

"I wouldn't if they weren't offered."

"When someone offers you a beer do you feel obligated?"

"No."

"Why?"

"Because I know that it isn't good for me."

"Right, so when people offer you other things, why don't you just do what you do when they offer you a beer?"

"You mean it's up to me to say no?"

"You have the choice to accept or reject anything that comes your way," Jimmy said, as Flo walked through the back door and up the stairs. "I've got to get back to work," he said, heading for the kitchen.

Choices seemed to be the greatest cause of my suffering. I'd had enough success in life that I had choices. I thought that by then I would have come to a place of peace and contentment, having mastered my life. I never dreamed that realizing my pursuit of freedom and autonomy would reward me with the treasures of paradox.

I had another choice to make, check on the MG or leave the old fart to linger all alone in his little heaven. I decided to go sniff around.

"How's things looking, Okie?" I asked, walking into the shop.

"She'll be ready tomorrow," he answered, rummaging through his toolbox.

"Had any troubles?" I asked, knowing that he wouldn't tell me if he had.

"Nope," he answered curtly.

"Sounds good. See you tomorrow," I said, following my cue to leave the magician and his trade secrets to himself.

"A, huh," Okie grunted, as he scrunched himself back under the bonnet of the roadster.

I wanted to piss in the old fucker's thirty-three-gallon barrel behind the seat of his cash register, but I still had a few more days to deal with the old fart. I also had a bill to settle with him, so I let my pocket book be my conscience. Flo was driving out in Ol' Reliable while I was on my way back to the diner. I laughed as I looked into the back window of the pickup, her head surging back and forth like one of those toy Chihuahuas as the Chevy did its choking act as it pulled out onto the highway. The remnants of my feisty mood from the previous day still lingered.

I was Sarah's only patron on that Friday's lunch rush.

"Something to eat?" Sarah asked, as I bellied up to the counter.

"I'll have the special," I answered, duplicating the fish and chips meal I had on the day of my untimely arrival.

"Tea?" Sarah asked, penciling my order onto a ticket.

"Lots of…"

"Ice."

"Please," I replied, feeling less at ease with Sarah than I had been the previous day. I was hiding my insecurity behind a justified sense of superiority.

"Here you go," Sarah said, setting my glass full of iced tea down in front of me.

"Thanks," I said, rubbing my temples.

"No problem. Everything all right?"

"Everything's fine," I lied.

"Whatcha got planned for your day?"

"No plans."

"It's so nice out. Always is after a storm like yesterday's."

"Yeah, it sure is." I answered, wrapped up in my inner turmoil, oblivious to the outer world.

"Bet it's a perfect day to fish?"

"Nah."

"Nah?"

"Water's probably muddy."

"What makes you say that?"

"Usually is after a storm like yesterday's."

"Why."

"Rain washes a lot of dry dirt down into the river from the tributaries."

"I see," Sarah said, following my mood.

"It hasn't been easy for you, has it?"

"What's that?" Sarah asked, trying to keep up with the pace of my shifting mind.

"Your life; living out here."

"Oh, that," Sarah said, her tone shifting.

"I guess if things had been easier, you wouldn't be here in the first place."

"Yeah, some life out here."

"Pretty shitty, I suspect."

"Lonely."

"Safe, too."

"It's been necessary. I needed to feel safe and to be alone."

"What do you need now?"

"I'm not sure."

"Do you need me to leave you alone?" I asked, expecting her to say yes and afraid of a no.

"I don't know."

"I don't get it," I said, as Jimmy slid my lunch through the window.

"I don't either. I mean, I want you, but I'm afraid," she said, getting up to retrieve my lunch.

"Afraid of what?"

"Of getting lost again. Afraid of you taking me over and running my life," she said, setting lunch down in front of me.

"Makes sense," I confirmed as she refilled my iced tea. She went back into the diner to collect the salt and pepper shakers.

I pounded the stubborn catsup bottle and finally got it to pour. After a few bites, Sarah returned and sat next to me at the counter.

"Will you?"

"What?"

"Try to run me?"

"Doesn't matter how I answer."

"Yes, it does," she said, as she started unscrewing the tops off of the shakers.

"No, it doesn't. Because I'm gunna be what you make me."

"What?"

"I'm gunna be what you make me. If you believe that I'll put you into a box, I'll put you there."

"Why would you, if you know I don't want to be put there?"

"Because you'll put yourself there: I'll just be the man in your life who's reflecting what's really going on inside of you."

"So this is my fault?"

"I don't think it's anyone's fault, but it happens all the time."

"I'm lost," Sarah said, going behind the counter to get the bulk containers of salt and pepper.

"Yeah, me too. It's just easy having preconceived ideas about how people are supposed to be. But it's how we see people most of the time. We see them the way we need them, instead of being able to see them the way they really are. I do it all the time. It's hard not to."

"Like how?" she asked, sitting back down.

"Like with your parents and your husband. They've made Mark into what they need him to be, the son they never had. You're the outcast since you aren't going along with them and their illusion. You're a threat, and it's easier to make you wrong and screwed up than for them to see things as they really are."

Sarah was quiet.

"What did you want from him?"

"Who?"

"Your husband?"

"His companionship: I wanted him to love me," she said, overfilling a saltshaker.

"Did you want him to make it all better for you?"

"No," she answered, wiping the spilt salt onto a serving tray.

"Are you sure? Maybe just a little bit?"

"Well, I wanted him to be a husband. I wanted him to be in love with me, and I wanted to have a family."

"How did he fail you?"

"Evan."

"He failed you because you lost Evan? You both lost him."

"I mean, after Evan died, Mark went away."

"How?"

"He just worked and fished. He left me. We lived together, but he was never around."

"So he wasn't what you needed him to be?"

"He wasn't anything to me," she said, screwing the last top back on the salts.

"I wonder what you were to him?"

"A nag."

"About what?"

"Anything."

"About him not being what you needed him to be."

"I was lonely. I just wanted to be close to him. He is my husband you know."

"Yeah, he is," I answered.

Sarah hesitated.

"I suppose if it wasn't Mark, it would have been another man unable to take away your loneliness."

"It wouldn't have been another man," Sarah replied.

"No, I don't believe that it would have been just any other man, but if it wasn't Mark, you would still have been with someone else. You needed someone."

"I don't know if I need someone."

"You don't, but you thought you did."

"I guess I did or I wouldn't have been with him."

"That's what I'm talking about. You needed him so that you could make him into what you needed him to be. Then when you found that he didn't fit your inner image, you left."

"I left because..."

"I don't care why you left, Sarah. I'm glad you did."

"Then why are we even talking about this?" she asked, screwing the last lid back on the peppers.

"Because if you don't figure this out, we don't stand a chance."

"Sounds like you want me to go back to him."

"I hope you dump his ass for good. I just don't want to become another Mark."

"What about you?" Sarah asked, as I swallowed the last of my tea.

"What about me?" I asked, setting the glass back down on the counter.

"Why me?"

"Wish I knew. Wish I could give you a logical reason, but you do something for me that I can't put in words."

"When that car of yours is fixed, you could just ride off into the sunset."

"I'm gunna ride off into the sunset," I said, standing.

"See!"

"What I see, is me stuck because of that damn broken down car of mine. There's no other reason for me to be here," I said, walking behind the counter to get the pitcher of tea.

"And when it's fixed, you're leaving?"

"You're damn right I'm leaving, and if you weren't married, you could leave with me."

"If I wasn't married you wouldn't be asking me to leave with you," she answered, as I refilled my glass.

"You don't know that," I answered, looking up to her and overfilling my glass.

"I think you're bold because it's safe to be bold," she said, returning the bulk seasoning behind the counter and getting a towel to wipe up my mess.

"Bullshit."

"So if I wasn't married, you'd take me with you?" she asked as she sopped up the spilt tea.

"Yeah."

"You don't even know me."

"Yeah, but I know how I feel about you."

"So you'd take me with you just because of how you feel about me?"

"Without a second thought," I answered as she wrung the wet rag out in the dirty dish tub.

"How do I know that you aren't making me into what you need me to be?" Sarah asked, turning the tables.

"I'm not," I answered confidently, with the instinct of a salesman trying to close a deal.

"Be careful of what you say," Sarah said, staring deep into my eyes.

Sarah's stare was overpowering, and I looked away. She walked off to return the salt and pepper shakers to the tables.

I longed for the day when I found the woman who I would ask to come home with me to stay, but I was also terrified of it actually happening. If Sarah was available, then what would I have done? She moved me like very few women ever had.

Thoughts of being monogamous made me cringe and made my head hurt. As much as I would have liked to blame my failed marriage on my ex-wife, it was me who couldn't live within the confines of my self-imposed prison. Marriage for me meant the loss of greater potentials. I dreamed of finding that special woman someday in whom I'd find peace and contentment, but the dream was more appealing than the reality. Behind the spirited longing for her, was a whispering voice warning me of a death that would accompany my realized dream.

Sarah had me and my boldness pegged. Lucky for me, she was still mixed up and tied to her past. She made me think though. She'd made me look at myself, the part of me who couldn't have what I thought I wanted. It came up periodically with women in my life, but I had hidden behind their lack of perfection; something was always wrong with them. I had always left myself an out, but for some reason Sarah could see through me.

Sarah came back with the sugar dispensers and set them on the counter.

"Sarah, I have to make a few calls," I said, really wanting to avoid more discussion.

"OK, I'll see you later," she said, as she started to unscrew the lids off the dispensers. She seemed calm, unaffected by all we'd just discussed.

"I'll talk to you later," I said, as I walked away.

I got off that hot seat before I bit off more than I could

chew. I kicked off my Tonys and lay down on the bed, my mind spinning like a drunk just before passing out. The storm whirling around inside was driving me crazy. I hoped to find peace and contentment in the direction that life was taking me. I longed to still suffer from the illusion that I actually had some sense of control over it. A rage and a depression were constantly simmering behind the mask I wore out in the world. Restlessness ruled me; it had even invaded my dream-life.

Somehow I dozed off in spite of my agitated state and fell into a dream about Lauren. She called me, and when I phoned her back, another woman answered. I asked the woman if Lauren was all right and also about her kids. Lauren wasn't home, but I asked questions to make sure that I'd dialed the right number. It was the housecleaner. I was assured that it was Lauren's number and that she had two young boys named Joshua and Nicholas. I called back again and a man answered. He seemed upset that I was calling. I told him that she had phoned, and I was simply returning her call.

The scene shifted to my visiting her. She was living in a really run-down neighborhood that almost seemed poverty-stricken. She told me that she was going to Mexico for over a month. She was living with a guy who seemed jealous. It was a mess around their place. She looked like she was healthy, but her environment had changed and it changed the way I saw her.

Her oldest son Joshua was there. Joshua had seemed to be the barrier between Lauren and myself. When I was actually seeing Lauren, Joshua was always trying to protect his mother and competed with me for her attention. In the dream, I introduced myself to him and shook his hand explaining how I used to go out with his mother. Joshua had grown considerably and didn't seem to remember me. I couldn't recall seeing Nicholas, the younger boy.

They were having a garage sale or doing something in the garage. It was not a place or neighborhood that I would live in. I left. I loved her still, but didn't necessarily want her. I might have wanted her a little bit, but something had changed. I was more upset to see the way she lived than concerned with having her back in my life.

I woke up saying "fear." Fear was leaving me unfulfilled, causing me to miss out on life. I drifted off back to sleep and this time woke to saying, "sadness" and feeling it. The sadness was about leaving behind an old way of being in the world. Whether I liked it or not, I knew that I had to let go of the past, or die.

Somehow, I had to find solace by pitching a tent in this wasteland of depression and surrender to its calling. I prayed that I would somehow find or stumble upon an oasis from which would spout the wellspring of new meaning and purpose in my life. I was tired of spinning off in a thousand different directions. I was tired of being torn between what my soul called for and the social duties and dogmas that had me in their grasp.

"No wonder I didn't have a woman in my life. I didn't have time," I thought to myself. "That's bullshit too," I said out loud, surprising myself. If the right woman came my way I'd damn well make time; might even rearrange my whole life. I was afraid of dying and missing out. It felt like I had so much left to do, but time was ticking.

I was a bucket of nerves. Unable to sit still, I was constantly wiggling my feet and ankles, stretching my neck from side to side and extending my spine to relieve the balled up tension caught between my ribs and backbone. I ran a hot bath. Within five minutes I climbed out feeling an unsettled driven urge to do something but found myself unable to home in on my calling. I felt like a useless man, unable to help myself, and in turn unable to contribute anything of value to a woman. There was no woman in my life, because I didn't feel worthy of her. I didn't feel worthy period.

CHAPTER 22
Saturday

The MG was parked in front of Okie's station. Her top was down and she looked as if she'd just had a bath and was waiting for me to climb in and drive her around the block a few times. I figured that I had better get scrubbed up lest she caught sight of my bed head and the roaring wind of my polluted morning breath and decided that she wasn't in the mood for a weekend, early-morning, run around the block. I got up, brushed my teeth, slicked my hair back, and dressed hoping that she'd still entertain me un-bathed.

"What's going on Jimmy?" I asked, as my Tonys led me to the coffee counter.

"Thinkin' about gettin' out of this place."

"What do you mean?" I asked, looking around for Flo and Sarah, but finding neither of them.

"I'm thinkin' about leavin'," he said, as I sat down next to him at the counter.

"For good?"

"Is anything for good?" he asked, both hands around his perspiring water tumbler.

"You know what I mean."

"It's time for a change," he said, wiping his hands on the front of his apron.

"Where?" I asked.

"Don't know for certain."

"Where do you want to go?"

"Remember when you said you just wanted to drive away?"

"And you said I was running from myself," I reminded him.

"Yeah, somethin' like that."

"That what you want to do, Jimmy, run?"

"Did it already."

"What do you mean?"

"I got in the car and ran from me already. It's how I got here."

"Of all places, how in the hell did you end up here?"

"Hell, I don't know. It's where my car brought me."

"How long you been here?"

"Few years. I finally caught up to myself though," he said, smiling.

"Took that long?"

"Guess so."

"Had to get lost to find yourself, huh?"

"I don't know, but I was supposed to be here for some reason."

"And now you're supposed to be somewhere else?"

"That's what it feels like," he said in a calm, peaceful tone.

"Guess you're the only one who can know that."

"And you're the only one who knows what you need, kid. Don't ever let anyone tell you any different, either."

"It's good to know you, Jimmy."

"Life's not about survivin', kid. It's all about livin'. They'd like you to think different, but it's all about livin' your life, your way."

"Who're they, Jimmy?"

"Anyone who's not you," he said, as he stood up. He was walking back to the kitchen when Sarah came in through the front door.

"Good morning," I said greeting Sarah.

"A great morning," she smiled back."

"Where you been?"

"Across the street at my uncle's station."

"Car troubles?" I asked, surprised that she referred to Okie as her uncle for the first time around me.

"No. Thought he might have had some mail for me," she answered, with a peaceful, almost relieved look. "Looks like your car's ready," she said, shifting the subject.

"I was about ready to walk over and take her on a test run.

With your uncle's blessing, of course."

"Want some breakfast?" she asked, still smiling about the blessing remark.

"No. Thanks, though."

"Just like a kid who won't eat until he gets to play with his new toy," she said, walking behind the counter and putting her purse away under the cash register.

"Something like that," I said, as I stood up and started walking to the door.

"Have fun."

"Yep," I nodded.

"And be careful!" she shouted, as I left.

I was approaching the car when Okie came out to meet me.

"Good morning," I said, as he walked up to the MG.

"Mornin', kid."

"What's up?" I asked, trying not to appear anxious about the car's repair status. If he had her fixed, he was losing his power over me. It was important to ease it, instead of jerking it away from him. That was also the real reason for him keeping me around until Monday.

"She's ready to roll," he said, with a serious and proud-of-himself expression for having her done when he said she'd be done.

"What do I need to do?"

"Take her on a test run."

"Wanna go?"

"No. Just tell me where you're goin' and how long you'll be gone. That way I can come after you if you don't make it back in time."

"I'll be back in thirty minutes... make it an hour," I said excitedly.

"OK, which way?"

"East, and I'll stay on the highway."

"Give her hell, but be careful."

"Of what?"

"I can fix the goddamn car. Just wouldn't know how to piece you back together."

"Thanks," I said, opening the door of the little convertible. Okie must have been aware that guys like me sometimes didn't survive the crises that overtook us.

I slid my body into the MG a lot like I slipped my feet into the Tonys. I knocked the loose armrest off the center console and after putting it back into place for it to fall off at the first bump in the road, I fumbled the keys into the ignition. I pulled on the manual choke, pumped the gas three times for good luck and turned the key. She purred, almost too smoothly. I wanted to second guess the mechanic, but knowing how moody my little red bomb was, I decided to enjoy her for as long as she'd last.

I pulled onto the highway and moved through the gears. Oil pressure was good, and the water temperature remained stable at 180 degrees. I clicked on the overdrive button, watching the RPM drop five hundred and feeling her smooth out as she glided down the highway. It felt so good to have my wheels back. I rolled along in the car feeling a freedom similar to the one I felt driving home to mom and dad the Wednesday afternoon before that last Thanksgiving.

I drove into town the back way that day. I descended the coast range and came into the Central Valley driving through the remote communities where I had started in the farm machinery business. I stopped and visited a guy who I once worked with in the early years of my career and then continued east to my friend Charles's ranch. Charles had died two and a half years before that Thanksgiving, his father a year before that. I sobered up in 1986; Charles didn't. His drinking and drugging didn't mix with his diabetes; we buried him in July of 1997.

Six months before Charles's death, I had taken a month off and rented a place in Carmel. I'd just turned thirty-six and was starting to question where I was in life. I'd been divorced for a few years and was nursing a broken heart from my failed relationship with Lauren. Something was already starting to change, but it was Charles's death that really shook my foundations. I realized that he could have been me. Why had I survived? Why was it me who sobered up? Why didn't Charles make it?

I had a dream about Charles a couple of weeks before that last Thanksgiving. He attacked me. I was a writer and he wanted me to write his death into a script. I told him that I would but was really lying to him. I had no intentions of writing him dead. In the dream, Charles overheard me telling two women, who were standing outside of the room, of my real intentions. He came screaming out of the room I had just left; wailing and swinging his fists at me like a mad man. That's when I woke up, my heart racing and scared half to death, believing that someone had actually broken into my dark solitary studio. I was relieved to find that the intrusion had only been a dream.

Freewheeling the way home to my parent's for Thanksgiving, I had somehow ended up at Charles's ranch. I drove through the fields that we had planted and cultivated together and then to the dairy where I always fed the cows because Charles had been too lazy or sick to feed them himself. I drove past the ranch house that his father let us live in. I continued my journey towards home driving past his uncle's dairy and spotting Charles's cousin, Danny, driving the skip loader in front of the barn. I turned around to say hello.

"Is that you, Danny?"

"Hey, man, how's the hell are you?"

"Good. You remember me?"

"Oh yeah, man. What're you doing out this way?"

"Strolling down memory lane; had a dream about Charles the other night. Was headed home for Thanksgiving and decided to drive this route on my way into town."

"Yeah, that's too bad about Charles. The rest of us all sobered up, but the poor guy didn't make it."

"Man, Danny, that's exactly what I thought as I drove down here from the ranch."

"Yeah, poor little guy."

"How's your family, Danny?"

"Good, man. Everyone's good."

"How about your father?"

"Still meaner than hell."

We both just laughed.

"Hey, man, I've got to get these cows fed. How long you in town for?"

"Probably through the weekend."

"There's a party Saturday night at the Dynasty. Seven o'clock. Come by."

"I just might see you there..."

After visiting with Danny, my drive led me past the bar I

frequented before sobering up. I stopped in, had an O'Doul's, and then made my way on home to mom and dad's place. I thought about stopping at Charles's grave before going home, but decided to wait for the morning. Instead, I chose to treat that night as a symbolic wake, in reflection and honor of my friend Charles, before the next day's funeral. I'm not certain why I treated this as a funeral, just as I'm not certain why Charles had attacked me in my dream. But I felt the need to treat this as some sort of death.

I went to the cemetery around eleven that Thanksgiving morning and after wandering around looking for his grave, I finally found it. His headstone was next to his parents. It had a picture of Charles. Below his picture, the stone was engraved with the words, "Fly Free."

Tears came when I first saw the grave. I sat and stared at the stone for a while, in some way hoping for a liberating experience: the same escape I had been seeking before I'd ever got involved with drugs and alcohol.

I wondered if that was the same experience Charles had been in search of, freedom from existential suffering. For a man who feared death so vehemently, it became clear to me that I had the same preoccupation that Charles had. Neither of us cared to suffer; we both sought an escape in drugs. Charles's escape turned into the ultimate escape, mine shifted from drugs to work. The drugs failed, and regardless of my material success, work eventually failed me as well. And still suffering, I continued to seek out this so-called liberating experience.

After my contemplation at the graveside, I felt it was time to move on. I started to walk around the headstone, but as I took the first step, I changed directions and stepped right over the center of the monument. It was an unconscious step. My body led me, and I stepped right over that "Fly Free" and then on to my car. I drove out of the cemetery and headed back toward my family home.

I had failed to look at my watch when I left and had lost track of time on my test drive. I figured I better head back to the garage. After turning around and settling in on my return, I drifted back to my daydream and the drive after leaving Charles's grave.

I passed another cemetery. It was where my paternal grandparents are buried. The same force that took me over the top of Charles' "Fly Free" was now guiding me back to my grandparents' grave. I walked straight to it even though I hadn't been there since my grandfather's service in November of 1985, fourteen years earlier; the headstone showed the dates of my grandparents' births and deaths. Engraved In the center of their stone was the inscription: Married 55 years. As I paid my respects, something that my grandfather said to me many years earlier came back to me.

My grandfather, my father's father was an American Indian. He was a quiet man, but when he did have something to say, it was worth listening to. His natural wisdom balanced out the rigid judgmental Calvinistic dogmas that I had inherited from my mother's side.

Eighteen plus years ago I saw my grandfather in the alley behind his house.

"Hi, Papa."

"Hello there," he said, greeting me as he carried a handful of weeds to the trash.

"Freeman's getting married," I announced.

"Yeah, I heard."

"Hell, he's crazy. He's only nineteen."

"It's a good thing. It will give your brother something to live for. It will give his life meaning."

That was years ago, but he spoke those words again to me that day at his grave. I think he had called to me as I was driving past his burial place. I didn't know exactly what or who was guiding me on the drive home that previous day, as well as on my Thanksgiving morning pilgrimage to the cemeteries, but I did know that it was a very significant day in my life and hoped that it would continue to become clearer as time went by.

When I pulled into Okie's, he motioned me to drive the MG into the repair bay. I, of course, followed his directions like a private taking orders from his Sergeant.

"How'd she run?" Okie asked.

"Great."

"You watch the temperature gauge?"

"The whole time," I lied.

"And?"

"One-eighty the whole way."

"Good. Doesn't sound like you have a cracked head. I want you to leave her with me for a few more hours. Once she cools, I'll look her over."

"Fair enough."

"You can pick her up later this afternoon."

"Talk to you then," I said, walking out of the shop. "Oh, hey, Okie."

"Yeah."

"Thanks."

"See you later, kid," he answered, happy that I'd acknowledged him, but not wanting to show too much emotion.

I walked back across the street for the diner. Flo was at the counter when I walked in.

"What's goin' on, kid?"

"Not much. Just getting ready to go. Sarah around?"

"When ya shippin' out?" she asked, ignoring my Sarah question.

"Not sure yet. Okie wants to give her the once-over before he sets me free."

"The ol' Okie benediction, huh?"

"You got it."

"Well, probably for the best anyway," she said, as she went behind to the register. She opened it and slid something under the cash tray.

"Oh yeah: I'd hate to get two hundred miles west of here and have her shit out on me again."

"Might stumble into another little gal like Sarah," Flo said, as she closed the drawer.

"God, I couldn't handle that again."

"Ah, come on."

"Come on, nothing."

"Don't give me that shit."

"What?"

"Five miles down the road you'll have forgotten Sarah."

"Bullshit," I said, grinning, but feeling a twinge in my gut.

"No bullshit. In five miles you'll be onto a new scent."

"We'll see."

"Don't have to, I already know," she said, crossing her arms.

"You just think you know."

"I know!"

"What do you care anyway? I'm leaving you your waitress."

"Like you have a choice."

"You don't think I do?"

"You're a dreamer," she teased with a smile.

"Whatever you say, Flo."

"Doesn't matter what I say."

"Yeah, right. What do I owe you, Flo?" I asked, changing the subject.

"What are you talkin' about?"

"My debt, for staying here, you know?"

"Oh, pay me whatever you feel's right."

"No way. What do I owe you?"

"Just pay me for the food."

"Have you kept track of what I ate?"

"No, have you?"

"No, but it's been at least two meals a day."

"Sounds good to me. Figure five bucks a meal."

"There's no way I'm only going to pay you a hundred-seventy dollars."

"That's all I want."

"Yeah, OK."

"Besides you've livened things up a bit around here," she said, smiling as she shuffled through some receipts that were next to the cash register. "Oh yeah, Sarah said to meet her at her house around seven," Flo said, as I took the stairs up to my room.

I kept on walking without letting Flo see that she'd jerked me down a few steps. My grandmother always did shit like that. She'd keep something to herself for fourteen years, something that I thought she had forgotten or never knew. Then at the right moment, in the middle of some subtle conversation, she'd pull it out of her hard drive and, like a computer crash, stop me dead in my tracks.

* * * * *

I watched the sunset in the rear-view mirror of the MG as I drove east to Sarah's place. My heart fluttered as I turned to follow the barbed-wire fence line back to the house. I took a deep breath of the dry, grassy, evening fall air, stretched my neck from side to side and tucked the fear into the back pocket of my Levis. At times, I hated how much I felt like a little boy around Sarah. I liked teasing her, I liked talking with her, and I loved making love with her, but I hated not having her wrapped around my finger.

Sarah walked out of the front door as I drove up to her house. She was wearing a pale yellow, one-piece, zip-in-the-back, jumper-type pantsuit with a small blue and green flower print. Her brown hair was down, her eyes glistening and her smile beaming an it's-so-good-to-see-you-look. She hadn't said a word, and I was already melting. I'd almost forgotten what it was like to have a woman look at me that way. My rigid, uncertain state softened, and I breathed her in.

"Damn, you really are a beautiful woman," I said, walking up to her.

"Nice to see you," was her response, ignoring my compliment, or at least not acknowledging it. She walked up and hugged me. "How's the little bomb?"

"Great! I took it for a run earlier and then left it with Okie to give it the once-over; just got it back."

"How's my uncle?"

"Seemed to be in pretty good spirits."

"He likes it when he's helped someone."

"Yeah, I can tell," I said, as an evening breeze started to kick up dust.

"Come on," Sarah said, taking me by the hand and leading me inside.

"Smells great."

"So, you're hungry?"

I smiled without answering.

"That's what I thought," she said, leading me into the kitchen. She poured my iced tea and set it down at the table. "Have a seat. I've got a few things left to do here."

I sat down and took a sip of tea admiring Sarah as she floated around the kitchen.

"I hope you like chicken," she said, testing my reaction.

"Love it," I said, staring at her ass cheeks.

"I bet you do," she said, turning to catch me in the act.

"Need any help?"

"Nope."

"You don't look like you do, but I thought it might be nice to offer."

"How gracious of you," she said, smiling as she pulled the chicken from the oven and placed it on top of the stove.

"What do you think Sarah?" I asked, as she began to set the table around me.

"About what?"

"Want to go?"

"Where?"

"Cali," I said, testing her reaction.

"California? I couldn't..."

"Yes you can." I cut in, correcting her.

"What about..."

"What about nothing," I interrupted.

"No, really what about..." Sarah stopped. "You're full of it," she came back, catching on to my flirt.

"About what?"

"Nothing I guess. Cut it out, you're just testing me," she said setting the roasted chicken on the table.

"Maybe, but let's pretend. What about nothing?"

"OK, what about my life? What about work?"

"Plenty of work there," I said, as she set a bowl of roasted potatoes and a tossed green salad next to the chicken.

"What about my home?" she asked, turning away for something else.

"You'll be with me."

"I mean, what about my stuff?" Sarah asked, setting a glass of water in front of her plate and topping off my tea.

"Leave it all behind."

"Leave it?" she asked, in an elevated tone, returning the pitcher of tea to the refrigerator.

"Not for good."

"I really don't have that much."

"Whose house is it?"

"My uncle's," she said, finally sitting down to join me.

"Will he let you keep your stuff here?"

"I don't know. Most of it is his or Flo's anyway."

"See?"

"I'm not ready for this."

"Me either, but so what. We're just pretending, remember."

"Yeah, that's right, just pretending."

"Besides, you're still married."

"More tea?" she asked, changing the subject.

After finishing dinner, Sarah began to clear the table. I followed suit and helped bus things to the counter. I found the dish soap under the sink.

"What are you doing?" she asked.

"The dishes," I answered, as I started rinsing them off.

"No you're not."

"Looks like I am," I said, continuing the task I started by plugging the drain and filling the sink with dishes, soap, and hot water.

"I'll do them later," she insisted, as she finished clearing the table.

I ignored her and kept at them. Sarah watched me for a few minutes, then gave up and walked off.

"Hey, Sarah," I yelled a few minutes later. I was almost finished and realized that she hadn't returned.

"Hey what?" echoed from another room.

"Come here."

"No, you come here," she yelled back.

"What about dessert?" I hollered, finishing the last dirty dish.

"I need some help with this zipper," she whispered, standing right behind me.

CHAPTER 23

Sunday

I snuck into the diner around six-thirty Sunday morning, or at least I thought I did. The back door was unlocked but could have been left that way from the night before. There was no sign of anyone up and stirring. I didn't get much sleep at Sarah's, so I lay down and tried to play catch-up.

I woke up around nine-thirty and ran my Sunday morning bath. One more day and I was out of never-never land. I started thinking about my drive home, wondering what I'd do once I got back. It would be nice to leave my Five Points loft above the kitchen and return to my studio in Carmel, but other than that I'd settle back into the routine of waking, walking down to the village for coffee, take in the morning beauties who came in for their lattes before scurrying off to their retail duties in the dress shops, art galleries, and countless other specialty shops that catered to the socially imposed demands of being unique.

I made very few purchases in Carmel, but had moved there shopping for a different life. I moved there to get lost, to blend into the beauty of the landscape and to escape myself and the identities I'd taken on up to that point in my life. Carmel needed a tractor-salesman like they needed another art gallery and that was exactly why I moved there. I didn't want to be an iron-peddler any longer. I simply wanted to be without the duties that an identity imposed.

Jimmy was sitting at the counter reading the paper and sipping his coffee. "Have a seat," he said, as I walked up. "The mornin' service is just about to get under way," he joked seriously.

"Let me pour a cup before you get started, Reverend."

"Hurry up son. You don't want to be late for judgment day."

"What's the sermon on today, Reverend?"

"Leroi!"

"Leroi?"

"Have you already heard my Leroi sermon?"

"Can't remember."

"Then you haven't," he said, folding up the newspaper.

"Looks like I am now, though," I grinned.

"Leroi was an old high school buddy of mine."

"Yeah?"

"Little bastard drove me crazy."

"How?"

"Couldn't think for himself. 'Hey, Jimmy, what do you think about this? Hey, Jimmy, what should I do about that?' Hey, Jimmy, my ass."

"Wore on you, huh?"

"I can still hear the echoes of that little fucker's questions."

"What ever happened to Leroi?" I asked, trying to shift Jimmy back from his agitation to the story.

"We all got drunk one day. Problem was, Leroi had no business drinkin'."

"Why not?" I asked, before sipping my coffee.

"'Cause he didn't know how to act sober, let alone drunk. Little fucker would start thinkin' on his own and not do a very good job of it."

"So what did he fuck up?"

"My dad's truck."

"Bad?"

"No. We were out at the lake that night, on my uncle's houseboat. Leroi forgot somethin' in my dad's truck, so I gave him the keys to run up after his goods."

"What did he forget?"

"A bottle of tequila, and his mind," Jimmy said, shaking his head from side to side.

"I see."

"You don't yet," Jimmy said, pausing for a breath. "Leroi strutted back down to the dock and hopped onto the houseboat, and we set sail for uncharted waters and a good old fashioned bender."

"A huh."

"We had about half a case of beer down when we broke the seal on the bottle of tequila. You know what it's like when you have a pretty good buzz?"

"Yeah."

"And you know its gunna get worse?"

"Better or worse."

"I mean, like you ask yourself: 'Is there anything I need to do before I get too drunk to do it later?'"

"It's been a while, but I remember."

"Well, I remembered the keys to the truck that Leroi hadn't returned to me after his tequila run."

"He locked them in the truck?"

"No, I wish," he said, pausing to swig some coffee. "I was behind the wheel, steerin' the houseboat when I thought of the keys, so I asked Leroi if he had 'em," Jimmy said, setting his coffee cup on the counter.

"What did he say?"

"It's not what he said. It's what he did. The dumb fuck fumbled through his pockets and when he finally pulled 'em out, they slipped out of his hands and flew overboard."

"And you didn't have an extra set?"

"We were in high school. Hell, I bought rubbers at the Greyhound bus station bathroom that was located halfway between home and the drive-in theater when I had a date and there were signs that I might get lucky."

"What's that got to do with Leroi?"

"Hell, no, I didn't have an extra set of keys to my old man's truck. My parents were gone that weekend, and I snuck it out. I wasn't even supposed to be drivin'."

"What did you do?" I asked, standing up to go for the coffee pot.

"We drank the rest of the tequila and I told Leroi he was the dumbest piece of shit that had ever been laid."

"How'd you get home?" I asked, refilling our cups.

"Called my uncle from the pay phone when we got back to the dock the next mornin'."

"What did you tell him?" I asked, returning the pot to the

coffee maker.

"That fuckin' Leroi tossed dad's keys overboard and that we needed him to bring us the extra set he had."

"So your dad never found out?"

"Yeah, he finally found out some time later."

"What did he do?"

"It was too late to do anything when he found out, but he never let me live it down."

"Oh yeah?"

"Yeah, before I could make-up an excuse, whenever I'd done somethin' wrong, he'd look at me and say: 'Don't tell me, it was that fuckin' Leroi, right?'" Jimmy said, leaning back and belly laughing over his youthful follies.

"Fuckin' Leroi!" I said, joining in with Jimmy's laughter.

I stood up a few minutes later remembering that I needed to get some miles on the MG or stand the chance that Ol' Deadeye might ground me for another day. He hadn't relinquished all of his power yet.

"Jimmy, I've goda put some miles on that little red bomb of mine before Okie will give me his final blessing."

"You better get to hoppin' then, son."

"OK, I'll catch you later, Reverend."

"Kid."

"Yeah?"

"Be careful in that little hot rod. I don't know the first thing about conductin' a funeral."

"I'll see you later, Reverend," I said, smiling confidently.

I drove west to Tranquillity. It was windy, so I'd put the top up on the MG before leaving Five Points. There was nothing like rumbling around in an MG with gusty winds. The winds had a way of heightening my sense of awareness just like when I was flying the Bonanza. I could feel every shift, right in the seat of my pants. Occasionally the gust felt like it lifted the little red bullet and set it over five feet onto the shoulder of the road.

Sunday in Tranquillity was lifeless. The hardware store was locked up tight. I turned into the drive-in planning on a burger, but was met with the disappointment of the CLOSED sign that sat just above the sliding window where you'd normally place an order. I stopped and got out anyway. The bathroom was unlocked, so I took advantage of my good fortune, not that I couldn't have found somewhere else to relieve myself in that little ghost town.

A tail wind pushed me and the MG back to Five Points, as if the Gods were seeing to it that I returned for unfinished business. I wouldn't have left without paying the old fart, with or without the help of the Gods. Flo was lounging in the booth where she normally sat during the evening watching television.

"Awfully quiet around here, too," I said, greeting Flo.

"Yeah, I sent Sarah and Jimmy home. Where've you been?"

"Tranquillity. Couldn't even buy a burger there."

"I could have saved you the trip."

"I needed to get the miles on the MG anyway."

"How's your little buggy runnin'?"

"Seems good."

"Sounds like you'll be off tomorrow, then?"

"Yeah, if everything holds together."

"I'm sure it will."

"Never know with that little bomb," I answered, sensing that Flo had more to say than she was saying.

"You've had more experience with it than me."

"What's up, Flo?" I asked, sitting down opposite her.

She hesitated and turned toward the kitchen service window. "He's leavin'."

"Who?"

"Jimmy."

"He's leaving?" I asked, acting as if I didn't know anything. I was surprised, though. He told me that he was going somewhere, but I didn't figure he really meant it or that it would be so soon.

"Yep, says it's time for a change."

"Where's he going?"

"Not sure."

"When?"

"Gave me a two-week-notice yesterday."

"What're you gunna to do?"

"Whatever I have to do."

"Ever think about closing up shop?"

"Yeah."

"Are you?"

"Don't think I can," she said, turning to look at me.

"Why?"

"Don't know anything else."

"All the more reason."

"What would I do?"

"Can you lease the place out?"

"Don't know."

"Can you afford to leave it?"

"Probably save money closin' it down."

"So why you still here?"

"It's who I am. It's been my whole life," she said, looking down and to the right.

"I know how hard that is."

"Do you?" Flo asked, appearing to be on the edge of breaking down.

"You'd be giving up every way you've ever been in this world."

"What little control I do have in my life," she said, regaining her composure.

"And giving it up without anything to replace it."

"I'd be givin' up everything I've lived for."

"Maybe it's time to say goodbye to your father Flo. Maybe it's time to start living your life."

"Where would I start?"

"Wherever you want, but I know where I'd start."

"Where?"

"By leasing this place out."

"You wouldn't sell it?"

"You can't."

"Why not."

"I don't think you're entirely ready to dispose of this part of yourself. Not yet anyway, but you could lease it out and test the waters."

"And then what?"

"Go explore. Go test the world. Find out where you'll fit in. Once you find it, then you can sell."

"All sounds good, but sayin' it and doin' it's two different things."

"Don't I know," I answered, thinking about how much my life had changed over the last year. "I've got to make a sandwich, Flo. Want one?" I asked, standing up from her booth.

"No thanks, kid," she said, as I walked back into the kitchen.

I returned a few minutes later and sat back down across from Flo. I ate in silence.

"Think I'm gunna try my luck out at the river one last time," I said, standing up after lunch, uncomfortable with the silence.

"Be careful out there."

"Always," I said, walking off toward the kitchen.

I threw my fishing gear into the trunk and climbed into the MG. This was the first river run for the little red bomb. We drove for the river road, the very road to sanctuary that the MG and I would soon forgo on our route home.

Returning home meant returning to the same emptiness that I was trying to escape in Five Points. There wasn't that much difference between my little room upstairs and my downstairs studio in Carmel. I had Tillie's coffee counter along with a few other coffee houses for my hangouts. I had befriended the waitresses and could run to them when my isolated life style turned into lonely terror and I needed the company of someone beside myself. Weekends were the worst for me; I couldn't wait for them to be over. I seemed to find more comfort and meaning during the week in the trivial duties of work or an evening college class.

I had moved to Carmel to take a break and then start over. I had signed up for a few college classes to keep me out of trouble and into the circle of younger, unattached women whose priorities were not getting married and having babies. For economic reasons, I had decided to return to the tractor business, no longer willing to dip into my retirement fund. I had physically tried to leave my discontent behind in that move, but it didn't work. My return to tractors was a grasp at hanging on to the past, something safe, but an identity that no longer suited me.

I knew exactly how Flo was feeling. I had surrounded myself with the California coastal community of people and possibilities only to withdraw into myself, except for those occasional bullshit sessions at coffee. For Flo it was a little different. Her withdrawal was into the solitude of Five Points where she occasionally found social contact with the transients who stumbled into her diner while on the road pursuing their own lives. These transitory patrons never developed into deep or longstanding friendships.

Jimmy's leaving was pushing her closer up against the wall of isolation that the remoteness of the diner provided. Sarah wouldn't be far behind Jimmy. It was no life for her either. Flo had hired Sarah to help Sarah, but Flo had also hired some companionship, a friend.

I rumbled over the cattle guard and thought the car was going to fall into a thousand pieces. Ol' Reliable was much more suited to off-road fishing hauls than the MG. The little bomb pulled itself back together, and we rolled on towards the river.

The earlier winds had subsided, but the river felt colder than it had on our previous encounters. I fished the same slot, perched on my under-water log. It was always nice to have a landmark to serve as a guide in hope of repeating a prior success, but it also narrowed my vision and robbed me of what the entire river had to offer. I considered moving downstream, but chose to continue fishing the same hole. I wasn't all that concerned with catching a fish; I was there just to be there.

I fell into my casting rhythm, but the chill of the river kept pulling me out of the trance that I was drifting into. The coldness discouraged me, and I decided to bow to Old Man River as well as the goose bumps that were overtaking me. I tiptoed backward off the log, turning in shallower water and heading back for shore. There she sat on the hood of her Jetta.

"Hey there," I said, surprised to see her.

"Hello," Sarah greeted with a warm smile.

"What brings you out this way?"

"You," she answered, with a look of hesitation.

"What's going on?"

"Missed you; I wanted to see you."

"I see," I answered, a little spooked. I longed for a woman to miss me, but it seemed that as soon as they started revealing their feelings for me, I locked up frozen solid, willing myself to be left alone in my wintry state.

"I mean... you are leaving tomorrow. I just wanted to hang

out with you some more."

"What would you like to do?" I asked, feeling as if an encroaching shadow was hovering over and about to devour me.

Sarah didn't answer. She just came over to me, wrapped her arms around me and pulled my wet wader-clad body into hers. I hugged her with my free arm as she tightened her hold. My heart started beating faster, and I began to catch my breath. I was feeling really scared, and then to my relief remembered that she was still married. I was able to breathe again.

"Come on. Let me shed this gear," I said, leaving my arm around her and making an effort to move towards the MG. She left one arm around me and turned to walk at my side.

I opened the trunk of the MG and sat down on its ledge to pull off my waders. Ol' Reliable's tailgate served much better when it came to providing a seat to finish off a day at the river. Sarah didn't say much. Actually, neither of us did. It was an uncomfortable silence. She just walked around while I stepped back into my Tonys, rolled up my gear and stuffed it into the trunk.

"I'm screwed up," I said, closing the trunk.

"What's that? I couldn't hear you?"

"I said I'm screwed up."

"Maybe not."

"You don't understand. I'm really screwed up," I repeated, hoping to scare her off.

"So what? We all are."

"Not like me."

"Oh, you're special?"

"Special? More like weird."

"You're weird all right," Sarah smiled.

"So what are you doing hanging out with a weirdo?"

"I like weirdoes."

"You've got nothing better to chose from."

"Excuse me?" she said, her smile fading.

"Well, I mean, who else did you have to choose from?"

"Look, I don't need a man in my life. I certainly didn't choose to be with you out of desperation if that's what you mean."

"Why'd you choose me then?"

"Who says I did?"

"You slept with me, didn't you?"

"It was more than that I hope," she said with a deflated look.

"You know what I mean. You chose me, or it never would have happened."

"Maybe it just happened. Maybe it was supposed to happen."

"Maybe."

"More than maybe."

"Guess I didn't think about it that way," I answered, reflecting on how I always tried to plot and manipulate my life and the events that surrounded it.

"You can't plan everything in life," she said, as if she knew what I was thinking.

"I'm beginning to wonder if you can plan anything at all."

"Maybe that's why you feel screwed up."

"Maybe you're right."

"So instead of planning anything, why don't you follow me home?"

"Why don't I?" I asked, with a smart-ass smirk.

"Because all we've got is right now, and you'd be a damn fool not to," she answered, walking for her Jetta. She climbed in and drove off without saying another word. She just smiled and waved goodbye.

I let the little red bomb catch the groove that led the way out of sanctuary. This time I slowed down and eased over the cattle guard. I pulled out onto the highway, shifted through the gears and into overdrive, allowing the MG to guide me past the diner. The fence line reeled me in the rest of the way to Sarah's and landed me up on her porch. The lump in my throat must have been the muddler I swallowed back at the river.

Chapter 24

Monday

Lying on my side, Sarah was curled up inside of me. The sun had yet to rise and her room was dark, but I could feel her. Her scent was so inviting that I couldn't resist. We melted into each other effortlessly. Our lovemaking seemed to flow as naturally as the river I'd stumbled upon when I first arrived in Five Points.

Sunlight finally started creeping between the gap of the shades and the bedroom window, a sign that it was time for me to get moving. It was the day of my departure, but for some reason I still felt the need to hide from Flo. I climbed out of bed and gathered up my clothes. I went to the bathroom, watered my hair down, and combed it back. Sarah was still in bed when I returned to her room to say good-bye. She had dozed off.

"You awake?" I asked, brushing her hair back so that I could see her eyes.

"Yeah, I'm awake," she answered, still half asleep.

I leaned over and kissed her forehead. "I can tell," I said, admiring her beauty and semi-unconscious condition.

"I'll leave my card so you know how to get in touch with me. You know, just in case you ever do get divorced."

"I'm already divorced," she answered groggily.

"Yeah, right," I said, as Sarah started to move. "Don't get up. I can find my way out."

"I am," she said calmly.

"Keep in touch," I said, kissing her one last time.

It was clear, a beautiful fall day. I opened the door and climbed into the MG. I unbuckled the two clasps that latched the convertible top to the front windshield and pushed the top back over my head until the hinged linkage that the ragtop was attached to collapsed. I climbed out to finish tucking the top back behind the seats and then snapped the cover over it so that everything looked as if it were in order. I wanted to breathe in all the scents of the landscape as well as feel the freedom of the wind whipping around me on my way home.

The fence posts had a different effect on me when I drove out of Sarah's place. They were still tugging at my heart, but they were also stirring up a sense of confusion. Why had she given herself so freely to me when she knew that I was leaving? After all, she wasn't going to get anything from me in return.

Flo and Jimmy were sitting at the coffee counter when I walked in.

"Guess he didn't crack it up after all," Flo said to Jimmy, on my behalf.

"Good morning," was all that I offered, trying to climb the stairs before anything else came at me.

"How's she runnin'?" Jimmy asked.

"Couldn't be better," I answered, dancing around on the bottom step.

"You hungry, kid?" Flo asked.

"Yeah, I sure am, but I want to clean up and pack my bags first," I answered, wanting to scrub off the guilt before Flo could sink her teeth into it.

"Suit yourself. We'll be here either way."

"I'll be down in a while," I said, climbing the stairs.

I bathed and packed my bags. Before leaving my room I went over to the corner with the windows. I wanted to climb out like I did as a kid, sneaking out to play without mom or dad knowing. There were a couple of problems, though. First, I was on the second floor, and I didn't think that my thirty-eight year old body would withstand a thirteen-year-old's leap. Second, they had all been good to me, and I owed them an honest goodbye. I grabbed my laptop computer case and pulled out my checkbook along with an envelope. I wrote a check and signed it, leaving the amount blank for Flo to fill in and stuffed it into the envelope along with my business card just in case she ever needed to contact me.

I carried all my goods down and out the back door to pack the MG before ordering breakfast.

"I'm gunna leave this here for you, Flo," I said, sliding the envelope between the cash register and the coffee counter.

"OK, thanks," she answered indifferently, standing behind the counter, leaning on the stainless steel serving station under the kitchen window.

"Whatcha eatin', kid?" Jimmy asked.

"Pancakes."

"You got it," he said, walking back to the kitchen.

"Coffee?" Flo asked, raising the pot in the air.

"Please," I answered, as she poured. "Flo, thanks for everything."

"No problem, kid... thank you."

"For what?"

"For bein' a pain in my ass and for lettin' me be one in yours," she said, as she walked around to my side of the counter. I stood up, and we hugged each other.

"Cut that shit out. The owner of this place might run both your asses out of here if she catches you two," Jimmy announced as he swung from behind the kitchen door and set the pancakes down in front of my seat.

"No shit. I almost forgot where I was," I said, returning to my chair.

"Maple or blueberry?" Flo asked walking back behind the counter.

"Maple," Jimmy answered as he filled his coffee cup.

"How long is the drive home?" Jimmy asked.

"Not sure, probably close to twenty hours," I answered, pouring the syrup over my hotcakes. "This is my first time on this route."

"Goin' straight through?"

"Don't know for sure."

"Wingin' it, huh?"

"Winging it... hey Jimmy."

"Hey kid."

"It's good to know you. Thanks, huh?"

"You're a real winner, kid."

"What did I do now?"

"I mean it in a good way. You got the blood pumpin' through me again."

"Well, I don't know what I did," I answered, uncertain of what I had provided, yet feeling a little proud of myself. "It was that fuckin' Leroi's fault anyway," I added.

Jimmy leaned back in his seat and started belly laughing. I joined him.

"What's so funny?" Flo asked, walking up to check on the commotion.

"Oh, the kid here thinks he's a comedian, is all," Jimmy answered.

"Sure thing, Reverend," I whispered to Jimmy as Flo walked off.

"Fuckin' Leroi," Jimmy said, shaking his head from side to side, his arms crossed, rising up and down on his belly as he laughed.

"Keep in touch, Jimmy. Let me know where you land next," I said, handing him my business card. "Keep me posted on ol' Leroi, too."

"You can count on it," he answered, sliding my card into his wallet. He stood up, extended his hand, but we embraced. "Take care of yourself, kid," he said, reaching for my dirty dishes and then taking them into the kitchen.

A few minutes later Flo and Jimmy came back out into the diner and walked me over to the MG. We said our final goodbyes, and I drove across to Okie's for his final blessing and to settle up with the old fart. I pulled up to the gas pumps, filled her up and was checking the oil when Okie walked up.

"How's it look?" he asked.

"About a half-quart low."

"How many miles you put on her?"

"Hundred and seventy-five."

"Burn oil before?"

"That's not burning oil in an MG. I thought you said you've owned one before?"

"You're right on that one," he said, chuckling to himself.

"Okie, I need to settle up with you."

"All right."

"How much?"

"Well, I figured I have about twenty hours into your little hot rod. You're already covered on the parts."

"Fair enough. How much?"

"Let's see. How about twenty hours at twenty bucks an hour. Yeah, four hundred."

I reached for my wallet and pulled out four, one-hundred-dollar bills and handed them to Okie. "Oh yeah, I still owe you for the gas."

"Call it even," he insisted.

"You sure?"

"Wouldn't have said so if I wasn't," he said in a firm tone.

"OK, thanks for everything, Okie."

"Not a problem, kid. It was actually kind of fun. Wrenchin' on your car brought back a lot of old memories."

"Yeah, no kidding," I smiled, thinking of all the memories that had been stirred up in me while waiting for the MG to get buttoned back together.

"Now, I've got to get this letter down to my niece, somethin' from a court in Florida. I don't know what the hell it could be, but she's off for the next few days, so I better get it to her in case it's important."

"Thanks again, Okie."

"Have a safe trip kid."

"Take care yourself."

I pulled out onto the highway westbound, thinking of the friends I'd made as a result of my misfortune. I never seemed to have a problem making friends. They just came to me. My problem was finding friends who didn't want something from me and who would allow me the space to have my moods. I didn't mind being there for a friend; I just didn't like it to be expected. All of my friendships that had a history of any length had been built on mutual respect and a time-honored space that allowed the freedom for each other to come and go as our lives called us. We were always there for one another, all it took was a simple phone call, but our devotion was never exploited.

I wondered why I really couldn't, or had yet to share this with a woman who was also my lover. Was it an illusion, or was I really missing out on something? Why at thirty-eight had I yet to form a lasting relationship with a woman? I suppose I had always feared being devoured as opposed to enjoying her loving devotion.

The MG was running so smoothly that she scared me. It was easier to have something wrong with her, just as long as it didn't stop me, because then I didn't worry about the big one hitting. I crossed paths with an eastbound champagne-colored Ford Explorer on the highway, just like the one Lauren used to drive. I thought about the dream I had of going back to see her and leaving because she wasn't as attractive to me in her state of poverty. It was a weird dream. I remember leaving her house in that run down neighborhood, feeling bad for her, where life had taken her.

I continued my drive west and decided to stop in Tranquillity for a burger. The pancakes were sitting in the bottom of my belly, but I was still craving a burger and didn't know where my next chance might be. I ordered an iced tea and a cheeseburger, less the onions. I skipped the fries. I sat down at the table on the side of the building and started reading the public's engravings. I wanted to carve my name to join the rest of the ass-ends of the community who had left their mark, and then a voice within discouraged me.

The woman inside the drive-in tapped on the side window summoning me to pick up my order. I walked to the sliding window to receive my prize and returned to the table where I unwrapped the burger and took a bite. Another Lauren dream image popped into my head. She was living in a nicer neighborhood, but was wearing a housecoat and looked run down, tired, maybe even sick.

I finished my burger, sipped the last of my tea, crumpled up the wrapper and stuffed it back into the little brown paper bag it came in. I walked over to the trashcan between the table and the drive-in, tossing in the bag as I passed by. I went to the window for more tea. Another Lauren dream flashed to me as I waited for my refill. She was in some professional building, possibly a courthouse. She had been beaten or abused. I wanted to walk up and help her, but before I could reach her another woman came up and escorted her away.

I thought that I was pretty much over Lauren, but for some reason these dreams were all coming back to me. I fired up the MG and headed west thinking about Lauren and what I could have done differently. I viewed woman as a debt who would occasionally fuck me if I walked the right walk and talked the right talk. I wanted to blame Lauren for my leaving her. Then a: "Don't tell me. It was that fuckin' Leroi!" and Jimmy's belly laugh echoed in my mind. My problem with woman was that I believed I had to trick them into giving in to me, and when this didn't work, I became angry, found something wrong and wrote them off. It appeared as if I was making woman into what I needed her to be.

I heard my cell phone ring over the wind as I tooled along in the convertible and reached down to answer it. It hadn't been ringing; I was hearing things. I recalled another dream. It was Lauren calling me on my cellular phone. I had caller ID and opted not to answer when I saw it was her calling. I looked at the temperature gauge and the oil pressure. Everything appeared to be fine. I looked at my gas gauge and thought of Okie and then Lauren leaving that professional building that might have been a courthouse. Okie had said something about a letter from a Florida court. Maybe Sarah was awake when she teased about already being divorced.

It was becoming clearer as to why my MG had shitted out when it had; the moody little convertible was doing me a favor. I couldn't go back to get Lauren in any of those sleeping dreams, but I couldn't leave Sarah back in the waking one that I'd just left behind. I pulled over to the side of the road, hung a U-turn, and headed back for Five Points and Sarah.

www.malcolmclay.com

Also by Mel Mathews:

Menopause Man

SamSara

Menopause Man

ISBN 0-9776076-1-5

"Over here," he announced, holding up her leash.

"Come on Diana," she said, walking over to retrieve the dog. Malcolm kept petting Diana to keep her from running off. He wanted to make sure Lance got a good crack at the master, not to mention that he desired the same for himself.

"Hi there," Malcolm greeted the master as she reached for the leash.

"Oh, hi there," she answered in a soft, listless-like tone.

"How are you?" Malcolm asked to hold her up for a few more seconds.

"Fine thanks. Come on Diana," she said, smiling half-heartedly as she led the pup away.

"See you later," Malcolm said, as the couple walked towards the parking lot across the way. "What do you think of Diana?" he asked, looking up at Lance with a big grin after dog and master had crossed the street.

"How do you know Diana's name?" Sheila was quick to ask.

"It's my job," Malcolm quipped.

"Yeah, right! Your job," Sheila said.

"She's got the most potential of any woman I've met around here, yet."

"She is pretty damn cute," Sheila conceded.

"Cute. Hell, she's hot!" Lance chimed in.

"I'm partial to the dog, myself," Malcolm smiled.

"You *are* a dog," Sheila snapped. "I know what you're really after," she added, punching Malcolm's shoulder.

"What's her name?" Lance asked.

"Diana," Malcolm answered with a smart-ass grin. "Weren't you listening?"

"Not the dog, the woman."

"I don't know."

"But you know her dog's name?" Sheila asked in a give-me-a-break tone.

"Yeah, she came and jumped up onto my lap one day."

"Right," Sheila said, shaking her head

"The girl or the dog?" Lance asked grinning.

"Really," Malcolm said, holding back his laughter to Lance's question. "I was sitting right up there on that bench," Malcolm said, pointing to the porch. "The pup just trotted right up those steps and hopped up into my lap."

"How do you know her name's Diana?" Lance asked.

"I asked."

"But you don't know the woman's name?" Sheila chimed in.

"I didn't ask," Malcolm answered in an impatient tone.

"Why not?" Lance asked.

"She wasn't ready to tell me."

"How do you know?" Sheila asked.

"I just know, all right? I can sense these things, you know."

* * * * *

Like a lot of people, he'd developed the habit of looking for love in all the wrong places. He really wasn't all that bad of a fellow. Yeah, he was selfish and self-absorbed, but Malcolm Clay had some redeeming qualities, too.

Something had changed, something he couldn't quite put his finger on, and it was driving him, as well as a few others, half nuts. He might have been chasing his tail, he might have been making mistakes, but he was still trying. One thing was certain: Malcolm hadn't given up!

Fisher King Books can be purchased online at:

www.fisherkingpress.com

or by calling:

1-800-228-9316

SamSara

ISBN 0-9776076-2-3

After settling his bill, Malcolm returned to the sanctuary to say goodbye.

"Well, Niamh, I probably won't be seeing you again."

"So, this is it, huh, Malcolm?"

"This is it," he answered, as she came out from behind the bar.

"It's good to know you Niamh," he said, reaching for her hand. Instead, she kissed his cheek.

"Say, Niamh, how do I get out of here and to the closest Dart station?" he asked, a bit set back by her gesture.

"Ah, Malcolm, that's an easy one," she answered, almost as if she had anticipated this very question. "When you walk out the front door of Samsara here, you'll go left down Dawson Street until you've reach Trinity College, then follow the wall around to your right and stay on that path. It'll wind a bit, but stay on that path and eventually you'll see the bridge where the train crosses. It'll take you about ten minutes."

"Okay, Niamh, sounds easy, and I can always ask for help if I get lost."

"Listen to me, Malcolm," Niamh commanded in a firm, direct tone. "Just do exactly as I say: follow the path and you'll have no problems."

"Okay, I'll trust you Niamh," he answered, and trust her is what he was about to do.

* * * * *

In **SamSara**, it seems that Malcolm Clay has finally broken away from the chains that once bound him, or has he? He's certainly on the path as he wrestles with those old ghosts from his past. But it just might be the kiss from an angel that sets him free.

LeRoi

ISBN 0-9776076-0-7

Le roi est mort, vive le roi! The black cover with the French title in thick, bright red letters as if applied with a bricklayer's trowel, and the crown that looked more like a jester's cap compelled me to take a look at *LeRoi* in a book store in Zurich.

At first it read like a simple story of this rather ornery but 'successful-in-life' character stuck in the middle of nowhere in his fancy MG, which had allowed him to limp into a gas station with a diner-cum-motel on the other side of the highway. I quickly realized that the simplicity was only skin deep, the writing a sort of self-analysis, the old mechanic and gas station owner a study in laissez-faire and cool disdain that tried the patience of our hero. As a matter of fact, all members of the cast including the Queen who rules the diner, the pretty waitress and the lanky fast-order cook are highly complicated human beings, which some may consider to be 'virtual' or a projection of the storyteller.

The enigmatic and moody old Chevy half ton pick-up truck he borrows is unreliable, but does give him the freedom to get away from the confines of the motel and the frustration of his broken down MG. Ol' Reliable guides him over a cattle guard, a mysterious unseen gateway into a deeply felt sanctuary. He has found the oasis of a river that cuts through this otherwise barren wasteland where he can cast a fly into adventure and misadventure, and beyond that, healing waters for the soul. Could this perhaps be a modern day model of the Grail Legend's Fisher King?

The depth of *LeRoi* is fascinating and frightening: it is full of magic, humor, but also inner suffering with terrible and seemingly perverted battles taking place that must be won to grant new life. It seems our protagonist needs this type of catharsis to free himself from the burdens of the past and restore his inner kingdom to prosperity.

As I came to the end of this satisfying and easy to read tale of redemption, I wondered if the author's future novels will be equally compelling sequels or completely different to the 'tongue-in-cheek' title of the novel *LeRoi*?

--Jack G. Moos - Küsnacht, Switzerland--